FOR Kevin
M K. Face
OF
PHONE AREA
MESSAGE
SIGNED

MTV's
MUSIC TELEVISION®

THE REAL WORLD

Diaries

PRODUCED BY MELCHER MEDIA / DESIGNED BY RED HERRING DESIGN

MTV BOOKS/POCKET BOOKS/MELCHER MEDIA

BASED ON MTV's THE REAL WORLD PRODUCED BY BUNIM/MURRAY PRODUCTIONS, INC. IN ASSOCIATION WITH MTV

THIS BOOK WAS PRODUCED BY MELCHER MEDIA
170 FIFTH AVENUE, NEW YORK, NY, 10010

EDITORIAL DIRECTOR: CHARLES MELCHER
EDITORS: AMY KEYISHIAN, SARAH MALARKEY
TEXT COORDINATOR: GENEVIEVE FIELD
ART DIRECTION: CAROL BOBOLTS AND DEB SCHULER, RED HERRING DESIGN
DESIGN ASSISTANT: ADRIA ROBBIN
PHOTOGRAPHY EDITOR: RUSSELL COHEN
DIRECTOR OF PRODUCTION, BUNIM/MURRAY: SCOTT FREEMAN

SPECIAL THANKS TO: MARY ANDERSON, LISA BERGER, ERIN BOHENSKY, MARY-ELLIS BUNIM, LYNDA CASTILLO, GINA CENTRELLO, ANITA CHINKES, OSCAR CREECH, AMY EINHORN, THOMAS EUSTIS, JR., CHRISTINE FRIEBELY, LISA HACKETT, JOHN-RYAN HEVRON, NATALIE HLADIO, BRIAN HUEBEN, MAUREEN JAY, SHERYL JONES, EMILY KEYISHIAN, MARK KIRSCHNER, GREER KESSEL, OLIVER KURLANDER, ANDREA LaBATE, STEVEN LICHTENSTEIN, CLAIRE McCABE, JONATHAN MURRAY, DONNA O'NEILL, ED PAPARO, RENÉE PRESSER, DONNA RUVITUSO, LAURA SCHECK, MAGGIE SHEARMAN, ROBIN SILVERMAN, DONALD SILVEY, CHRIS SNYDER, LIATE STEHLIK, DAVID TERRIEN, VAN TOFFLER, KARA WELSH, AND IRENE YUSS.

GRATEFUL ACKNOWLEDGEMENT IS MADE TO THE FOLLOWING PEOPLE AND INSTITUTIONS FOR PERMISSION TO REPRODUCE PHOTOGRAPHS AND ARTWORK: MICHAEL YARISH/MTV PRESS: PAGE 4. TIFFANY HOSS: PAGE 199. BILLY RAINEY: PAGES 7, 16, 56. ROBERT "FROG" MATTHEWS: PAGES 12, 13, 15, 17, 41, 58, 64, 71. JACINDA'S DIARY DESIGNED BY JIM MEYERS.

AN *ORIGINAL* PUBLICATION OF MTV BOOKS/POCKET BOOKS/MELCHER MEDIA

POCKET BOOKS, A DIVISION OF SIMON & SCHUSTER INC.
1230 AVENUE OF THE AMERICAS, NEW YORK, NY 10020

ISBN: 0-671-00373-9

FIRST MTV BOOKS/POCKET BOOKS/MELCHER MEDIA TRADE PAPERBACK PRINTING NOVEMBER 1996

10 9 8 7 6 5 4 3 2 1

PRINTED IN THE U.S.A.

Table of Contents

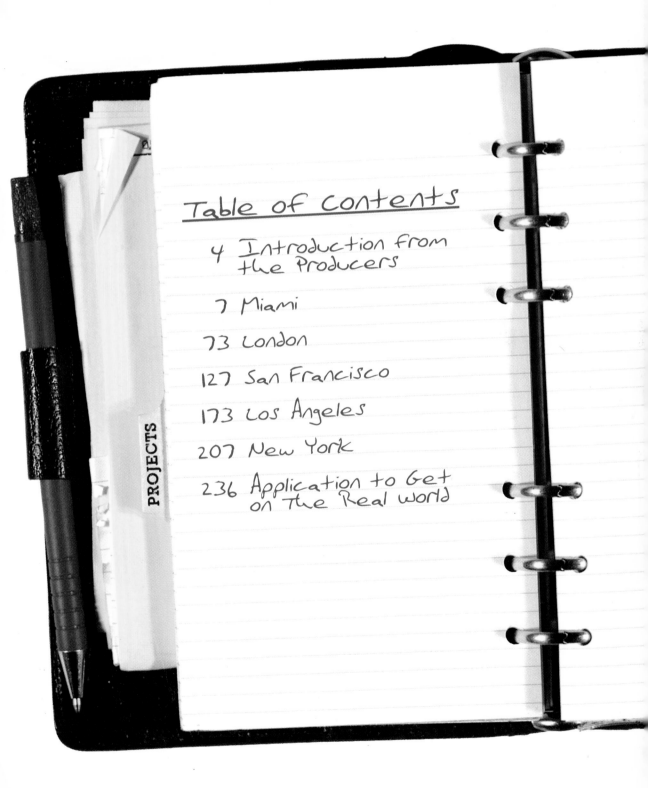

INTRODUCTION TO THE REAL WORLD DIARIES

BY MARY-ELLIS BUNIM AND JON MURRAY

WITHIN THE RECESSES OF A LARGE PRE-WAR MASONRY BUILDING IN HOLLYWOOD SIT THOUSANDS OF TAPES AND TRANSCRIPTS FROM THE FIRST FIVE SEASONS OF THE REAL WORLD. ONE BOX IS LABELED "JULIE — ALABAMA," ANOTHER "DAVID/TAMI FIGHT," STILL ANOTHER, "NEIL'S TONGUE." EACH ONE OF THESE LABELS REPRESENTS ALL THAT WAS RECORDED ON THAT SUBJECT. BUT AS EACH REAL WORLD EPISODE IS ONLY A HALF HOUR, THERE REMAINS MUCH THAT THE AUDIENCE HASN'T SEEN OR HEARD.

IN THE PAGES THAT FOLLOW, OUR CAST SHARES DETAIL AND INSIGHT INTO THE STORIES THAT MADE UP OUR FIRST HUNDRED EPISODES AND REVEALS SOME STORIES THAT HAVEN'T BEEN TOLD UNTIL NOW.

READING OVER SOME OF THE EARLY TRANSCRIPTS, IT SEEMS LIKE ONLY YESTERDAY THAT WE SET UP THE FIRST REAL WORLD LOFT AT BROADWAY AND PRINCE IN NEW YORK'S SOHO DISTRICT. EVERYONE WHO HEARD THE IDEA HAD STRONG OPINIONS ABOUT WHAT WE WERE PLANNING TO DO: FIND SEVEN YOUNG ADULTS FROM DIVERSE BACKGROUNDS, MOVE THEM INTO A FANTASY LOFT, FILM THEIR EVERY WAKING MOMENT, AND CUT THE RESULTS INTO THIRTEEN WEEKLY EPISODES OF A "REALITY SOAP OPERA" FOR MTV. THOUGH CONVENTIONAL WISDOM WAS THAT WE WOULD FAIL, INDUSTRY INSIDERS WERE ROOTING THAT THIS BOLD EXPERIMENT WOULD CREATE A NEW FORM. WE HOPED THAT IT WOULD, AT THE VERY LEAST, GET SOME POSITIVE PRESS, AND OURSELVES SOME MORE WORK.

AS NO ONE HAD YET HEARD OF THE REAL WORLD IN 1991, WE HAD A DIFFICULT TIME FINDING THE FIRST CAST. WE STARTED IN NEW YORK, FLIERING LAUNDROMATS, RECORD STORES, CLUBS AND SCHOOLS. WE PUT AN AD ON THE BACK OF THE VILLAGE VOICE. THE CASTING ASSISTANT ROLLERBLADED DOWN MAJOR BOULEVARDS PUTTING NOTICES ON

HYDRANTS AND PULLING PEOPLE OFF THE STREET. THE RESPONSE WAS SMALL, ONLY A THOUSAND VERSUS THE TEN OR SO THOUSAND THAT YEARLY RESPOND NOW. WE USED THE SAME CRITERIA FOR CASTING THE FIRST SEASON THAT WE DO NOW: DIVERSITY, INTELLIGENCE, HUMOR, VERBAL ABILITY, WILLINGNESS TO SHARE THEMSELVES, CHARISMA, AND A DESIRE TO GROW THROUGH THE EXPERIENCE.

WE ALSO WANTED A "FISH-OUT-OF-WATER," SOMEONE WHO WOULD BE NEW TO THE CITY AND THROUGH WHOSE EYES WE COULD INTRODUCE THE SERIES. WE HIT GOLD IN BIRMINGHAM, ALABAMA. SHE WAS FRESH, INTELLIGENT, AND HAD A GREAT SENSE OF HUMOR. HER NAME WAS JULIE, AND ALTHOUGH SHE DIDN'T KNOW IT, SHE WAS OUR CHOICE FROM THE MOMENT WE MET HER.

THE FIRST SEASON WAS A ROLLER COASTER RIDE FOR BOTH CAST AND CREW. NONE OF US HAD EVER DONE THIS BEFORE. IT'S EXHAUSTING TO HAVE EVERY WORD AND ACTION SCRUTINIZED. AND IT'S EXHAUSTING TO KEEP UP WITH SEVEN 18- TO 25-YEAR-OLDS, ESPECIALLY WHEN YOU'RE CARRYING THIRTY POUNDS OF TELEVISION EQUIPMENT. BY THE TIME JULIE AND KEVIN HAD THEIR BIG FIGHT A WEEK BEFORE MOVE-OUT DAY, ALL OF US, CAST AND CREW, WERE COUNTING THE DAYS TILL "THE EXPERIMENT" WOULD BE OVER. WHEN THE EXPERIMENT TURNED OUT TO BE A BIG HIT, WE WERE FACED WITH DOING IT ALL OVER AGAIN IN LOS ANGELES, SAN FRANCISCO, LONDON, AND MIAMI.

TO TELL OUR STORY IN THE MOST CINEMATIC WAY WE CHOSE TO HAVE THE CAST NARRATE THEIR OWN LIVES. IN WEEKLY INTERVIEWS, INITIALLY CONDUCTED BY US AND LATER BY GEORGE VERSCHOOR AND THOMAS KLEIN, WE PROBED FOR EVERY DETAIL OF WHAT HAPPENED TO THE CAST DURING THE PRECEDING WEEK. WE ASKED THE CAST TO TALK INTO THE CAMERA, IN COMPLETE SENTENCES, AND WHEN POSSIBLE, IN THE PRESENT TENSE. WE WANTED IT TO APPEAR AS THOUGH JULIE OR ERIC OR KEVIN WERE TALKING DIRECTLY TO YOU, THE VIEWER AT HOME. FOR A WHILE, ERIC ACTUALLY THOUGHT HE WAS. HE'D BEGIN HIS INTERVIEWS OFTEN BY SAYING, "SO YOU GUYS PROBABLY WANT TO KNOW WHAT HAPPENED THIS WEEK ...."

IN THE SECOND SEASON OF THE REAL WORLD WE ADDED THE "CONFESSIONAL." EACH WEEK CAST MEMBERS WERE TO GO INTO A SMALL, SOUNDPROOF ROOM AND TALK; THE SUBJECT WAS UP TO THEM. IT WAS INTIMATE AND COMPELLING. FOR MOST OF THE CAST IT WAS A CHANCE TO SOUND OFF, EITHER ABOUT THEIR ROOMMATES OR THE PRODUCTION. BUT SOMETIMES, IT WOULD PRODUCE INSPIRED LUNACY. IN LOS ANGELES, DAVID, HIS FACE COVERED WITH WHITE COLD CREAM, TALKED ABOUT BEING MISUNDERSTOOD BY OTHERS IN THE HOUSE. TAMI, JON, DOMINIC, AARON, BETH S., AND GLEN ATTEMPTED TO DO A "LAST-DAY-IN-THE-HOUSE" CONFESSIONAL TOGETHER IN ORDER TO FINALLY APPEAR LESS CONTENTIOUS BUT ENDED UP ARGUING AND STORMING OUT. IN SAN FRANCISCO, JUDD DONNED A NUN'S HABIT TO GIVE HIS CONFESSIONAL A LITTLE MORE WEIGHT; WEEKS LATER PUCK, JUDD AND RACHEL USED THE CONFESSIONAL TO COME DOWN AFTER A DRUNKEN NIGHT ON THE TOWN. IN THE LONDON CONFESSIONAL, JACINDA AND HER DOG LEGEND DANCED THE NIGHT AWAY TO THE SONG "SON OF A PREACHER MAN;" LATER, JACINDA RETURNED TO THE CONFESSIONAL WITH NEIL AND KAT TO SPECULATE ON WHICH ONE OF THEM SHOULD GIVE THE SEX-STARVED MIKE A "GOOD LAY." FINALLY IN MIAMI, FLORA AND MELISSA APPEARED AS "WOMEN OF THE NIGHT" AND CONFESSED THEIR WONDERMENT ABOUT WHY THEIR ROOMMATES HAD SUCH A PROBLEM WITH THEM. NONE OF THIS WAS EXACTLY WHAT WE HAD PLANNED FOR THE CONFESSIONAL, BUT ALL OF IT WAS CERTAINLY AMUSING.

THE STORY THAT YOU ARE ABOUT TO READ IS A COMBINATION OF THE CONFESSIONALS AND THE WEEKLY INTERVIEWS. THEY ADD A DEPTH AND PERSPECTIVE THAT IS NOT POSSIBLE TO ACHIEVE IN A MERE TWENTY-TWO MINUTES PER EPISODE. WE HOPE YOU ENJOY THEM AND THE STORIES THEY TELL.

This is the true story of thirty-eight strangers, picked to live in five houses and have their lives taped to find out what happens when people stop being polite and start getting real...

MANATEE ZONE
SLOW SPEED
MINIMUM WAKE

THE REAL WORLD

MIAMI

CYNTHIA

Cynthia: You have to be off the wall to even try to do something like this—you know, having people follow you around twenty-four hours a day, all in your business, in your everyday life. It's sort of like making a pot of goulash—you really don't know what it's going to taste like until you taste it, until you put it all together and mix it up and stuff.

DAN

— FLORA

Flora: I'm sure I'll get along with most of them, but I'm sure I won't get along with one or two; it always happens that way, and that's what I'm a little uncomfortable about.

PROJECTS

Dan: The best thing about this entire experience is that it's like a roller coaster, I guess. Because you're terrified and you're so scared of what's going to happen and you have absolutely no idea of what's going to happen to you from moment to moment, but you can't wait to see what's going to happen and what's around the next turn. I am so happy that I'm gonna have new friends, and I'm also scared that it's gonna be six complete jerks who are going to hate me.

Joe: I've never been so scared. And I'm so concerned about how people are going to be affected by my leaving New York. I'm trying to clean that up so that it's as smooth as possible in terms of work-related, friend-related, and family-related issues.

JOE

MELISSA

MIKE

Melissa: Everyone has an opinion as to how I should act or what I should say. People thirty-plus, all they tell me is, "The only Cuban person they've had on the show is Pedro, and he was gay and had AIDS, and what does that make us look like to the rest of the United States? You've got to show a nice, clean-cut, straight girl going to college." And then I have people my own age, saying "Oh, my God, I would hate to be in your shoes—Pedro Zamora was like the perfect person. He was honest, he was kind, he was clean, he was considerate...how the hell are you going to follow in his shoes?" And so right now I'm just, like, going crazy. I don't want to forget who I am in this whole mess.

Mike: Only thing that's going to worry me is the fact that I am kind of a crazy person. I tend to get under some people's skin, and I just don't want to get kicked out. Looking forward to maybe having a cute girl in the house, one that I at least get along with. And just looking forward to finding some ideal friends to hang out with and become really good friends with.

SARAH

FIRST
IMPRESSIONS

Sarah: I have no problem fitting in with other people, or their lifestyles. Once in a while I cut on them, 'cause I just think it's kind of daft to see people lying around on the couch, watching TV all day; I like to be active. So I might wind up cutting on some people, but I think I'm just going to try to behave myself and give everybody a chance. I just hope they like toys, and candy, and skateboards, and jump ropes, and Pee-wee Herman.

Dan: Sarah is very strange. But I really like it. She claims she's a superhero who can shoot ice cubes out of her butt. I mean, how could you not like that? When I'm standing next to Sarah I feel like I'm Mister Rogers because I'm so plain compared with her.

Flora: Sarah's quiet, she's very sweet, a little messy, a little strange. And she has all these toys. She's definitely a weird girl, but I love her; she's great. I didn't think I was going to at first, but she is just great. Anything I ask, she does, she gives. I mean, she's a very giving person.

Mike: Sarah looks like the poster child for Wendy's hamburgers. I thought she was somebody's daughter at first. Found out she had about three suitcases full of toys...things to play with, candy. I figured she was probably the youngest of the group, maybe seventeen, eighteen years old. Turns out she's the oldest. Whatever.

Joe: The moment I got into the house, we jumped in the pool together with our clothes on, and that was awesome. I was like, "Oh, I got a little mate in the house." She's wild. She's absolutely wild, but at the same time, she's cool. She's got multiple personalities, that one.

100% **Page 1** ▶

Melissa: Sarah's so open to everything. That's why I love that girl so much. I mean, she asked me about my city. And I was telling her how I love Miami, how I think it's the best city, because it's like the whole world, it's like the greatest melting pot, and she was so into it. I mean, that chick's so fascinated, she's like, "I want to learn Spanish, I want to try your food and go to all these places."

Cynthia: Sarah's, like, really free-spirited. She's not like the average white girl at all. She's down-to-earth. Her friends pretty much match her, too. She has all types of friends. All colors, all different kinds. And they're all the same—cool, you know? She just reminds me of a grown child.

Cynthia: Dan, he's just crazy. He's extremely hyper, okay? Extremely hyper. He's full of energy all the time.

Flora: Dan, very outspoken, he'll tell you exactly what's on his mind. He's funny, he's hilarious, I love him, he's great.

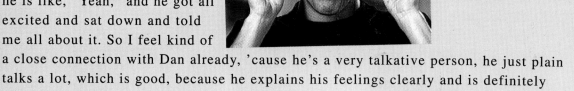

Joe: Dan asked me if I had a girlfriend, and I told him a little something about Nic, and I said, "Hey, what about you?" And he was like, "Nope," and I knew that he was a man-on-man type of guy. So I said, "You got a man?" And he is like, "Yeah," and he got all excited and sat down and told me all about it. So I feel kind of a close connection with Dan already, 'cause he's a very talkative person, he just plain talks a lot, which is good, because he explains his feelings clearly and is definitely a trusting and open guy.

MEMORANDUM

DATE: RE:
TO:

Mike: Dan is going to be very, very different. I see a little friendship happening with Dan, and I'm not sure exactly what's going to come of it as far as becoming closer or, you know, maybe not liking each other that well in the future.

Sarah: I know lots of clowns like Dan, you know, and those are the kinds of guys you just want to push into the ocean.

12

Cynthia: Melissa, she's really...she's more prissy than all of us. From my understanding, she doesn't pay any bills, she has no concept of paying bills or paying rent or car notes or anything like that. She's a student, she doesn't work, and she has money. So that makes her a little different from the rest of us.

Dan: With Melissa I'm going to have a lot of conflict. because I think that she's really controlling. and I think she's used to getting her own way.

Flora: Melissa. I usually go by first impressions. And my first impression of her: She's a stuck-up bitch. Because we were sitting there talking about all the bills we have to pay and how we pay for rent and about how all of us struggle to pay for our school. And she goes, "You pay for rent? Oh, my God, I never heard of paying for car payments like that." And everybody just looked at her like, "Girl, you gotta come down to reality. Not all of us are as fortunate as you."

Sarah: Melissa's awesome. She likes to club, and I just thought that was a bonus right there. This girl never gets tired. And that's exactly the type of person I need to hang out with: somebody who will stay out until six in the morning and then stay up for another couple hours just to talk and talk about what happened that night. I just really like her energy.

MIKE: JOE IS TOTALLY DOWN-TO-EARTH. IF I CAN BECOME REALLY GOOD FRIENDS WITH ANYBODY HERE, AND HANG OUT, IT'S GOING TO BE JOE. HE'S JUST ALWAYS SMILING, ALWAYS HAS POSITIVE THINGS TO SAY. TRIES TO COOK...HMMM, DOES OKAY. BUT HE'S JUST GOT A GREAT ATTITUDE, AND I THINK THINGS WILL WORK OUT WITH US.

Cynthia: I liked Joe right off the bat; Joe was cool. I love the accent—I copy him all the time. He's such a sweetheart; he's smart, he has a lot of sense, he's really low-key, he doesn't really bother anyone, he is sort of the hermit of the group.

Dan: Joe is so cute. He is the cutest little guy. I heard the accent, I saw the goofy grin, and, I just thought, He's such a great guy. I mean, he's so sweet and so funny. He's a little timid. His girlfriend is the luckiest girl in the world.

Flora: When I first saw Joe, I knew right away that he's a nerdy kind of guy, and when he told me he's a computer dude...I definitely knew that I was right. But when I think of a New York person, I think of, you know, hip-hop pants, those kinds of New York people. When I saw Joe, he totally didn't strike me like a New York person,; he strikes me more like a Long Island type of person. He has potential to be cool. But I don't know, he might need a lot of help.

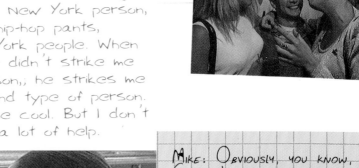

MIKE: OBVIOUSLY, YOU KNOW, CYNTHIA'S GOT HER LITTLE ATTITUDE ABOUT EVERYTHING— THAT'S PRETTY POSITIVE. I CAN JUST TELL RIGHT NOW, THAT'S ONE GIRL I'M NOT GOING TO PISS OFF, 'CAUSE I DON'T WANT TO DEAL WITH THOSE FINGERNAILS AT ALL.

Dan: Cynthia is absolutely hysterical. She is totally from the other side of the tracks, different from anything that I have ever, ever seen in my entire life.

Flora: Cynthia is a riot. She's a petite little thing. She's cute. She's lots of fun, but she's a tough cookie. You know, you can't step on her, because she'll tell you off without blinking.

Joe: She's really open about sex and I really appreciate that. She's an extreme challenge, the kind of woman I would definitely go for.

100%   Page 1   ▶

Sarah: Cynthia seems real cool. She called me Willy Wonka, because I'm obsessed with candy and toys, and I took that as a compliment.

Flora: Michael, he is also a sweetheart. He's very kind, he's nice, he's cute. He's adorable, like, "Oh, boy." I get along with him.

Joe: I thought Mike was going to be a beer-drinking, frat-party-going, babe-banging guy.

Melissa: I really like Mike, 'cause he really likes my mom. He thinks she's really pretty and really nice, and he was rapping with her. But Mike needs to get laid. That guy's a walking hormone.

Cynthia: Mike's funny. He's an impressionist. He can do Wanda, he can do Fire Marshal Bill, he can do all kinds of characters. He does a really good impersonation of a black chick, too. It's not like he's making fun, but it's just...he has a lot of the mannerisms of some of the black chicks that I know, so that's why it's really funny to me.

Dan: Oh. I thought Mike was hot when I first walked in. He's this big, simple, happy, funny guy. He's a guy. You look up guy in the dictionary and there's this big picture of Mike with a can of beer in his hand, grinning.

Sarah: Mike seems somewhat active, and he claims he dances, but when I asked him to bust a move, he declined. I just thought that was kind of bogus. He jumped on my bed this morning, trying to be funny, but he doesn't have a very good sense of humor. He likes to be superdramatic about stupid stuff, and I think it's really chapped.

Cynthia: I really like Flora, but when I first met her, I felt like this is the person that I am not going to get along with—me and her is going to be funking in this house. Someday, and someday soon, too.

Joe: Flora's attractive. She's definitely a partier. She's definitely a strong woman. She didn't even want me to carry her bags. That's difficult for me. I mean, she'd rather haul the bags and wobble all over the place while I'm standing there with a whole free hand to take her bag.

Sarah: There are a lot of things about Flora that normally would bother most people. You know, like her being loud and obnoxious and pushy and whiny. But it's just, like, hilarious; I mean, it's just funny to watch her. She's a sitcom.

Melissa: I have to be careful around Flora, because if you get on her bad side, you're really, really on her bad side. So with her I'm just, like, very patient and very quiet.

NOTES

Mike: Flora just says whatever the hell's on her mind. And she's the kind of girl who's going to walk around in her panties and not really give a damn what anybody else thinks. Flora is Flora. That's that.

Dan: Flora's very nice. A little hyperactive. But she is kind of cool.

FEBRUARY 11, 1996
(WEEK THREE)

Cynthia: I talked to my ex-boyfriend last night, and he was really surprised to know that I was in Florida. Well, he was more surprised that I would leave California without telling him anything. I told him how I was male-bashing him and how I did not have one good thing to say about him, except that I still cared about him, and that's true.

Joe: Nicole—Nic—is the woman I'm currently spending most of my time with. That's going to be one hell of an issue, man. Should we stay together, are we going to stay together, is the relationship strong enough? This is the strongest I've gotten with a woman, the closest I've gotten in the shortest period of time.

Flora: My boyfriend, Mitchell, definitely trusts me more than I trust him. On a scale of one to ten, he probably trusts me a four, or four and a half. On a scale of one to ten, I trust him one. Maybe one and a half.

Melissa: It's just unfortunate that now is not the time for me to be with Cesar—or anyone else, for that matter. I just wish that I had met him about five years from now. It would have been perfect, but right now I'm only twenty-two, and there is so much that I wanna do. But we never really talk about that. We just continue trying to make it work. I just wish that I could really let him go. And every day, I tell myself I'm gonna do it, I'm gonna do it, but I have a feeling I won't. I guess he's kind of like my security blanket.

Dan: Arnie's my pal. Arnie's my friend. Arnie is a criminal defense attorney for a local law firm whom I met at Bar None when we all went there to hang out. He is a very mellow, quiet, well-grounded individual and that is such an incredible rarity in this entire city that I just had to snatch him up as quickly as I could find him, 'cause he's great. He's really—he's a really great guy. I mean his name's Arnie. How can you not like a guy named Arnie? He's just a really great guy. I just—he's a lot of fun to be with. He's just—he's very intelligent, you know. He's just really fun to talk to, very interesting and he's great.

MIKE: I WENT TO SEE MY EX-GIRLFRIEND, HEATHER. PROBABLY THE SINGLE MOST HEART-WRENCHING THING I'VE EVER DONE IN MY ENTIRE LIFE, KNOWING THAT THIS WAS JUST A REALITY CHECK, THAT WE ARE OVER. AS MUCH AS IT HURT, IT REALLY DID ME SOME GOOD.

Sarah: I'm in love with Matt Dillon. I mean, everybody thinks he's kinda booted, 'cause he was in The Outsiders like ten years ago; and he's not really what people would consider the hot catch, but I still like him. I've been faithful for about ten years now. And then when I saw him in Drugstore Cowboy, I was convinced. He's the one for me. I haven't met him though, so he may turn out to be real low, but as of right now I think he's pretty cool.

MIKE: FLORA DECIDED SHE WAS GOING OUT ON THE YACHT WITH HER NEW BOYFRIEND AND HIS FRIEND. IT WAS KIND OF AMUSING, BECAUSE THE BOAT CONKED OUT ON THEM AND THEY ENDED UP DRIFTING FOR A WHILE. AND WHAT CAN YOU DO BUT LAUGH? SHE MADE AN IDIOT OUT OF HERSELF, AND SHE NEEDS TO LEARN TO KEEP HER MOUTH SHUT WHEN SHE DOESN'T KNOW WHAT'S GOING TO HAPPEN.

Melissa: The main thing of this week has been Flora and the whole Louis situation, his money, his status—if I have to hear one more time how rich this man is, I think I'm gonna puke.

Joe: It's all about image to her. She had Louis come over on his boat, telling everybody, "Hey, Louis is coming over on the yacht." And she got really depressed when indeed the yacht was a small boat.

Flora: Louis asked me if I wanted to go for a little ride. So we went out, but the engine of the boat got flooded and we couldn't get it started and everybody was laughing and making funny jokes. I was ready to jump overboard and swim back to shore.

Personally, I don't care that it was just a small tub. I definitely would prefer a larger, nicer...that kind of thing, but hey, it doesn't mean he can't afford to buy one later. Whatever. I don't even have that kind of a boat, and I'm not really materialistic. I come off as being so, but it's all funny to me. It's a joke. Everybody likes it, so I keep going.

THE ROAD RULES INVASION

Cynthia: We had a very interesting encounter with the Road Rules people. Of course, we didn't figure this out until much, much later, but they came in and took the eight ball from our pool table, and I'm kind of pissed off about it, because I don't like to be made a fool of. But Mike and Dan were the real fools, because I was the only one asking questions—I felt very uneasy about the situation.

You see, they all came into the house with brand new overalls on, claiming that they were the maintenance crew, and I mean, they went as far as having buckets, mops, dusters, all kinds of bulls**t. At first it was okay, because it was only one of them. But I went outside to show him the pool area and the Jacuzzi area, and by the time I came back in, it seemed like there were about eight people in the house, all over the entire house. I mean, they were all over the place, and that's when

Maybe about five days later, after they had come and gone, we were told that they were the <u>Road Rules</u> people, which kind of pissed me off because I had called and I asked our contact, Billy, about it and he claimed that he didn't send them over and they didn't know anything about it, so I guess the joke was on us. But Mike came up with a very interesting retaliation plan, which would be to find out where the <u>Road Rules</u> is and flatten all of their tires, including their spare tires, and leave a note on the window that flat tires are a bitch in the real world. It was a pretty good idea, but I doubt they'd have let us do it.

I got a little bit suspicious. You would think that the men of the house would have said something. Being that I only weigh like a hundred and three pounds and I'm only five-two, you'd think that the guys would try to take over and protect. No, not our guys. I was the one to ask questions.

But by that time they had already taken the eight ball, which I hadn't noticed until, like, much later. Actually, I didn't notice; Mike did.

I'm kind of mad at this. I'm not the type of person who really knows how to take a joke, but I guess that's just my own problem. I'll get over it eventually, but I didn't like the idea of being a part of someone else's gag. I just don't like it, period.

PRODUCERS' NOTE:

AS THE CAST OF **THE REAL WORLD, MIAMI** YOU HAVE BEEN GIVEN A UNIQUE OPPORTUNITY—TO FORM A BUSINESS. EACH CAST MEMBER WILL BE A SHAREHOLDER OF THE COMPANY. A BUSINESS ADVISOR WILL BE APPOINTED TO HELP WITH LOGISTICAL DECISIONS, BUT OTHER THAN THAT IT'S UP TO YOU, THE **MIAMI** CAST, TO FIGURE OUT HOW TO MAKE A SUCCESS STORY OUT OF A $50,000 DONATION FROM **THE REAL WORLD**. THERE AREN'T TOO MANY RULES, EXCEPT THAT CASH EXPENDITURES WILL BE CHECKED BY AN APPOINTED ADVISOR, THE TYPE OF BUSINESS CHOSEN MUST BE ON THE UP-AND-UP (OF COURSE), AND IF A SOLID BUSINESS PLAN IS NOT DEVELOPED, AND THE BUSINESS INCORPORATED, WITHIN TWELVE WEEKS, THAT'S JUST TOO BAD, TIME'S UP. IF ALL GOES WELL, THOUGH, IT'S UP TO YOU TO TAKE THE BUSINESS TO THE FUTURE. IT'S ALL YOURS.

Document1

Joe: The clock is ticking, and no one wants to address that issue, as it is a very sensitive issue to all. Whoever mentions it is basically looked down upon by the group. For me to bring a reality check to the group, though, I feel like they're gonna think I'm Mr. Business-Educated Snob Man who thinks he knows all. Maybe they think that, but hey, if they want a business to happen, we oughta get crackin'. If I'm gonna be the one to crack the whip and say, "Hey, let's roll," I'm gonna do that.

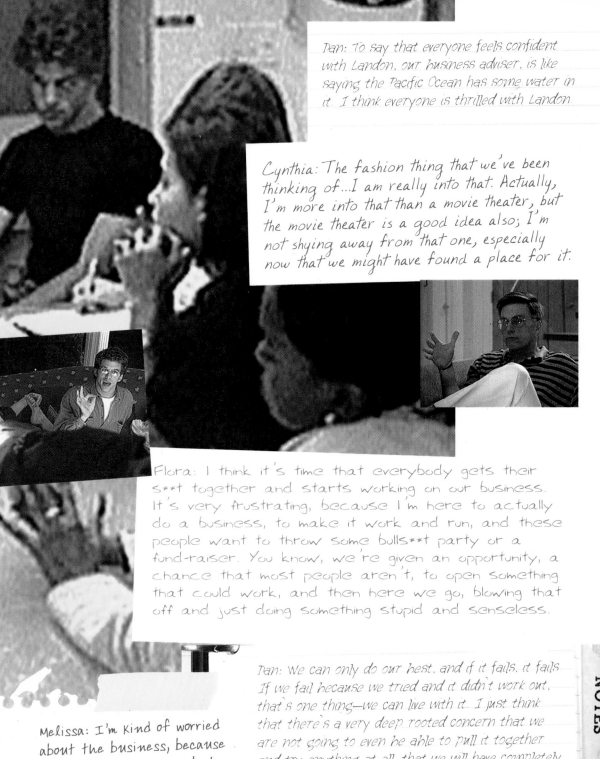

Dan: To say that everyone feels confident with Landon, our business adviser, is like saying the Pacific Ocean has some water in it. I think everyone is thrilled with Landon.

Cynthia: The fashion thing that we've been thinking of...I am really into that. Actually, I'm more into that than a movie theater, but the movie theater is a good idea also; I'm not shying away from that one, especially now that we might have found a place for it.

Flora: I think it's time that everybody gets their s**t together and starts working on our business. It's very frustrating, because I'm here to actually do a business, to make it work and run, and these people want to throw some bulls**t party or a fund-raiser. You know, we're given an opportunity, a chance that most people aren't, to open something that could work, and then here we go, blowing that off and just doing something stupid and senseless.

Melissa: I'm kind of worried about the business, because I don't think anyone but Joe is taking it seriously.

Dan: We can only do our best, and if it fails, it fails. If we fail because we tried and it didn't work out, that's one thing—we can live with it. I just think that there's a very deep rooted concern that we are not going to even be able to pull it together and try anything at all, that we will have completely lost that opportunity and will be able to do nothing but sit there and think, What if, what if, what if.

R
NOTES
ST
UV
WX
YZ

Sarah: This is really confidential. I've been meaning to tell you guys this for some time. I have two identities. I am Sarah the comic book editor; but with the comic books go superheroes. And among superheroes there are superwomen. And I am one of those. I am Snow Leopard. And this is a very rare moment for me, because I have never, ever, ever been taped or filmed as Snow Leopard. I'm in a fraternity of superheroes, and if anyone should find out about this, I will be kicked out of the galaxy. This means a lot to me.

But anyway, you're probably wondering what I can do. Well, my gas is lethal. I can shoot ice cubes out of my ass. I can freeze the ocean with a touch of my finger. And I can get any guy I want. Anywhere, anytime. When I don't live in La Jolla, I live in the Milky Way.

It all happened when I drove out to California from Illinois. I was in my car, driving through the Rockies, and I was going about a hundred miles an hour. And I drove into an avalanche. Actually, the avalanche leaped over the Continental Divide and more or less landed on me. The snow consumed me. I was frozen for about two weeks straight, until a couple of hicks came over and chopped me out of it. I found myself wrapped in leopard, and my hair was frozen white. The mask is actually burned on my face and my hair. I can't take it off without one of my assistants.

So I'd appreciate it if you'd keep my superhero identity mum, not say anything about it. Seriously. Just don't tell anybody that I am Snow Leopard.

FEBRUARY 25, 1996 (WEEK FIVE)

Sarah: Cynthia is a supersensual girl, and any guy would have interest in her. And Joe may be one of 'em.

Cynthia: The first time I discovered that Joe was very comfortable with nudity was when we were all in the hot tub together and Joe said that he was "hot as balls" and he was gonna take his shorts off. I automatically assumed that he must have a jock or some swim trunks on under the shorts, but he didn't.

And then we turned the bubbles off in the hot tub—and you know, when you turn the bubbles off you can see directly through the water—and we saw what he had going on down there. At least I know I did, 'cause I was looking.

We were all trying to find out what Nic saw in Joe. I mean, we know he has a brain, he has a personality, he's a good-looking guy and all, but what exactly was it about him that a six-foot-one blonde model chick would want with Joe? I kind of know now, and it was to my surprise, actually. He's got a little something going on down there.

Joe: Wow, did I enjoy hanging in the Jacuzzi naked. And Cynthia trying to get her foot up my butt. I don't appreciate the turning off of the bubbles, but hey, whatever. Everybody's trying to take my pants away, and all that stuff. That was an unnecessary part of the whole production; I just wanted to be naked.

Dan: I'm sorry, but I'm going to come out with it. I've always been very attracted to Joe. He's such a sexy little guy, this little goofy Italian Guidoesque thing from Brooklyn. That's why I like Arnie. Physically, Arnie reminds me of Joe. But Arnie has a better name. Arnie. Arnie. Arnie. Arnie. Arnie.

Mike: Joe is a little showboat. He decided he wanted to take off his shorts, for what reason I have no idea. I know when I get in the Jacuzzi I like to be naked, but I don't do it in broad daylight when there's six other people sitting around. When Joe took off his shorts, I decided to turn off the bubbles and let the girls get a peek at what Joe had to offer, and Cynthia started putting her foot down there and people were trying to grab at him and it was a weird scene. It was one big wanna-be orgy. Cynthia loved the fact that Joe took off his shorts. I think there's a little jungle fever going on there maybe. She definitely wanted to see what he had to offer, so she was putting her foot down there and checking it out. I was definitely not gonna stick my foot down there.

baaa-ionno: _interj._ the answer you give when you don't know the answer.

bar: _adj._ ugly, as in, "He needs a bar of soap."

bolt: _v._ to leave hastily or with urgency, to exit

booted: _adj._ something material which is lacking (also rigged, low, chapped, chipped, chaffed, rigortoid, cheap, legged).

box: _n._ car

C, C-wee: _n._ someone who says something stupid

chapped: _adj._ tired, old, no longer full of the vital essence of coolness

There's only a few people who actually use these terms, and they all live in Kenosha, Wisconsin.

All right. Basically, _bow_ is a sound that a guitar makes. When something bad happens to you, you wind up getting the strings, or the _ba-wow_, or the _bow_, and those are just different sounds that the guitar makes.

Let's say, for example, that this chick's walking by the pool and she slips on a banana peel. She gets a six; she gets the six strings.

Now say this chick is walking by the pool and she slips on a banana peel and her top falls off; then she gets a twelve, a little bit more serious than the six.

And now let's say this chick is, like, walking by the pool, she slips on a banana peel, her top falls off, and it's all in front of Brad Pitt. Then she is actually getting the five-neck Rick Neilsen. Rick Neilsen's a guitarist in Cheap Trick, and he has a guitar with five necks, so it's just like the major _ba-wow_ if that happens to you. So that's the most severe.

Ba-wow. Let's say, for example, that somebody's carrying a bunch of flyers, and you take their hand and you, like, wiggle it and the flyers, like, go all over the place: "_Ba-wow_." Instead of saying, "Ha-ha," and letting them catch on and know you're making fun of them, you just say, _Ba-wow_, 'cause nobody catches on and you can make fun of this person and they'll never, never even know what you're talking about. It's just like your own secret way of like making fun of them.

cookie: *n.* a cute boy

daft: *adj.* dumb, uncool

dork: *n.* male sex organ; geek, nerd, unhip person

duck: *n.* guy; a person typically in the background, as scenery

filth: *n.* best friend

fins: *n.* money (also scratches, bread)

fresh: *adj.* cool

__-good: *adj.* not good—fill in the blank with something you think is bad, such as <u>Aero-good</u> if you don't like the band Aerosmith.

gince: *v.* to freak unnecessarily

get the Jackson: *v.* to have something terrible happen to you

jizzy: *adj.* excited to a spastic degree, derived either from an elated state of orgasm, or by combining <u>jumpy</u> and <u>busy</u>, depending on your prudishness

jonesin': *adj.* filled with desire for something, a near-obsessive need

lid: *n.* a hat or cap

mama: *n.* a cute girl

melon: *n.* head, place to put your lid, as in, "Man, look at that guy's melon."

morphodite: *n.* an adult with childish qualities; for instance, a grown man who enjoys <u>Mighty Morphin' Power Rangers.</u>

munch: *v.* to wipe out, fall, eat dirt

pile: *n.* an unattractive person

'puter: *n.* computer

rad: *adj.* a heightened level of cool that noticeably stimulates the pleasure centers of the brain

ride: *n.* car

Satan's lap dog: *n.* someone who betrays you

smooth: *adj.* pleasing to the eye

spastic tundrum: *n.* a person who is "kinda loopy," characterized by flailing arms and other signs of lost motor control brought on by an excited state of mind.

tommin': *v.* lying, derived from a kid in Kenosha, WI, who fibbed a lot

useless pile of breathing flesh: *n.* someone you hate

Van Halen warehouse: *n.* something so bad that you don't even want to know.

wheel: *n.* pizza

wicked: *adj.* someone who doesn't have it all upstairs (also tormented)

27

MITCHELL

Flora: I talked to Mitchell. Me and him are still fighting 'cause I keep picking fights with him for no reason,. I'm just that way—I'm being a bitch, and I admit it. I am definitely being a bitch to him, which is not cool. I miss him.

I'm hanging out with Louis and having fun with him. He's an awesome, unbelievable person, and I thought I was using him at first for a job and stuff, but you know, right now I'm realizing that I'm really glad I know him, and I'm totally not using him now.

I'm having fun with him, and you know what? If he didn't have a dime, I wouldn't give a s**t at this particular moment, because I'm having lots of fun with him and he's just a great person and a great friend, and I know I can count on him.

Cynthia: That girl Flora has no respect for herself with the Mitchell situation. Everybody knows that she should leave him. She even has friends back in Boston who say she should leave him. He's messing with some of her friends...people that she calls her friends. You know, I don't understand how she could even give him the time of day. She's worth so much more than that, and she just doesn't even know it.

LOUIS

Flora: Mitchell is coming tomorrow. I don't know what's going to happen, how everything's going to turn out. I'm kind of freaking out about the whole situation. I don't know what to do. He's coming to bring my car and I'm kind of...I don't know. I kind of want him to come, and I kind of don't. I mean, I've been away from him for three weeks, and I think I'm a little bit beyond his stage right now. I've moved on, and he's still on the same level, so I don't know how this is going to turn out.

I mean I do love him, but I know I don't have a future with him, and it's kind of hard, because I was with him for five months. I mean, it's not very long for some people, but I really do love him, even though I f**k around and stuff like that. But whatever—what can I do, right?

Melissa: Flora and Mitchell have the most interesting relationship I have ever seen. Flora and Mitchell are meant to be together. To hear them fight is like music. It's like, back and forth and back and forth; I mean, there's rhythm to it. Listening to them fight, I feel like I'm at the opera sometimes. They're hilarious. They hang up on each other, they hate each other, they love each other, they fight, they make up. I think they're just exactly the same kind of people: They're both jealous, they're both possessive, they're both crazy. They come from the same school—two different backgrounds, but they went to the same school. It works for them.

Sarah: Flora and Mitchell are just a walking, talking disaster, man. Horrible relationship. I just think he's like a little remote control plane, you know? And she just flies him around. She's having fun just jerking his chain.

Flora: Mitchell just left the other day, and it went pretty well when he was here. But I have this bruise on my chin. Everybody thinks that Mitchell beat the s**t out of me, but no, the fact is that I fell. I fell stepping onto the jeep and scraped my elbow and hit my chin on the little step, going onto the jeep.

Sarah: Flora, she hit it when she tried climbing into the jeep. I mean, that happened to a kid I babysat before, so I know what it looks like; it looked pretty similar. I mean, it seems like maybe some people in the house might think she got slap-boxed or something by Mitchell, but I think she was just trying to climb into the jeep and hit it. I don't think she got punched or anything. But I do think Mitchell is C-wee, Mitchell is low.

Dan: As far as Flora's concerned, I really hope that she got those scratches tripping. I really hope that she was drunk and tripped trying to get into her jeep. I think it's a crock of s**t, though. I mean, she's a grown woman—it's her life, and she won't, there's absolutely no way in hell she's going to listen to anyone. Especially me. Oh, God, I'm like her nemesis. But the fact that she has scratches on her face and her elbow, coinciding with the time that Mitchell was here and was getting into fights with other people—it's awfully fishy.

March 10, 1996 (Week Seven)

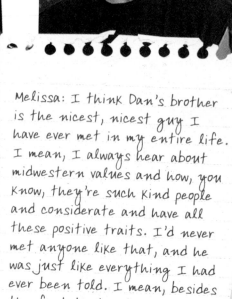

Dan: My brother's in town. He's the one who is much larger than me and makes Melissa swoon "Your brother is so f**king fine." That's what she said. You know, my brother, he's a good guy, he's fun; we're not very close, but when we're together we're brothers.

No matter how old I get, I will always thrive on driving my older brother crazy. I will be eighty years old, in a home, crank calling my brother. And hiding his dentures. And coating the bottom of his cane with Vaseline. And then he'll take his cane and whack me over the head and beat me up, and I'll just laugh. You never grow out of that.

Melissa: I think Dan's brother is the nicest, nicest guy I have ever met in my entire life. I mean, I always hear about midwestern values and how, you know, they're such kind people and considerate and have all these positive traits. I'd never met anyone like that, and he was just like everything I had ever been told. I mean, besides the fact that he's gorgeous, a very good-looking guy, with a great body, he's so nice, so incredibly...I liked him a lot.

NICOLE

Melissa: The big question in the house was, "Is Joe going to act differently once Nicole comes?" The answer, within the first two minutes they walked in through the door, was yes. He was not porno Joe, or nymphomaniac Joe at all. He was like, "Nicole, Nicci, I love my life," looking into her eyes longingly. I mean, it was ugh. It was, like, so sweet. Everyone was getting cavities from this, and we knew it, we knew that there was no way he could possibly be the same—and he's not at all.

Sarah: He's frontin' like he's some dedicated boyfriend, when he's not at all. And it sucks for Nic, because she's his girlfriend, and she should probably know this guy inside and out, but instead, six strangers are getting this whole other view of this guy, a whole other side to Joe that she'll never even know, 'cause she's not supposed to know... She's not allowed to know the secret Joe.

Melissa: Joe's girlfriend is very, very tall, and Joe's very, very short, so it just looks awkward. We have, like, all these theories as to why they are together, and we were just taking shots at the poor girl the whole entire night. She's easy to take shots at. She gives us lots of material.

makes her more ugly. If she was like a really nice, sweet, genuine person, you would be able to tolerate her, but you know, she complains, saying, " I was coming here to go on a vacation, and this vacation sucks, so I'm going home, and blah, blah, blah," and, " Joe didn't tell me that it was going to be all this." Give me a break, okay?

And then the way she dances. Oh, I don't even need to go there. You better be glad my hair's not all down my back and stuff. I mean, she did more movement with her hair than any woman I've ever seen in my whole life! And the fashion police need to come and arrest her, because you don't wear a damn bright-pink chiffon bra with yellow stripes when you can just see straight through the shirt. I mean, she's just like tacky as hell.

I feel really bad about this, but you know how I am. And Joe, I'm really sorry, but he could do much better than that.

Cynthia: The way Joe described her before she got there was, "Oh, I love my woman, I love my woman, she's gorgeous, she's tall." I thought it was going to be Claudia Schiffer or one of them Revlon chicks or something like that. But then she comes in, and she is ugly, just period. I'm really sorry, but Joe can do a lot better.

Plus, she complains, she's bossy, and she's obnoxious, just completely obnoxious. And you can tell that Joe spoils her, because she's just like, " Go do this, go do that, I want this, I want that." You know, you just want to climb the ladder and smack her. She just gets on my nerves. I mean, she complains way, way, way too much, and for her to look like that and act like that—it just does not match. It

Dan: Many moons ago I mentioned that Nicci was the luckiest girl in the world because she had Joe as a boyfriend. I stand by that so forcefully, not only because Joe is such a nice guy but because she is so damn lucky that he puts up with her crap on a daily basis and will deal with that. She has no idea how good she has it.

Joe: Nic is gorgeous. Nic is many, many men's dream. I mean, walk down the street with her and ten guys, you know, out of twelve, will make rude or nasty comments or will be passing her their phone numbers or will just be on top of her trying to touch her. It's so pathetic, but it's true. It's totally a reality, but it's something I have to deal with—and it's something she's got to deal with, and it just sucks for her. She doesn't want to go outside because of it, so we have gotten to know each other inside really well.

FLORA'S TOE

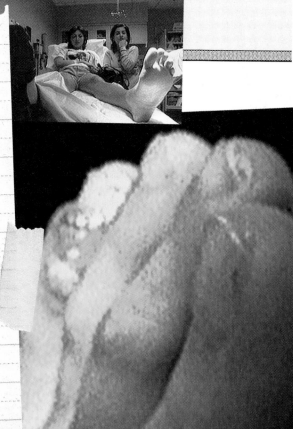

Melissa: Flora's toe was bit by something; we don't know what. She says maybe a spider, an ant—we don't know. But I came home one day and she had her leg up, and her toe was huge and red and disgusting, and there was pus coming out of it. It was just nasty. I told Flora I would take her to the hospital and the drama queen went into effect. The whole way there, she was showing it to anybody who wanted to see. In the hospital, she acted like it was a heart attack or like her arm had been cut off or something. It was just so much theatrics—she left on crutches, with her foot bandaged. She got bit by an ant, you know. She got bit by an ant, so she milked it.

Dan: I'm not belittling, and I'm not attempting to minimize the extent of Flora's injury in any way, shape, or form. But I will go to my grave believing that Flora was so excited about the prospect of all the wonderful things she could do with that injury. She's so funny. I like Flora. I don't know why I like Flora, but I like Flora.

Flora: If the same incident, an ant bite on my toe, had occurred when Mitchell was here, I could have called him in the middle of the night, and no matter what he was doing or where he was, he'd come here to take me to the hospital. Whereas Louis said he had to go to Home Depot, I could have been dead by the time he got back from Home Depot. It is very important to me that someone's there for you, at any time, especially when it's an emergency or something like that.

BUSINESS DECISIONS

Dan: Joe is just getting a little out of hand with this whole business thing. I find it really shocking that he has so much management experience because he's very un-diplomatic. I am somewhat bewildered by the fact that he would be in charge of manipulating the actions of other people. You don't have to be friendly, you don't have to be cute and charming, but you do have to be approachable, and you have to be able to discuss things on the same level. He just doesn't listen to people at all.

As far as the business, I guess we have an idea, and I'm not unhappy about the idea of making golf clothes. I really don't know what golf clothes are. They could be something entirely different than what I'm expecting. I may like them. For all I know, maybe I would wear them. But I like this idea. It's ready to go. We should just do it.

DAN VS MELISSA

Joe: The meeting with Landon and Flora was very good, basically, with Landon making it clear that Flora and I, who are the only ones who seem serious about staying down here in Florida, should really take the business by the reins and just go with it—get the accountant, get the attorney, and just do it. Whoever doesn't join the bandwagon, screw 'em. But it's hard for me to go with that philosophy.

You know, I like working with other people, and I want to learn to work with other people while I'm here. So doing this on my own, or with just one or two other people, is not something I was planning on. But hey, if that's the only the way the business is going to work, that's what we're gonna do.

`100%` | **Page 1** | ▶

Dan: The underlying issue that precipitated the explosion was Melissa's complete and utter disregard for the value of someone's personal space. That infuriates me to this day, and it always will. People keep going into their food cabinets, and discovering that their food is gone. We know who took it. We've brought it up a zillion times to Melissa, and she knows that it drives us crazy, yet she looks us straight in the face and says, "Well, I'm going to do it anyway."

I'm aghast, and at a loss about what to do. In the course of the discussion, she acknowledged that she understood why I'd be upset by that. She didn't say she would never do it again, but at least the acknowledgment of why something would upset me was a start. The really important issue at that point was that we both flew off the handle. We both admit that we shouldn't have done that. As strongly as I may believe in something, and as angry as I may be about something, I never have any desire to hurt somebody. I may have a lot of problems with what Melissa does, but I have no intention of ever being the catalyst for her momentary loss of self-control.

We both apologized, but I think she's going to do it again. And there's nothing I can say, because I certainly don't want a fight like this to happen again. I don't even want to talk to her anymore. But at least some good came out of the fact that we've both apologized and admitted that we really don't want to act like that toward each other.

Cynthia: Landon asked all of us if we wanted to go out and get some dinner. So all the roommates agreed to go. Sarah also had Hank and their other two friends down for the week, and so Sarah just asked all of us if it would be okay if her friends came. Everybody was like, "We don't care." But Melissa said, "Only if they can afford it, because it's very expensive," and that pissed Sarah off. It would have pissed me off, too, if she had said that about my friends. She was like, "What do you mean, 'If my friends can afford it'?"

So Sarah was like, "What does that have to do with anything? That doesn't have to do with my friends." And Melissa was like, "The last time we went out, you didn't have your tip and your tax, and we had to pay for this and that." She was just pretty much bein' a real bitch to Sarah. So Sarah was very pissed off. As far as Sarah's concerned, you can insult her, but don't insult her friends.

So once we had gotten to the Van Dyke, we were all going to sit at the same table. All of a sudden Sarah got up and said, "And where do you get off talking about my friends and stuff like that? Do they look like a bunch of scrubs to you?

They probably make more money than you do." Which in reality, they did—all of 'em have very good jobs. I mean, Melissa totally underestimated all three of 'em. She just assumed that because of the way they looked and the way they dressed, and because they were Sarah's friends, that they didn't have any money. So they had an argument. Melissa was totally wrong.

So Sarah got up and took her friends and sat at another table. We had dinner and everything, and then when we asked for the bill, the waitress came back and she said, "Oh, the bill has been taken care of by Hank and Tubacca," who is Sarah's other friend.

I looked at Melissa, and she just looked so stupid. I was like, "You oughta be feeling mighty stupid right now." And so as we were all about to get up and leave, Melissa walked over to Sarah and her friends, and she apologized to them. And when we left the restaurant, I was like, "I'm very proud of you, Melissa. That was very big of you."

Dan: I think a lot of Melissa's motivation was not necessarily that she didn't like Sarah's friends, but that she wanted to take a shot at Sarah. No buts about it: taking a shot at Sarah's friends was just a way for her to get at Sarah, and she did very well, I might add.

Melissa: I just said to Sarah, "If I remember correctly, you were the one that went to Hard Rock with us, ordered a hamburger with everything on it, threw out whatever money you had, and said, "I don't have tax or tip money." You didn't say, "I'm short, can anyone spot me?" Nothing. You ordered the full load, then said, "This is all I have—you guys gotta pay the rest.

I told Sarah, "I'm sorry if it came out wrong. Usually when we go out to a restaurant, I tell you guys if it's expensive, because we're usually on a budget." But she didn't want to hear it. And I didn't hang out with them the rest of the weekend, because I had to work. But I guess she accepted that apology. She was kind of cold with me for a few days, but Hank and Abe and Paul, they were cool, so it ended up being okay.

Joe: The fact that Hank picked up the check was just such a delight, like, you know, a "screw you" to Melissa.

STAYING REAL

Melissa: Landon had a talk with me about what qualities come to mind when I think of Cuban people. Everything he said completely made sense. He asked me, "How would your parents feel if they saw that you were just doing the minimum amount required to run a business? Do you want everyone who sees this TV show, people who maybe have never met a Cuban, to think that Cubans are just slackers?" When he started talking about my family and about the hardships that they suffered when they first got here, it just hit so close to home. From that moment on, not a day has passed that I haven't done something for the business.

Cynthia: I definitely feel closer to Melissa than to anyone else in the house. We are the minority in the house, and there seems to always be a tendency to bring a lot of negative things out about the minority. Stereotypes and things like that. You know, we're very afraid of that. And we're trying our best not to fall into any of those categories. I'm really not interested in becoming a black stereotype. It may bring ratings or whatever, but I am not interested in being a black stereotype or a damn fool or anything like that.

I try to be as real as I can, but there are limits. There are some things that I'm not gonna display on TV. Melissa feels the exact same way. She doesn't even feel like she can really be herself, because she's so self-conscious about her future. She wants to go into television, broadcast journalism and all that, and that's why she's so set on not going to the nude beach. She has a fear that we could be followed there and somehow, thirty years from now..... She doesn't want any kind of dirt on her, period.

Melissa: Sarah, Cynthia, Hank, Abe, Paul, myself, and Dan, we started playing a game of truth or dare on their last night here. You don't want to mess with Sarah's friends in truth or dare. They throw out some serious dares. I was playing it safe, truth every time, but Hank ended up running around the pool buck naked, singing the theme song to <u>Chariots of Fire</u> with an ALF doll between his legs. Abe ended up doing the backstroke naked in the pool. Sarah went out to Jon Secada's house in pink underwear, a black bra, and her Snow Leopard wig, and she rang the doorbell. It was definitely a crazy night.

Sarah: The dare was to get Jon Secada to come to the door and see me standing there in my Snow Leopard outfit.

They really freaked out, 'cause I jumped in the pool with clothes on—like that was a really big thing—and they didn't think I was going to do it. Sarah was high-fiving me, and I realized that the way to win Sarah over is to just do something nutty. She just loves it. She was like, "That's so cool. I have such respect for you."

I think they think I'm some nerd or something. They told me that I have definitely been watching myself since I've been here. My friends outside of the house would just be like, "Big deal."

Dan coming down in his red underwear was an image that will cause night- mares for many, many years. It was just weird. He came down in his red underwear, and he has these long legs and this skinny little torso, and he was just being very Dan— and it was horrific. Flora couldn't even bear to look.

APRIL 7, 1996 (WEEK ELEVEN)

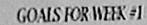

GOALS FOR WEEK #1

WEEK #1 Monday the 21st to Sunday the 29th
-corporation formed
-shareholder agreement draft
-Insurance proposals
-bank arrangements
-lease draft at attorneys

PURCHASING
Mark and Sarah are attaching this
match invoices to budget
John McGlynn, Cole

Cynthia: I didn't realize that we had up until, like, the twelfth week to get a business started. But now that I know this, I really kinda find it hard to believe that by next Friday there will be an up-and-running business.

Landon made me feel really good about a lot of things. Landon also opened up Melissa, so I know that I believe in whatever it is that he's saying. But as time winds down, it's really, really shaky.

I feel like we've done so much, but there's still so much more for us to do in order to get our business started. I mean, we've shucked and jived all the way up until the eleventh week, and now all of a sudden, we have only a week to get all that done. That's going to take a lot of commitment from a lot of people, and it's gonna take more than talk, which is what we've been doing most of this time—just talking, talking and talking.

Flora: I didn't know the deadline was in a week. A few of us did not know. And now, since I know the deadline is a week from this Friday, I know nothing is going to happen. Nobody's doing anything. I truly believe that if other people had this opportunity, this business would have been off the ground a long time ago.

Dan: I have to admit, I'm kinda disappointed in myself, about the whole thing, 'cause when I came into this situation twelve weeks ago, I was ready to do something. I proposed the fashion idea, and I really liked it because I thought it was something that could be grandiose and really wonderful and that could work out really well, make us a huge success. When that didn't work out, it nauseated me. How in the hell are seven people who have nothing in common supposed to come together and do a business?

39

Cynthia: No one except Joe sees the possibility of doing this in eight days. And except Sarah. Sarah's just a nut, period. She's like, "Oh, that's great, I do everything at the last minute anyway." A lot of people do things in the last minute, but start a whole business? I mean, hello? It seems like it's dissolving, like an Alka-Seltzer in water or something.

The reason why I get so agitated with the business is because, yes, it could potentially work, but to be totally honest, this is not something that I see myself doing. This is not a career move for me.

If it's huge, I would like to be a shareholder; that's fine, but I don't see myself trying to work there and bein' behind the counter.

Dan: We really would've liked our ideas to have worked, but I knew they weren't going to; I knew that weeks ago. We bit off way more than we could chew, and we had to eat a little humble pie, no pun intended. We had to come crawling back with our tails between our legs, going, "You know what? We can't do this, we cannot do it, we don't know anything about it, this was a bad idea." Plus we didn't do any research. We really should have looked into what we were getting ourselves into. It's never easy to take a step back, but a step back is a step forward.

Mike: As far as the shareholder agreement goes, basically we're almost there. We had a little back-and-forth with us and this guy Mark, who we brought in as an eighth partner, and I think we all came to agree on something. We're just waiting for Dan's final glimpse at it, and then, hopefully as of this week, it'll all be done, taken care of, kaput. Flora and Melissa were completely against Mark being an equal shareholder. Their reasons I really don't know. I think they were just there to contradict anything we had to say. When I first met Mark, back in February, I really didn't know him too well, and he came off as the kind of guy who was sorta lookin' to get some publicity. But now that I've gotten to know him, know his ideas, the way he works, I'm totally for him. I think he's a good asset to the company.

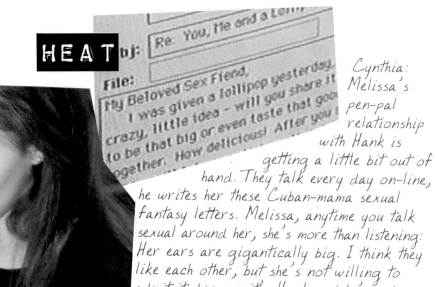

HEAT

Subj: Re: You, Me and a Lolli...

File:
My Beloved Sex Fiend,
I was given a lollipop yesterday,
crazy, little idea – will you share it
to be that big or even taste that goo
together. How delicious! After you s

Cynthia: Melissa's pen-pal relationship with Hank is getting a little bit out of hand. They talk every day on-line, he writes her these Cuban-mama sexual fantasy letters. Melissa, anytime you talk sexual around her, she's more than listening: Her ears are gigantically big. I think they like each other, but she's not willing to admit it, because it's Hank and he's gringo.

Mike: I'm twenty-four years old, Heather's twenty-eight. A lot of her friends and relatives are married, they even have kids, and I think at this time Heather needs to be part of that. She feels like she's aging fast and wants to have a family and is ready to settle down, whereas I'm twenty-four years old. I still have a lot to learn, a lot to do. It's not the commitment thing I'm actually scared of, it's the marriage and kids thing right now; I just couldn't give that to her.

Flora: I was unhappy with Mitchell at first, because I was here and he was there, and this and that. Louis and I were friends, we were very good friends, we hung out, we went out to dinner, everything was peachy-peachy. Then I found out some things about Louis that make me not wanna be his friend any more. Louis never had intentions of gettin' into a serious relationship with me; it was all use, use, and use. He used me, and I used him right back. There were a couple of times when

I would get into a fight with Mitchell and then I'd get into a fight with Louis, so I was by myself, and I was like, Man, what am I to do? But I always knew that Mitchell was gonna be there. I really, truly believe that he loves me and that he will be there. So no matter what screw-ups I do, I think he'll be around.

Mike: One of Dan's friends invited us to a party at his apartment the other night, and I had a few beers before we went. Once we got there, I started getting real comfortable, and somebody started breaking out shots of vodka. Well, after about seven or eight of them and about four beers, I got to the point where I said "I'm in Miami and I really don't give a rat's ass what happens from now on. I'm just going to enjoy myself."

So I just started hanging out. I figured since I don't have a girlfriend anymore, I was just going to enjoy that while I could and get what I could. Things sort of went on from there. We went to a couple clubs, and my mind kind of went blank after that.

All I remember is two girls asking me to go home, so I went home with them. The next thing I knew it was about eleven o'clock in the morning, and I told them I was going to check outside to see what the weather was like.

The one thing I do remember was that I put on a condom; it was a colored condom that Dan had given me, and it was a very dark color, and when I put it on and looked down, it sort of scared me, because I thought I had changed into an African-American. That's embarrassing.

Dan: I have no idea what to do about Arnie. Arnie and I are having some problems. We are in sort of different spots in our lives right now. Unfortunately, Arnie is still in the closet. That is a somewhat significant problem considering we have to constantly sneak around and lie to people. He's not at a point in his life where he can be in the presence of another man and be comfortable with it. It's still a big deal with him. I have no desire to put myself through that again; it's a torturous situation to be in. I totally respect him and I totally respect the choices that he's making, if that's the way he wants to lead his life. But I cannot be expected to walk around and lie when I'm trying as hard as I can to simply be who I am and not make a big deal out of it. As a result there are just certain things that are always going to keep Arnie and me apart and if he chooses to live this way, there's nothing I can do about it, but I also have to look out for myself. And it really, really sucks.

Sarah: Joe got this fax the other day from somebody at Fordham, somebody looking for his project, and I felt sorry for him, because Joe is working hard to get his masters. But I believe that he's not doing everything in his power to graduate. He's letting his girlfriend and his family consume him, and they're overwhelming anything that has to do with school. It's just like me and this comic book: I'm havin' a tough time, but I am contributing to Gen 13, I'm still editing the script, and I'm still writing the letters page. It's definitely not easy, but I'm finding time to do it. I'm sure Joe is not working as hard as he could toward his degree at Fordham this last semester, because man, that kid messes around just as much as we do.

Cynthia: Joe quit the business. He copped out on us at the very last minute, forty-eight hours before it was time for us to sign our names on the dotted line. All of a sudden, out of the blue, he just wanted to quit, because of personal reasons. I was highly, highly upset about him quitting the business, but I knew there was nothing I could do.

He said that he was not happy with the business and that we were not a challenge for him. But then he would say something like, "I still want to help." I'm like, "I don't want your help, I don't want your advice, I don't want s**t from you." I think I was more upset than anyone else in the house about him leaving the business. We all went through our own periods of time where we all wanted to leave, and who was the one to keep us in the business? It was Joe every time. He was like, "Don't give up, you can do it, it's gonna work, it's gonna be fine, it's gonna be all right, we're gonna kick ass," and all this other type of bulls**t, and then he turns and quits, and can't nobody talk him back into it.

I think that Joe would return to the business if we, as a group, asked him back, but we're not going to, because Joe walked out on us.

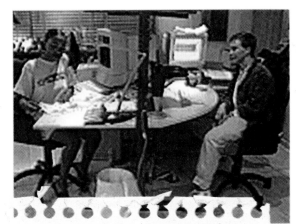

Melissa: Joe dropped out. He's a loser, and I'm very pissed off. He quit; when it was the absolute worst it could be, he pulled out and quit.

Dan: At the time that Joe quit—in case you don't know—I was really ready to pack my bags. I was just like, "Damn! He beat me to it." 'Cause I was really getting ready to say the same thing.

MIKE: DELICIOUS DELIVERIES IS AN UNUSUAL CONCEPT, SOMETHING I THINK CAN WORK WITH THE RIGHT MARKETING AND THE RIGHT PEOPLE. BUT WITH THE PEOPLE WE HAVE RIGHT NOW, I DON'T SEE IT AS ANY BIG FORTUNE 500 COMPANY. BUT THERE'S ALWAYS HOPE AND LUCK, SO I'LL TRY AND COUNT ON THAT.

PRODUCERS' NOTE: WHEN THE FASHION BUSINESS FELL THROUGH AND JOE DROPPED OUT OF THE LEADERSHIP POSITION, SARAH AND HER BOSS, MARK, STEPPED IN WITH A DESSERT-DELIVERING BUSINESS CALLED "DELICIOUS DELIVERIES."

Document 1

Joe: Well, this has certainly been a challenging week. I feel like I've entered a new stage in life as far as decision-making and confidence in myself as an individual. I am so happy right now: Number one, that I left the business, and everything that surrounded that; and number two, that I was able to communicate openly and honestly the reasons that I left. How they take it—for better or for worse—is up to them.

My mental capacities have left me incapable of concentrating or focusing on schoolwork and writing papers for some time; I've had so many other things that were priorities.

I've learned just in my time down here that it's impossible to please everyone, that you have to cut your losses short, that you've gotta do what you can, but not kill yourself, that you've gotta move ahead, not backward. You've gotta feel right about your decisions and do the morally and ethically correct thing.

I didn't come down here to run a business on my own. I came down here 'cause I had six other people who supposedly were going to be running the business with me. I didn't have the heart for this particular project. I feel like my heart was ripped out of me by my roommates.

APRIL 13, 1996 (WEEK THIRTEEN)

Leroy Bow Know Jackson

Cynthia: We have a new dog in the house: His name is Leroy Bow Know Jackson. Sarah brought him home from work one day, 'cause a homeless woman or someone gave her the dog, and so when I came home from work, everyone was like, "Oh, s**t, Cyn is home," 'cause they know how I feel about animals and kids in the house. It took me a while to be able to accept him, but now he's part of the family. He's really cute, and he's grown a lot. He s**ts and pisses all over the place, but that's the only thing that bothers me; other than that he's a great dog.

Sarah: Flora is completely miserable, because she needs a man in her life at all times to function, which is pathetic. So I got a dog. And I figured, out with Louis, in with Leroy, and now she's 100 percent healthier. I think she just needs a hobby, and I got her one. The dog does not talk back to her. The dog doesn't cheat on her, either.

SHIFTING TIDES

Sarah: I haven't talked to Cynthia for about a week now. The last time Cynthia and I talked was about two weeks ago, and she was actually asking me to turn back into a goofy sixteen-year-old again. I mean, that's the last time we talked—when she thought I was getting way too serious about the business—and she didn't think I was being that much fun anymore.

Cynthia: Melissa and I lately have not been as close as we used to be. She's been involved in her own thing and I've been involved in my own thing. She and Flora have had a chance to bond a little bit closer, which is cool.

Melissa: Cyn is still very distant. I tried everything. I cleaned up the whole bathroom, I washed all the towels, I cleaned up the room, I left everything spick-and-span. I continue to take her to work, and I took her to the airport at seven o'clock in the morning. She still doesn't say thank you. I'm going to get a thank you out of that girl if it kills me. If I have to clean her feet, I'm going to hear the words <u>thank</u> and <u>you</u> come out of that girl's mouth.

Maybe when the show comes out she'll realize all the things she was doing that were pissing me off. But basically it's just, like, her using my every-thing without asking. It started with her using my mascara. And now she's using my eyeliner, and my lipstick. And eating everybody's food. The girl has not bought food since January. And she's gaining weight, so she must be eating something. She comes in the house and she doesn't say hi to anybody, she just goes upstairs. It's like she's always pissed off, but she's not.

Flora: Melissa and I have been hanging out a lot. She's awesome. Me and her get along; we're just casual. She's not cheap—she'll give anything to a friend—and I'm the same way. To me, that's more important than absolutely anything. Cynthia's been really weird lately. She has a chip on her shoulder about something. She's always pouting. She's always in a bad mood.

She's been so retarded and moody since that chick LaShondra, her best friend, left. I don't know, maybe LaShondra said something to her, like, "You're black, you stand up for your rights," or something like that. When she first got here, she was acting like a lady. Everybody was like, "Man, you're such a lady." Now all of a sudden you got this chick who's snapping all the time. She was going to kick my dog, and I said "If you have a problem with my dog, you tell me and I'll take care of it."

And she went off in my face and all that. So this is exactly what I said—and it wasn't a prejudiced comment—I said, "I'm sick and tired of your black attitude." So she says, "Well, I hate your Russian attitude." I'm proud of my Russian attitude, so it seemed to me that she got offended about her black attitude, but I didn't get offended about my Russian attitude. So we just went back and forth: She called me a bitch and this and this and that, and I just stood there.

I'm like, "Listen, if I start calling you on things, you're going to get embarrassed, and you know I don't want to embarrass you, so don't push me." And she goes, "Go ahead." She was in my face, provoking me to call her on something. Everybody knows Cynthia is a mooch, and I didn't want to embarrass her, but the girl hasn't shopped since the first week; and she's been eating everybody's food, and after four months, it's gettin' a little expensive. So I was like, "Well, maybe you should start buying your own food and stop using people's stuff." She used up my whole bottle of perfume, which cost me eighty-five bucks. So I had to call her out on these things. And the only thing she had to say was to call me an _E_-something bitch, because she had absolutely no response. Everybody knew that this is what she does.

MIKE: FLORA AND MELISSA SEEM TO HAVE THIS LITTLE BONDING THING GOING ON RIGHT NOW, BUT I THINK IT'S DUE TO THE FACT THAT IF THERE'S ANY TWO PEOPLE IN THE HOUSE WHO ARE GOOD AT TALKING ABOUT OTHER PEOPLE AND BEING TWO-FACED, IT'S THOSE TWO.

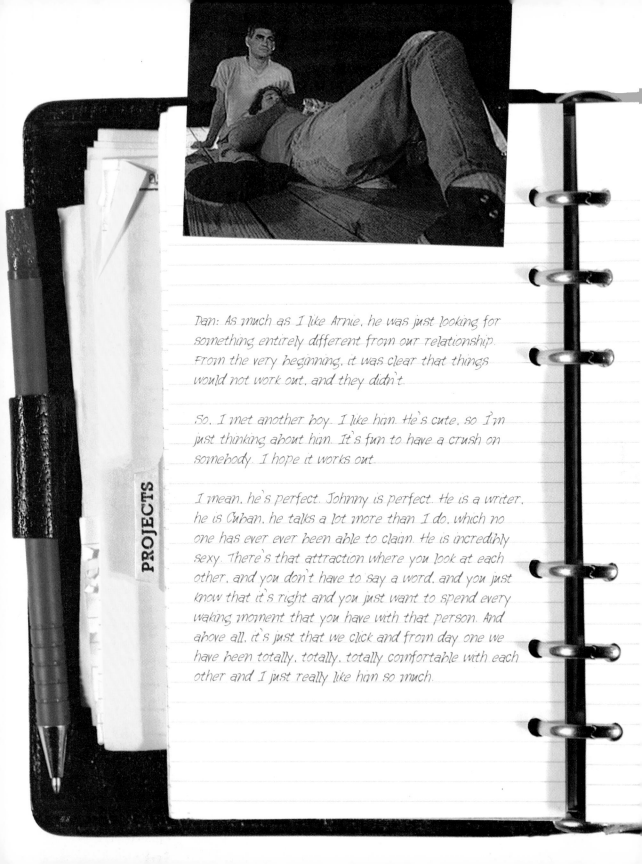

Dan: As much as I like Arnie, he was just looking for something entirely different from our relationship. From the very beginning, it was clear that things would not work out, and they didn't.

So, I met another boy. I like him. He's cute, so I'm just thinking about him. It's fun to have a crush on somebody. I hope it works out.

I mean, he's perfect. Johnny is perfect. He is a writer, he is Cuban, he talks a lot more than I do, which no one has ever ever been able to claim. He is incredibly sexy. There's that attraction where you look at each other, and you don't have to say a word, and you just know that it's right and you just want to spend every waking moment that you have with that person. And above all, it's just that we click and from day one we have been totally, totally, totally comfortable with each other and I just really like him so much.

PROJECTS

DATE: RE:

TO:

MIKE: MITCHELL'S COMING TO TOWN FOR LIKE A WEEK. AND JOE, DAN, SARAH, AND MYSELF ALL DECIDED THAT WE DON'T FEEL COMFORTABLE WITH MITCHELL IN THE HOUSE. THE GUY CALLS AT FIVE-THIRTY AND SIX AND SEVEN AND SEVEN-THIRTY EVERY MORNING, LEAVING FIVE MESSAGES ON THE ANSWERING MACHINE. WE'RE PRETTY MUCH JUST SICK OF HEARING HIS VOICE. JOE SAID THAT HE'S GONNA TALK TO FLORA AND JUST BE STRAIGHT UP WITH HER, TELL HER WE'VE ALL DECIDED WE DON'T WANT MITCHELL IN THE HOUSE.

FLORA HAS A HEART OF GOLD, AND I'VE LEARNED THAT, AND I'VE REALLY BECOME CLOSE TO HER, EVEN THOUGH SOMETIMES I CAN'T STAND HER. I HATE TO SEE HER HAVE TO GO THROUGH THIS PUNISHMENT. I DON'T THINK THAT HE DESERVES HER, AND I JUST REALLY WANT HER TO BE HAPPY, 'CAUSE I THINK THAT'S

SIGNED: HER GOAL FOR EVERYBODY ELSE—TO BE HAPPY.

SHAREHOLDERS

Joe: I had thought about how I could somehow still be a part of the business, help the group, without being part of the business. And I didn't really know how to do that, because it didn't seem like the group was accepting me as an advice-giver. Then I thought about the dog. I thought about the bills that were coming up for the shots, the worms, everything that was going on, and it was expensive. It occurred to me that it would be kinda cool to have the dog as part of the business—or in some way get compensated through the business—and I could make the decisions for the dog. I thought that it would bring me back on the board as a voter and an advice-giver.

Sarah: I don't know what Joe was trying to accomplish. Maybe that's his way of being part of the group, through Leroy. He wanted Leroy to have shares, and it seemed really retarded, but if it makes Joe feel happy, then let him do it.

Saul, the lawyer, thought it was kind of goofy, too. I mean, every time I want to talk to Saul, Joe says, "Hey, remember, time is money. Every time you talk to Saul, it's going to cost money." But then Joe wanted to actually have shares through Leroy, which would cost more time and money than we need to spend.

Joe: I was very surprised at Saul's reaction, actually. He was like, "Oh, that's ridiculous." And I'm like, "Just get it done, you're the lawyer, you don't tell me what's ridiculous, just get it done."

Melissa: Oh, victory is such a sweet thing. We go to the lawyer's office, and the dog's in, right? Wrong. I guess Joe's memory failed him in the sense that you cannot make an animal a shareholder. It has to be a living, natural person. The lawyer thought the whole idea was so absurd that we had to be joking. I know revenge is a bad thing, but oh, it felt so good. I was looking at everyone at the table with such a smirk—I felt like Joan Collins on Dynasty.

It gets better. Not only was it lovely to hear those words come out of Saul's mouth, but when it came time to put our names on the agreement, everybody gave their full names. And then at the end, I think Mike or someone said, "Leroy Jackson," and Saul said, "Not the dog." So then Joe murmured under his breath, "Joseph."

That was Joe's wussy-, pussy-ass way of getting back into the business.

MAY 5, 1996 (WEEK FIFTEEN)

Joe: I absolutely knew when I was playing with her finger and sizing up her finger  that I was really gonna do it. I was in Tiffany, and I had no questions whatsoever. I just went right to the ring section, and I was all confident that that's what I wanted. I saw the ring, and I was like, "Oh, my God, it's the perfect ring," 'cause it matched the ring that's already on her finger.

 I was dying during the graduation ceremony. I was sweating and was all tight and cramped between two people who had no idea what I was about to do.

I finally saw my sister in the audience, and I said, "Get Nic, get Nic, bring her up to the front." The whole time, I was thinkin', What is my plan, how am I going to give her the ring without being too disruptive? But at the same time, I wanted to make it really, really special. I had no idea what I was really gonna do until I actually did it. I went up, got my diploma, kissed and hugged the deans, and then totally zoned out.

I went straight to Nic. And everybody in the audience was like, "What happened? What's he doing?" I didn't hear a thing. I was focused on going up to Nic and doing the best thing I've ever done in my entire life. I was so confident about it, even with the difficulties that we've had. I knew she felt the same way. I would never have done it otherwise.

Cynthia: I started to talk to Joe about his engagement, but why even bother? I don't give a s**t; it's his life he's ruining. And she's too young—she's a baby. I don't know where they came from. I just thought it was pulled out of the sky somewhere, you know? He's engaged? How dumb. If you want something permanent, get a tattoo. But he's happy.

Melissa: I think it was good timing on Joe's part. He proposed to Nic and made sure she said yes—before the show airs. And she's conveniently moving to Italy and he's conveniently moving over there with her. And they don't show The Real World in Italy, do they?

PRELUDE TO A TRIP

Cynthia: Flora and Melissa showed the most negativity about the trip of any of the room-mates in the whole entire house. It could be because they're both monkey-see, monkey-do. So it's like, if Melissa didn't want to go, then all of a sudden Flora didn't want to go.

Flora: I am not an outdoor person: I get bit by grass. I'm very glad I didn't go, because I would have suffered on that trip. I'm allergic to anything that bites me, and I would have been miserable, I probably would have been taken to an emergency room in the Bahamas. I'm really affected by these flies, the tropical bugs here, and I'm not very much of a sporty person, so I just would have sat on the beach and fried my ass off, which is probably not a very healthy thing. I'm glad I didn't go; I don't regret it one bit.

Melissa: We got this paper that said what we were to bring: Everything you bring has to fit in one small bag. Don't bring any nice clothes. Don't bring anything electric, like blow-dryers. You don't need any makeup, either. Everything was, like, anti-Melissa. It said to bring jeans. I don't own a pair of jeans. It said to bring a bathing suit. I don't own a bathing suit. It said to bring lots of baseball caps. I don't own baseball caps. I was like, "I don't even have anything to wear—how am I going to go on this trip?" I didn't want to spoil it for everyone, I didn't want to have a bad weekend, so I just didn't go.

Sarah: Melissa stayed home because she didn't want to be seen in a swimsuit. And Flora stayed home 'cause she thought it was cool that Melissa was staying home. That's why they stayed home.

Dan: Thank God Flora and Melissa didn't go, because they would have complained the entire time. That's all I have to say.

Cynthia: I'm gonna be a bad bitch if I came all this way and we don't at least go on a trip. From my understanding, it was that we were not going to go on a trip if the trip interfered with our getting the business up and rolling. I've sacrificed my life to the world for five-and-a-half months, so at least give me some type of reward besides the business, which gives me nothin' but f**kin' headaches. I want to go on the trip.

I didn't actually think that we were gonna go camping or anything, so I told the roommates, "We're not going camping." And somehow we ended up going camping.

Dan: It seems Miss Cynthia had a little too much to drink at Joe's birthday party the night before. Johnny and I were dancing with her all night at the bar, and we thought that she was just in a really good mood. We didn't realize that she had imbibed enough alcohol to kill a whale.

Cynthia: The morning of the trip, I was sick as a dog. I had a hangover, I felt like s**t. I'm so serious—I was so so sick. It was all my fault. I couldn't blame anyone but myself. But this is the first time that I had a lot of fun being sick. I threw up twice before I even left home. And then when I got on the bus, I threw up twice. Then I threw up once on the plane. Sarah called me Barfarama. It was really funny, though. Nobody wanted to sit next to me. It was just so funny. I just laughed through the whole sickness, and Sarah just kept on taking these really bad photos of me while I was sick. I just felt like I was going to die. I had a massive headache. I just felt very, very bad.

Mike: CYNTHIA WAS A LITTLE APPREHENSIVE AT FIRST. I DON'T THINK SHE LIKES LITTLE PLANES LIKE THAT, AND ONCE WE GOT UP IN THE AIR, SHE WAS SCARED TO DEATH. ALL WE COULD DO WAS BASICALLY TRY AND MAKE HER THROW UP SOME MORE TO TRY AND MAKE HER FEEL BETTER, SO ALL WE COULD TALK ABOUT WAS THINGS THAT MIGHT MAKE HER SICK: HOGBALLS, WARM BEER AND CIGARETTE BUTTS, DIARRHEA WITH PEANUTS IN IT—ANYTHING IT TOOK. AND WE SUCCEEDED: SHE FILLED UP A NICE LITTLE BAGFUL OF VOMIT.

Cynthia: After I got off the plane in the Bahamas, the sickness suddenly lifted. I don't know if it was the clean air, the clear blue water, but I felt much better. I was good to go.

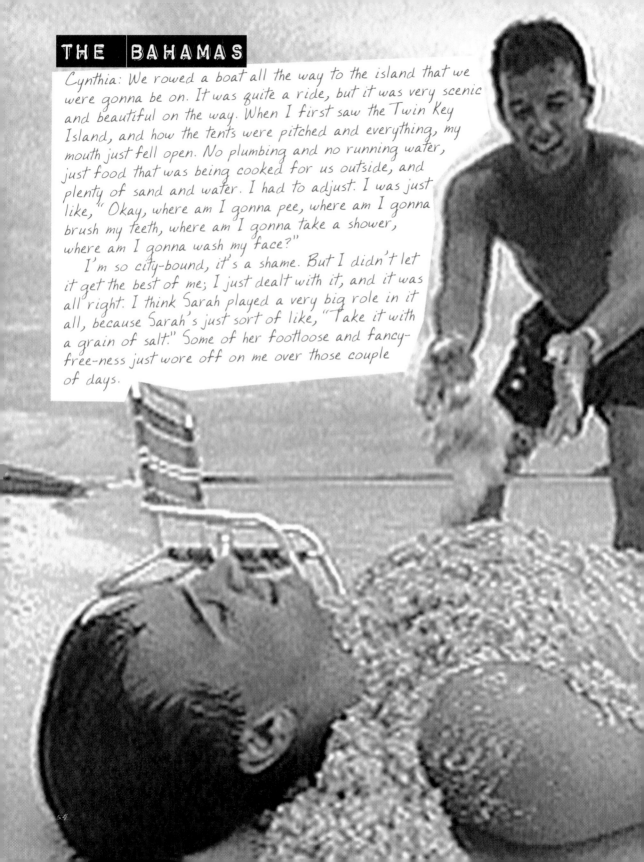

THE BAHAMAS

Cynthia: We rowed a boat all the way to the island that we were gonna be on. It was quite a ride, but it was very scenic and beautiful on the way. When I first saw the Twin Key Island, and how the tents were pitched and everything, my mouth just fell open. No plumbing and no running water, just food that was being cooked for us outside, and plenty of sand and water. I had to adjust. I was just like, "Okay, where am I gonna pee, where am I gonna brush my teeth, where am I gonna take a shower, where am I gonna wash my face?"

I'm so city-bound, it's a shame. But I didn't let it get the best of me; I just dealt with it, and it was all right. I think Sarah played a very big role in it all, because Sarah's just sort of like, "Take it with a grain of salt." Some of her footloose and fancy-free-ness just wore off on me over those couple of days.

MIKE: THE ONLY THING WE HAD TO SHARE THE ISLAND WITH WAS BASICALLY HERMIT CRABS. IT REMINDED ME OF <u>GILLIGAN'S ISLAND</u>. NOTHING THERE. SURROUNDED BY WATER AND SOME TREES, AND THAT'S PRETTY MUCH IT.

Sarah: Every time Cynthia went to the bathroom, she'd have to take me by the hand and whisk me down the beach to squat with her. We'd talk and giggle and chitchat. I don't know. It was pretty funny. Cynthia likes company; she got mad at me when I wrote in my journal.

Dan: Sarah was so scared of being in this tiny little kayak. I guess she was scared of being in this big ocean with nothing but a layer of canvas to protect her from all the sharks and killer ocean things that were gonna come up and eat her. So she power-paddled the entire way there. At one point I had to stop her from rowing, because I was like, "Sarah, everyone else, including the tour guide, is back there, and we're up here and we don't know where we're going." She was like, "I don't care, we'll figure it out, we've just got to get there. I don't want to be in this ocean anymore."

Sarah: Dan was trying to steer, but he wasn't paying attention. I just don't go for those lounge-type recreational activities, so I kept paddling and paddling and paddling 'cause I had to go faster. Dan was like, "Quit paddling, 'cause they're trying to film us just cruising." I'm sorry, but I can't cruise at half a mile an hour, so I just paddled on purpose to get him mad at me.

Joe: I felt isolated, alone, at one with myself and the universe and the beauty around me. Absolutely. It was wonderful. It was a tropical, secluded paradise. It's something I've always wanted to experience. It even hooked me with a stronger spiritual connection and a crossing-a-bridge type scenario—from one stage of my life to the next. It was a little interlude of reflection that was really necessary, a needed and welcome retreat. It was more of a sign of God's presence than I've ever experienced in my life, and I took it as both, "Hey, wake up, here I am, appreciate me, appreciate yourself, appreciate the others around you," and "You're absolved."

Dan: Joe's a really romantic, emotional guy, and he'd obviously been really affected by what he had been going through. This entire camping experience just really awakened something in him. I don't know what it was, but it was really, really beautiful to watch.

Cynthia: The only reason why I was, like, glad to come home was so I could actually take a shower and lie in a bed. I could be inside, in air-conditioning, and stuff like that. But other than that, I wish I was still in Twin Key Islands. You know, I had a lot of fun there. I'll never forget it.

HIV SCARE

Dan: In two days I get my HIV test back. I'm very nervous. I've always been so careful about what I do and who I do it with, but as careful as you are, you never know. In retrospect, it makes you wonder: "Was it really worth it?" Obviously, it's really not.

I don't know what the hell I was thinking, getting my test done during the show, because whatever the test results are, they're none of anybody's business. My name is not Pedro Zamora. As wonderful a guy as he was, I don't have the strength that he did. I'm not ready to take on that s**t.

I haven't done anything that would put me at high risk for HIV transmission, but I certainly have, you know, had sex, and that's enough, even if you are really super-careful and use the thickest condom in the world with every single spermicide known to man. It's still possible that it could get through; you never know. There's nothing more frustrating than the uncertainty of not having any control over whether you get it or not. It would be real easy if I just slapped on a condom and said, "Okay, I'm not going to get it now." But unfortunately that's not the case.

ADDRESSES
EF
GH
IJ
KL
MN
OP QR
NOTES ST
UV

[PRODUCERS' NOTE: DAN'S TEST CAME BACK NEGATIVE.]

THE BUILDUP...

Dan: Mike dragged me into an argument, because he can't have an argument by himself.

Flora: Mike didn't have the guts to come up to me and say, "I don't want Mitchell in the house." If he had talked to me, we could have cleared it up right there and then, but him being gut-less and him having absolutely no balls, he just didn't confront me.

If he had come out and said, "I don't want Mitchell in the house," I would have told him to go f**k himself and kiss my ass, because he brings disgusting crabby whores to our house, and they use our bathrooms, they use our kitchen and our silverware. It makes me really nauseous that we don't say anything.

MIKE: WHEN WE WERE IN THE KEYS, DAN HAD SAID THAT FLORA HAD FINALLY ADMITTED TO MELISSA THAT MITCHELL HIT HER. HE REALLY DIDN'T GIVE ANY SPECIFIC DETAILS, BUT WE JUST TOOK IT THAT HE WAS

Sarah: All I know is this: Mike meets some very low, rigortoid women, brings them to the house, gets drunk, runs around naked, sends them home. They're just another group of chapped chicks. That's all I know about 'em. Yeah, just these two chicks came over, got in the hot tub with Mike, went into the bathroom, poked, and left.

RIGHT, AND WHEN IT CAME DOWN TO IT, I GUESS HE WAS WRONG. FLORA NEVER SAID ANYTHING. IT WAS JUST ANOTHER ONE OF THOSE DAN LIES THAT COME BACK AND HAUNT HIM.

WE'RE ALL A LITTLE CONCERNED FOR FLORA. THE LAST TIME MITCHELL WAS HERE, HE GOT INTO A FIGHT WITH TWO GUYS, SO THERE'S NO TELLING WHAT THE GUY'S GOING THROUGH. HE SEEMS TO BE REALLY NICE, BUT WHEN HE COMES TO TOWN, WE'RE ALL A LITTLE NERVOUS TO HAVE HIM IN THE HOUSE, ALTHOUGH IT'S SOMETHING WE JUST DIDN'T BRING UP TO FLORA. FLORA FOUND OUT THAT WE WERE ALL A LITTLE CONCERNED ABOUT MITCHELL STAYING AT THE HOUSE, AND SHE WAS ANGRY THAT WE DIDN'T CONFRONT HER WITH IT. SO THAT BROUGHT A HUGE FIGHT BETWEEN FLORA AND ME.

Melissa: I think they just didn't want Mitchell in the house because they didn't want Mitch in the house. I got really pissed off when I heard that, because they bring in every bimbette from A to Z, and we never say anything.

Dan: Everyone is really concerned with Flora and at one point or another has voiced their opinion on what is going on with her relationship. It's none of our business, but you can't help but be concerned when you think something is going wrong. Unfortunately, Mike, in his infinite wisdom, decided to pull out some information that was given to him confidentially and use it as a weapon in his argument with Flora.

THE EXPLOSION

Cynthia: Mike told Flora that Dan told him that Mitchell had hit her. So she got mad at Dan about that. But Dan said that Melissa told him that. Melissa said she didn't say anything about it. In the end, Dan did admit she didn't say it.

Flora: I knew that Melissa didn't say that, but I just wanted to hear it from her. And she said, "Are you crazy? I don't even like Dan, I don't even talk to him, I avoid him." And I said, "Would you mind standing there when Dan gets back while I confront him in front of you and Mike and everyone else, just so everyone else can see what a big fat liar he is?" And she said, "I actually would want to be there, so there's no way he can lie again."

Cynthia: But anyway, when Dan got home, Flora was like, "Dan, I want to talk to you, and I want all the roommates to be around." He was like, "No, I'm gonna eat right now. You can wait." And I was like, "Yeah, good for you. Don't let this girl punk you like that."

So we all went outside. Flora was asking him if he had said this, and he said that it was taken all out of context. And he explained how he had said it, and he made her understand that he really cared about her as a roommate and as a friend, and that not only Dan but Dan and the boys all felt very uncomfortable about Mitchell being in the house, because they felt like he was beating on Flora.

Flora: I believe that Dan has a lot to worry about. I made sure I told Mitchell exactly what happened, that all the roommates didn't want him in the house, because Dan was spreading rumors that he beat me up. I told Mitchell he has my permission to do whatever he wants with Dan when he gets here. I know Mitchell, and believe me, if Dan even thinks of lying to his face, he will bop him, and I'm going to stand there and I'm going to cheer him on.

MIKE: DAN JUST TRIED TO GET HIS WAY AROUND IT BY SAYING, "FLORA, I CARE ABOUT YOU," AND FLORA DIDN'T BACK DOWN. DAN KNEW HE WAS BUSTED RIGHT AWAY. HE HAS THIS WAY OF GETTING AROUND EVERYTHING, AND IT WAS A PRETTY NASTY SCENE. HE REALLY HAD NO WAY OF GETTING OUT OF THIS ONE.

Sarah: I guess Flora's on this mission to call Dan out. Just call anybody out for anything. Flora doesn't have any hobbies, that's the bottom line. I mean, you just gotta occupy your time better than trying to change six people who are not gonna change for you, you know?

Dan: Flora was really, really, really humiliated by the entire subject and was just looking to embarrass someone as much as she was embarrassed. She thought that she could do it by dragging me onto the porch and reaming me and confronting me with something that she knew I was going to deny. Unfortunately, I'm not denying anything, but she still is calling me a liar and still refuses to listen to what I say.

Melissa: I don't know how Dan got out of it. He did say, "Melissa never told me that, I never said that."

Cynthia: Flora's pretty much moved out of the house now. She has her apartment. She has the key. Mitchell will be here at the end of the week to move in with her.

Melissa: Flora moved out of the house first because she had her apartment and because her boyfriend was here—and why are you going to sleep alone when you can sleep with your man? Cynthia moved out second, because she got her own apartment. Private, to herself, no cameras, no mikes, and rent-free, so why wouldn't you go there? And I moved out third, because I did not want to be in the house anymore— I was very unhappy.

Dan: Flora has every intention of staying down here and getting something going for herself. More power to her. I mean, let her just go, let her do whatever she wants to do, and of course, we're going to end up with that beautiful, trendy coffee shop that was proposed on day one. If that's what she wants to do, then let her go for it.

Cynthia: Well, once again, the business has changed. We're like, what? I mean, it's changed again. As far as I know, we're gonna have a café. We're back to the café thing again. Isn't that something? We're back to the café thing again. Mark doesn't want to have anything to do with the business. Sarah's upset. The boys have nothing to do with it. I'm just pretty much not doing anything. It's just totally ridiculous.

Flora: We're doing a café now. I hate my roommates, every single one of 'em, including Melissa and Sarah, who were the only roommates I did like. I hate them all. I had the café idea from week two, and if everybody wasn't greedy and stupid and retarded like they are, they would not have nixed my idea of a café and we would have had four months of free advertising. We would be rolling in the money right now. They're all losers, and they were the wrong people to pick for this project, because they don't give a s**t. It's going to be a waste. It is a waste; we wasted too many months doing nothing.

Joe: Hank's movies have caused much controversy in the house. I think they are great. I think they depict each and every individual of the house very well, very eloquently and funnily. The whole thing is funny, but people have taken it the wrong way.

Mike: When Hank was here last time, he shot all this footage of everybody and told everybody that he was going to make a video. Well, Hank finally got back down and brought the video and showed everybody, and it turns out that it was a huge, huge hit. He put everything together—everything was perfect, and it was really, really entertaining.

Hank touched on everybody's personality, what they have to offer. I was Handy Boy in the film. It showed Dan in full gayness. He showed Flora and her breasts, Joe talking about computers and relationships and all the other stuff. He really touched hard on each person's true essence. I guess, some people were offended and some weren't.

Melissa pretty much came off looking like a slut. I think she heard about it and was a little hesitant to see it. I don't think she wants anybody else to see, but you know, Melissa, you act like that and people are going to see.

Sarah: Joe and Mike seemed to really love the video, and Flora really loved the video, but when Flora watched it a second time and saw how lewd they were being, she realized how much of an ass she had made of herself and that maybe she was just a little bit too revealing. But it was perfect, 'cause we captured Flora, we captured everybody, and everybody was pretty much happy with their part. Cynthia's was probably the best part, but she didn't get to see it.

Joe: Flora, was laughing the whole time and saying, "Oh, I love the way I flash my breasts here and there and all the time, that's so hilarious, ha, ha, ha." But the next day, she's like, "I'm gonna sue you, man, I'm gonna sue you, Hank. I want copies of the tape." The tape clearly portrays Melissa as a sexually liberated woman. It is Melissa in full effect, it is who Melissa really is, and Hank just got it on film and made a funny little story about it. But Melissa doesn't want people to remember her as the way she was a couple months ago.

MIKE: FLORA LIKES TO SHOW HER BREASTS. I THINK IT'S PRETTY OBVIOUS FROM HANK'S VIDEO THAT SHE LIKES TO FLASH EVERYBODY, AND SHE DIDN'T SEEM TO MIND AT FIRST, BUT APPARENTLY NOW SHE'S A LITTLE UPSET ABOUT IT. FLORA SAID SHE WAS GOING TO CALL HER MOM AND GET A LAWYER AND HAVE THE VIDEO SEIZED. I DON'T KNOW WHAT SHE'S THINKING. SHE LIKED IT BEFORE, SO WHY NOT NOW?

JUNE 2, 1996 (WEEK NINETEEN)

DELICIOUS DEFUNCT

Cynthia: Sarah just sort of fell by the wayside after Flora introduced her idea to Mark, given that Sarah and Mark had done all this work for Delicious Deliveries, you know, and then all of a sudden they're changing the idea because Flora doesn't see how we would make money selling cakes. I've been saying this all along. How in the hell are we gonna make money selling cakes?

Yes, Flora's definitely pushing to try to make the business happen, and yes, I will help Flora out for the next ten to twelve days on whatever it is that she needs help with. That's the least that I can do.

PROJECTS

Dan: The only mistake we made was not going with the coffee shop from the very beginning. We had these concepts that were going to be new and exciting and innovative, but when you have seven different focuses all kind of floating around, it's kind of hard to get anything going in the same direction. All we really need to do is just find something that we could really work on together and just focus all our energy on being successful rather than being hip and cool.

Cynthia: I'm definitely gonna feel bad that we didn't get a business started. It's a shame, but there were just too many chiefs and not enough Indians. I kind of figured that it wouldn't happen.

MIKE: I WOULD DO THIS AGAIN IN A HEARTBEAT. I ENJOYED EVERY MINUTE OF IT.

Dan: There has been a veritable cornucopia of unpleasantness in this situation; to single one out would almost be an exercise in futility.

Melissa: It's been quite an experience. Not something that I would ever repeat, but if I told you that I didn't learn a million and one things from living in this house, I'd be lying.

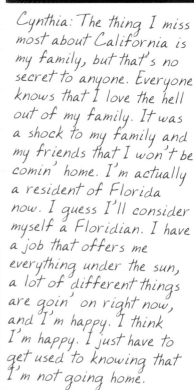

Cynthia: The thing I miss most about California is my family, but that's no secret to anyone. Everyone knows that I love the hell out of my family. It was a shock to my family and my friends that I won't be comin' home. I'm actually a resident of Florida now. I guess I'll consider myself a Floridian. I have a job that offers me everything under the sun, a lot of different things are goin' on right now, and I'm happy. I think I'm happy. I just have to get used to knowing that I'm not going home.

Flora: There would be nothing that I would do differently if I had to do it again. I would do the same things. There is nothing that I've done that I'm ashamed of or that is not normal for me. But if I had a choice of doing this thing again: never.

Sarah: I guess some of my roommates think that this is the beginning or end of life, you know, and they're making all these preparations, like getting married and getting apartments with people and just trying to put some kind of order in their lives. They're trying to solidify these relationships so that when the truth comes out they can sort of vindicate themselves. They'll already be safe.

Dan: I'm really gonna miss Leroy. I mean, I will really miss playing with Leroy, with those little floppy ears. If I had to clean up his dog poop, I wouldn't miss him at all, but I didn't so therefore he's cute. Uhm, I'm really gonna miss Leroy.

Melissa: My fondest memory would have to be the first week, when we just went clubbing every night. The differences in my roommates fascinated me. I mean, I just couldn't know enough about them. We were having the best time. There were no personal differences yet, there were no problems, there was no envy or jealousy or what have you. We were all equal— seven people who did not know each other or the circumstances. That had to have been the absolute best time, that week.

PROJECTS

65

Cynthia: The happiest moment I've ever had would definitely be snorkeling during the Bahamas trip, even though my ass got bit by a damn piranha. I'm convinced there was piranha in the water. I don't care what anybody says—I'm convinced of that.

Sarah: My most unpleasant moment was when Mike farted in my face six times in a row in one day.

Flora: There's absolutely nothing positive that would stick in my mind, that I remember.

Sarah: This is just an episode in my life. It isn't the beginning or end of my life, and I don't understand why everybody feels like it is, like they're closing a chapter of their life or something. I'm kind of in the middle of a lot of things, you know? This is just sort of something in the way of me accomplishing my goals.

Joe: Absolutely, positively the best experience I had in my five-and-a-half months here was when I was on the beach in the Bahamas when it started pouring rain and the double rainbow came out. It was beautiful water, beautiful sand, beautiful sky, nature, spiritual God, the whole thing. I was one with it all, and I was just totally happy, in bliss, and psyched to be on this earth. That was the most wonderful, most special private moment of my entire life. It was perfect. It was absolutely perfect, and for that moment, and that moment alone, this whole five-and-a-half months was worth it.

LAST LOOKS

Cynthia: Sarah is the person I think I'll miss most. But I have a feeling that I'll see Sarah often. She's the traveling queen, so she wouldn't have a problem with coming back here. But man, I'm gonna miss her a lot.

Flora: I don't really care about Sarah, and I don't care to think what's going to happen to her in ten years. I really don't care about any of these people except Melissa and Leroy. I don't care if they die. I'd be sad, but I wouldn't cry, basically. That's how much they disturbed my life, and that's how much these people made me hate them. I do not care what happens to them, ever.

MIKE: SARAH AND I WILL DEFINITELY KEEP IN TOUCH. SHE'S REALLY BECOME A STRONG PART OF MY LIFE. SHE'S GOT THIS ENERGY AND...I DON'T KNOW WHAT IT IS ABOUT HER. SHE'S JUST GOT THE ONE THING THAT I'VE ALWAYS WISHED I HAD, AND THAT'S, LIKE, TOTAL PEACE OF MIND. I LOVE THE GIRL TO DEATH.

Joe: I believe that Flora, deep down, is a decent individual who's caught up in a difficult situation with her man and her life.

100%   **Page 1**

Melissa: I think what's most ironic is that if there was anyone I thought I would never click with it would probably be Flora, and she's the one that I ended up being the closest to. I still can't figure out why, because I still see us as such complete opposites. I just remember thinking, there's no way I will ever have anything in common with this girl, and I was wrong. She comes across as this backstabbing, conniving, out-for-herself kind of girl, but with me she was always honest, she was always up-front. We just ended up becoming closer and closer regardless of how different we may seem.

Dan: Flora's interesting to watch the same way that it's interesting to watch someone with Tourette's syndrome, 'cause you just don't know what they're gonna do.

Sarah: Flora is pretty nutty. I like Flora, but she reminds me too much of my sister. She knows how to get me riled up and just makes me want to kill her.

Melissa: I think Joe has changed the most in terms of emotion. From day one till now, he seems to have changed a lot. His goals, the way he saw things, the way he thought about things, his private life—all have definitely completely changed. He seems to be the one that has grown the most, and that's exactly what he wanted to get out of this. One of the first things he told me was, "I'm doing this because I want to grow and learn about myself," and he definitely accomplished his goal; he changed a lot.

Dan: I think the rest of us sunk to this level of little petty squabbling a long time ago, and Joe was always miraculously above it. Within five years Joe will have written a book about something simply because he wanted to express his love to the rest of the world. It doesn't really matter what it's on; he'll just have written a book. It'll be a beautiful thing; it'll have his picture on the back, smiling for the girlies.

Cynthia: As far as Joe goes, I don't want to see him ever again if he has to come down here with Nic. But if he's, like, on a solo trip, we can hang.

Flora: Mike. Where do I see Mike? Mike is a great salesperson, so he would...he'll be selling cars. I could see Mike selling these expensive Porsches and stuff. He thinks he's gonna be some movie star, but I wouldn't even go there.

Cynthia: Mike lives here in Florida, but I have a feeling that Mike has bigger and better things waiting for him, and I wish him the best in life, because he's, like, hella cool with me. I don't have a problem with Mike, and I'm definitely going to miss him doing the Handy Boy thing for me.

Sarah: It is kind of cool to have Mike around, because he's the only person who really likes to play.

Melissa: I see Dan so differently now. When I first met Dan, I really liked him, and then he really became a pain in my big Cuban butt and I couldn't stand him. Then I don't know what happened, but, he just completely changed again. He started speaking up, and he stopped doing the things that bothered us so much about him in the beginning, like talking too much. And in the business, he was one of the few people that spoke with half a brain and made valid points.

Flora: I don't think Dan's gonna accomplish anything in his life, because he talks too much bull. He doesn't know how to approach people properly. He gets annoying really fast, and he thinks he's going to be a supermodel.

Cynthia: I wish the best for Dan, who's gonna be the supermodel. I'm gonna miss him, too. Dan is hella cool, too. He's hella cool.

Flora: I love Melissa to death, she's great. I think Melissa is going to be the best gossip columnist in the United States.

Dan: I think Melissa's really scared about the public perception of the things that she's done, and she thinks that simply by concocting a bunch of lies and making a bunch of stories, she's gonna somehow absolve herself of all her own actions. She's the most backstabbing, backhanded evil person I've ever met in my life.

Joe: We have last, and certainly least, Melissa, who I plan never, ever, ever in my life to go out and seek communication with in any way shape or form. I wish never to hear of Melissa again.

Flora: I see Cynthia working at a little coffee shop, seriously serving coffee, as a waitress. I wish her happiness and success in the job that she's got now, but I truly don't see Cynthia in that job. She's a 'hood kind of girl. It's not a prejudice thing or anything like that.

Cynthia: The person in the house who I think has achieved the most—not to sound cocky—I think would be me. Because when I got here, I had a limited amount of experience in some things, and over this period of time, I've learned more and more and more and more and more. I have a job that could turn into a career, I have an apartment down here, and I've established a life for myself out here

MIKE: Cyn IMPRESSED ME THE MOST. I THOUGHT SHE WAS GOING TO BE THIS LITTLE Miss Goody Twoshoes, BUT Cyn CAME OUT, AND SHE WAS A DRINKER, A PARTIER, SHE GOT IN THE WATER, DID SNORKELING AND, I THINK, REALLY AGED A LOT MENTALLY. SHE JUST BECAME MORE INVOLVED WITH WHAT SHE WAS INTO.

Sarah: I really like Cynthia a lot. I think Cynthia is awesome and has a lot to offer. It's just that she has to be around the right people. When she opens up, she's just an incredible person, and I really appreciate her a lot.

Joe: I am so proud of Cynthia. It couldn't have happened to a better person than her. I am so happy for her. She's worked hard. She's always been straightforward about the business and straightforward about her life. I am so happy she's not going home to California, and I'm so happy that she has a professional opportunity here and that someone has believed in her and given her a chance.

Dan: Cynthia's got it goin' on.

Cynthia: This is the way I would describe all of my roommates in the house to someone who didn't know us yet: I would describe Joe as the genius, Mike as the sporty all-American dude, Sarah as the crazy comic-book, skateboardin', freelancing, freehearted, free-spirited type of chick, Melissa as the salsa queen, Flora as the Hooters girl, Dan as the outrageous gay dude that's hella cool, and me myself as the mama.

Mike: Ladies and gentlemen, you are free to take off your seatbelts and return your chairs and tray tables to their full, upright position. We have landed. It's been one hell of a ride, we're done, and I'm out of here—see ya.

ADDRESSES EF GH IJ KL MN OP QR NOTES ST UV

LONDON

18

NEIL

Neil: Well, being both misanthropic and xenophobic, I find it a bit tricky to deal with the possibility of meeting new people. Hopefully they'll be nice, but they might be complete bastards. As long as they give me some reasonable arguments, I'll be happy.

I think typical Oxford students are a bit more studious than I am. There's a lot of quite wealthy people around here, people who come from quite privileged backgrounds, and that's not really me. Generally they're sort of upper-middle-class people who've had too much education and want some more.

Originally I'm from Devon, which is on the south-west coast of England. A small town. A few friends, lots of sheep. Oxford was a bit of an eye opener. When I was eighteen, I had two choices: Either I went to Oxford University and pursued my dream of studying philosophy, or I went to art school and painted. And I chose Oxford. And having done that for five-and-a-half years now, I quite fancy doing something a bit more creative again. I'm currently dropping out of a Ph.D. in psychology to pursue my career in rock 'n' roll.

I'm involved in lots of different sorts of music, at least two or three bands at the same time, to keep my options open. One of them I like to describe as progressive assquake, the idea being to create the right frequency of noise to cause people to s***t themselves. And the other one is TROLL, my house band, which is sort of nose-bleed techno with a strong seam of psychology and hard science in it. The idea being to induce psychotic incidents in the listener. I'm not planning on growing up. My father is sixty-five and he claims he doesn't know what he wants to do when <u>he</u> grows up.

Jacinda: I've been traveling and modeling full-time for five years. When I first started, it was fantastic—seventeen, straight out of high school, thought the world was at my feet. But a lot of time has passed, and I've seen a lot, and it's not really my love anymore. Mentally I'm somewhere else when I'm doing the job. But it's fantastic money, and I continue to do it for the money and the wonderful lifestyle, to travel the world. I think it's silly when people are jealous of models, because every person is different and every person has got something to offer.

I have a boyfriend now. We're really happy together, but he's going away anyway. That's the difficult thing about the lifestyle I lead. We're always traveling, and no matter who you're with, whether it's friends or boyfriends or family, you're always saying goodbyes. Always leaving each other.

It's a bit sad. We've spent the last five months together. And I mean, even in that time, we've had to go away. We're kind of getting used to goodbyes. But this is a long one.

JACINDA

Jay: Alicia, my girlfriend, is a lot younger than me. She's sixteen. I'm nineteen. I met Alicia when I was a junior and went to see a soccer game. I look over, and I see this girl wearing a Boston College sweatshirt, standing with her parents, right? And I'm like, oh, man. 'Cause I figured she was the older sister of one of the kids on the team. And it turned out she was in the eighth grade! I was like, oh, no. So, I put her out of my mind. And then two and a half years passed, and I finally asked her out and all that.

The first date Alicia and I went on was so much fun, 'cause I got asked to speak at a fiftieth reunion at my high school. So it was the class of 1940, and she was my date. We went and we hung out with a bunch of sixty-seven-year-olds and had the time of our lives.

I'm a writer. Right now I have an outline for the next show that I'll write. But it's kind of tough to write a show when you've got a girlfriend—there's not too much motivation. So getting away from home and away from the girlfriend, will give me time to write again.

The biggest thing about living on my own is that I'm gonna really have to learn how to pick up after myself. I'm not too confident about that. I'm going to be sloppy and lazy, I think.

— JAY

SHARON

Sharon: My relationship with my mother is a very close one. We really are very good friends, which mainly stems from the fact that we were a single-parent family for eighteen years. I'm twenty now, but for eighteen years there was just the two of us. So we forged almost a sisterhood, 'cause we relied solely on each other and 'cause I'm an only child. We're just very, very close, and I love her dearly. She's been my mentor in a lot of ways. She's a very intelligent woman, and I have gleaned a lot of knowledge from her. She's a very strong woman. I think she's a good role model. She's always given me belief in myself, and I think that's a healthy thing—especially for women nowadays.

Lars: I plan on working in the music/nightlife scene, which could mean working for a record label or a radio station, or doing special events for clubs, something like that. I run a business with a friend of mine, and we do events—we organize parties for other people. We've also done some marketing jobs before, for magazines, radio, things like that.

The only thing I can expect is that my roommates are not like me. There are not going to be seven Larses in that apartment, because that's not what this show is about. Big loves and big laughs and heavy discussion is pretty much what I think will happen.

I'm a person who you can really go out and party with, but I can also really get into serious talks about politics, about culture, about those types of things.

LARS

— **KAT**

Kat: I was born in Alaska, and we moved for a while to Hawaii. And then we lived for a while in Idaho with my grandparents. We moved to Washington and lived in Seattle for a while. And then when I was probably about seven or eight we moved out to Yelm, Washington, and I've lived there ever since.

My mother is very open-minded—"All right, I can understand why you're doing this; just be sure that you do it right." My ethnic background is English, so she's open about my living there.

My father has two priorities, which are my priorities also: fencing and school. I could be walking on a tightrope in Jamaica, as long as I were also fencing and in school. He's like, "Why do you have to go and sit in front of the camera and talk about yourself? Don't come to me crying that you don't like London, because I'm not coming to get you." But he's just teasing me. My dad knows that people have got to take big leaps.

MIKE

Mike: I drive race cars, and I've been doing that for three years. It's more for fun right now, but my father's been doing it for about seven years. I started in Oklahoma, where I led my first race from the second lap on, until the very last lap, when I spun off and finished seventh. But I was pretty pumped up that first time. I set the fastest lap of the race, too, and I thought that was really neat.

This is kind of like a fraternity, in that it's a bunch of people my own age living with each other and dealing with each other. But I've never lived with girls before. I've spent the night at a couple of girls' houses, but I've never lived with girls. That's going to be a whole new experience in itself, because I don't have a clue what they're like to live with.

I had this scary dream the night before my flight: I was walking up these stairs and the other six roommates were already there, just sitting there laughing at me. I couldn't recognize any faces or anything, but I could see them all, like when you have a dream and you can't describe anybody but you can see them. All six people were up there as I was walking up the stairs, and it was like they were already best friends, they'd hung out forever, and they didn't want to talk to me. They were just kind of laughing at me as I was walking up the stairs. Then I woke up, so I was okay.

FIRST IMPRESSIONS

Jacinda: I'm rooming with Kat. She's really sweet. Sharon said that at first, when we went to bed, she could hear us talking, and she knows that when you get into bed, you talk about everything. So she felt a little bit left out. But she said she loves having her own room, and Kat and I get along really well, so we are enjoying having that room.

Mike: When Kat's around, it's so much more relaxed. And we've talked about everything from Seattle to St. Louis to how to give good head. It's great, because I could talk to her just like that, right off the bat.

Neil: I've been hanging out with Kat quite a lot. She's nice. She's kind of old beyond her years, yet pleasingly non-cynical, which is quite refreshing to a jaded old bastard like me. She's sort of attractive 'cause of her naïveté. She may end up suffering from the pernicious anemia of the soul, which is a bit dangerous, but hopefully she'll get streetwise enough to see when people are using her. I'm curious to see how she copes here. She seems to fluctuate quite a lot between knowing what to do and being completely lost.

Jacinda: Jay is so sweet. And he's been so quiet, although I think he was just feeling a little bit down. It's his first time ever away from home, and on top of that, he missed his girlfriend. I think he's in love with her, and I know how hard he's finding it. I was trying to tell him that I know how he feels because I've been there before.

Kat: I really like Jay a lot. He's the kind of person that you feel that way toward. I grabbed him this morning, and I'm like, "You went to bed early last night—what was wrong?" He said, "I think it's harder for me than it is for everyone else." It's his first time out, and in some ways I think Jay left more at home than the rest of us did.

Lars: Jay sleeps twelve, thirteen, fourteen hours every night. And then he gets up and has some disgusting bacon breakfast, making everything filthy in the kitchen, and then he'll play billiards all day. What's the point? I can't really dig that.

Mike: I think that Jay wants everybody to think that he's this really nice, couldn't-hurt-anybody, never-done-a-bad-thing-in-his-life kind of person. I don't think he's a criminal in disguise, but I think there's a hidden side that he's not letting out yet. I think he's still holding something back.

Jacinda: Mike is really American; he's oozing American-ness, the way he conducts himself and the way he talks and everything. I think that of all the people here, he's really set, he's sure about what he wants. He only liked one type of toothpaste. And he only liked one type of girl. A girl with long hair and lipstick. He says, "I never want to live anywhere else but America. I love America. I'm American." It's sweet.

Kat: Mike looks like a J. Crew ad, you know? I feel bad for him, because the rest of us have this level of sloppiness that he just rises above.

Sharon: Mike's cheeky. By cheeky I mean "cocky." He's funny, too. He's a man's man. He's got his attitudes on certain issues, and you won't change him. He's a fun guy.

Jay: Mike is a frat boy.

Jay: When Neil comes walking into the entryway, you just see this hair walking in.

Kat: It's not very flattering to be told that you look like you're twelve by someone who claims to have completely figured out the depths of your personality in two days. But that's okay. If Neil has, he's just going to be in trouble, 'cause then I'm going to ask him, "What do you think I should do? Tell me, Neil. I don't know."

Lars: Only with Neil can I have conversations like I'm used to having back home. I mean, after you've gone to university for a couple of years, discussions are different. You're more focused on the scientific way of discussing a problem. And with Mike and Jacinda and all of the rest, you can't do that.

Kat: Jacinda is a laugh. She's lived this lifestyle that you expect would create a certain type of person, and she's not any of that. She seems to have come out unscathed by a lot of what people suffer when they go into modeling. She wants to be a princess. That's what she told me: that if she could be anything, she'd be a princess.

Sharon: Jacinda is very well-traveled. I mean, even though she's a model, that's not the biggest thing about her. I'm more interested in her for her cultural and traveling experience, and for all her stories. When people travel, it really opens their eyes to so much. We both agreed that it's such a humbling experience. It teaches you not to be too attached to too many material objects.

Neil: I like Lars. It's good to have a kind of elder European ally in the house.

Mike: I'd like to take Lars back to the States and just watch the women crawl all over him. He's just such a smooth guy, and he's easy to talk to.

CORREO AEREO

PAR AVION

VIA AIR MAIL

Kat: I like Lars. He has got a subtle sense of humor. He's very patient. He seems pretty accepting, not very judgmental. But he kind of keeps to himself a little bit.

Mike: I liked Sharon right off the bat. She's got outrageous energy and excitement for everything. Right when I met her, I was like, "This thing is going to be great. I don't have anything else to worry about 'cause if Sharon is here, everything is going to be great."

Kat: Sharon is really friendly. She's very gregarious. She talks so fast, and she's got so much to say that she just can't fit it all in. But she does listen, you know. She'll talk and say her piece and then she'll pause and look at you, and then you know that she wants to hear as much as she's given.

Neil: Sharon is probably the one I'm going to have the most conflict with in the end. Not because of any strong opinions she has, but because of the force of her personality; she really does pile it on. She shouts until she's heard, which is kind of anathema to my approach. If you've got a point to make, make it. If not, then shut up and listen to someone else. And she doesn't seem to do that. It's most un-English. I'm surprised she's taken as a representative of England. Hey, it takes all sorts, but I'm always dubious of people who are certain about the way they feel, particularly when they're only twenty years old.

FLIRTING

Sharon: At the moment, the place is sexually charged. Everybody has got too much sexual energy. And all the innuendo—this and that and the other. It's just like they all need a shag, basically. I don't want to be crass, but they just need to get it out of their systems.

Kat: You have, what, one club baby, three musicians, a writer, and Jacinda, an artist—I mean, she's modeling right now, but when you listen to her talk about writing or about costumes, you know she's artistic.

And it's a group of people who are going to stay up later and are going to get a little funky.

Lars: Mike is basically out to have a good time and get laid. And that's basically all he talks about. I'm really having a fun time hanging out with him, and I've enjoyed the way he talks about women. It's not my perspective, but I think it's hilarious. I kind of go along with it and play along. When we're together, we talk about "them bitches," you know, talk like that.

Mike: The women are starting to look better, or maybe my standards are dropping.

Kat: Yeah, I guess I'm a flirt. I don't always know when I'm doing it intentionally. I'm a physical person. When I'm friends with someone, I hug them. It's how I am.

Mike: I thought I was clicking with Kat, but all of a sudden she's kind of gone the other way. I'm not cutting on Kat, I'm not putting down Neil; I think that if they want to get together, that's fine. I just don't think there should have been this splitting up, 'cause Sharon, Lars, Jay, and I just kind of feel like we're not a part of it.

Kat: I'm irritated with Mike because he's making comments about Neil and me. I don't think that there's any reason why I shouldn't be friends with someone, and I don't think that there needs to be comments made about it. I'm just Neil's friend—that's it. I'm an affectionate person.

I like to relax and be friends with people. And I have more in common with some people than others. It's just how it is. I'm really tired, and it actually hurts my feelings.

Neil: I'm not in the mood to deal with the group situation, and particularly not after Mike's crass comments about me and Kat. I'm not exactly sure what his problem is, or what he thinks he knows about what's going on. I can't be sussing that. Maybe it's jealousy, or maybe he's just goading us for the hell of it. I'm not sure. I shouldn't let it bother me, but sometimes it does.

This whole situation is just getting to be too much for me. I'm a control freak who likes to put myself in positions where I'm out of control. But it's a bit too much of a challenge at the moment. I'm not really sure how to cope with it at all. It seems that people like Mike just say, "Well, f**k it. They can film me. I'll just do my normal stuff and deal with it." I just can't do that. I'm constantly aware of the situation, aware that I am being observed. And that's not something that I think you can ever prepare for. I just need to come to terms with it and then start living normally. But at the moment it's very, very, very hard.

Mike: I'm a little bothered. Maybe it's early, maybe nobody knows anybody, maybe nobody trusts anybody, but there's a lot of stuff that's not being said. There are a lot of secrets being kept, and nobody wants to open up. They'll tell you how they feel on an issue, but no one is saying who they are yet.

Jacinda: Mike says that, if you don't say something, you're embarrassed about it. But I don't think that everybody has to tell their whole life. I think it's just a matter of saying, "Well, fine, if you believe in always saying everything, that's great. But that doesn't give you the right to expose other people's business as well, unless they say that it's okay."

FEBRUARY 26, 1995 (WEEK FIVE)

Jacinda: I remember when I was in Japan, and I was, like, seventeen. I was so skinny. I was like a stick. I had nothing, no shape or anything, but I had a really chubby face and I wore thick clothes. And they would say to me, "Ah, Jacinda, be careful you don't get beefier." And I was like, "Why are they saying that to me?" And it's just because they're scared that you will. I just think it's a real narrow perspective. I mean, I know some girls who became anorexic 'cause of the way they perceived themselves in this business—it focuses so much on your looks.

I guess a lot of people want to do it. They think it's fast money and a fast life and all that. But the fast life is not there, and the money is there only if you can work it really good. And basically that's got nothing to do with you. It's got to do with people liking the way you look, which you can't thank yourself for anyway. I mean, that's your parents. Modeling is a superficial business, and I'm just playing the game.

Neil: A Unilever gig should be like a good splatter movie. Very cheap, very cheesy, and full of fun and horror. I see it as cabaret, perhaps. Noisy cabaret.

Lars: Neil seems to be a bit schizophrenic. I mean, he's this nice guy back home, and then you see him up there on the stage—it's like two different people. But it didn't surprise me; I knew that he had this side to him.

When we went to hear him play at this gig, I didn't quite understand the lyrics. The whole atmosphere was, like, they were trying to make a point, but since no one understood the lyrics, no one got that point.

Jay: Neil dedicated a song to us, and I started getting all excited—what is this going to be about? Then he just went crazy, and I couldn't figure out what he was saying, so that made me a little nervous. I was trying not to make eye contact with him, because I figured that if he saw me, he might come down and start singing to me or something.

Mike: All in all, I thought the Unilever show was pretty cool. I mean, I wouldn't buy the CD or anything. I wasn't walking out inspired. If I was inspired to do anything, it might have been to kill somebody. But I enjoyed it.

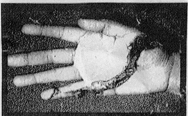

UNILEVER

1 March - The Dublin Castle - Camden
3 March - McMillans - Deptford

STRIFE

Mike: Since everyone is so weird about the cameras here, it's kind of hard to get to know anybody. Like, we went to this thing the other day. I sat on the bus with Kat, and we shared a chair. I was asking her questions, and she wouldn't talk to me. It was weird. I was like, "So, did you have fun at the Junior Olympics?" She was like, "Yeah." So I said, "How did you do?" "Eh." "Did you have a good time?" "Yeah." "See your parents?" "No." I was like, "Oh, nice talking to you, Kat, you have a real nice personality there." Frustrates me.

That girl is too...high-strung, I guess. Tense. Nervous. Moody. Maybe it's a chemical thing, I don't know. But in one conversation she can go from totally laughing to being totally pissed. Once I dated a girl like that, and it was the most frustrating thing in my entire life.

Kat: Sometimes I wish I weren't such a moody person. I think it would be easier for me to make decisions and to know what's going on in my life if I didn't have such extremes, but I do. Yep. Sure do.

Neil: I think my girlfriend Chrys is unhappy about the situation I'm in at the moment. It's changed our relationship quite substantially, which I don't think she was expecting. She saw it as me moving to London and being closer to her, whereas in reality I've moved to London and hardly ever see her, because of the nature of the project.

The Kat thing is a bit of a thorny one. I imagine that if this was a different environment Kat and I would probably be having sex by now. I mean, there's a sexual vibe between us, and I must admit I take advantage of that. I enjoy flirting with her. I think she does, too. But I don't think it would be suitable for us to have a sexual relationship. It's tricky. I like her a lot, and she's a very attractive girl in a number of ways. And as she chooses to climb into my bed at three o'clock in the morning, it's quite difficult to be appropriate in my actions.

My concern is for everyone involved. And Kat is not in the most stable position at the moment. And for me to take advantage of that situation would be inappropriate. Similarly, I don't know what is going on in my relationship with Chrys. It's not fair to cheat on her, particularly with someone I'm living with. It's just not the sort of thing to do. And I'm not sure how to react. I'm not happy about a camera coming in and filming me interacting with Kat in that way—for Kat's well-being and for mine when Chrys comes around and cuts my bollocks off.

Sharon: Jacinda, Neil, and I went to a protest with the Coalition Against the Criminal Justice Act, a bill that takes away a lot of people's civil rights. So we went on this organized trespass on a path along the bottom of Queen Victoria's Garden. We walked along this path that the plebes hadn't walked along in a hundred-fifty years. You felt a little proud. It wasn't that the act itself was any great thing; it was more what it symbolized.

It was peaceful for the majority of the day, but toward the end of the march, there was a girl walking along the road. And I will swear in any court that she wasn't doing anything other than walking down the road. All of a sudden I saw three policemen in full riot gear running in her direction. They got this girl and they tapped her on the shoulder from behind. She looked around, saw the policemen, and started to run. One of the policemen just got hold of her ankle and yanked it so forcefully that she fell to the ground. She went down and of course she's wriggling to get free. There were six policemen grabbing her hands and legs and her feet and arms. And she's struggling violently, so her head is, like, being continually banged on the concrete.

I rushed towards her, yelling, "Get off of her!" They were treating her like an animal, like a carcass being dragged along the ground. I have never seen anything so horrific. And the thing is, there was no provocation. I just totally freaked out. I don't say this casually: It really was evil.

Anyway, Neil and I ended up on the news 'cause I'd lost it, and he grabbed hold of me just to kind of control me, 'cause I had this adrenaline. I was shaking. I've never been like that in my life; I was just so horrified.

MARCH 12, 1995 (WEEK SEVEN)

NEIL'S TONGUE

Neil: Here is the story. There was this guy at our last gig who had been heckling me during the song "Satan." He stood right at the front of the stage and waggled his tongue at me. I waggled my tongue back, then I decided to give him a surprise. I kissed him—hard. I stuck my tongue right into his mouth. That was my mistake. He bit me. He bit me *hard*. Then I kind of fell off the stage on top of him. All the while, he was fighting me. We ended up on the floor, and it felt as though my tongue was being wrenched out of my mouth. I pushed him away and ran to the toilet. Blood was everywhere. My mouth was full of blood. And my tongue was kind of hanging on a thread. After much confusion, I managed to get in a car and go to the hospital. By the time I got to the hospital, my whole mouth was filled with blood clots. Not very nice.

Jacinda: After Neil left, everybody was just kind of standing there, shocked. Nobody knew what had happened. So I went downstairs and he was just a mess. There was blood everywhere, and nobody was really doing anything. So then Chrys came down, and we finally organized and called an ambulance. Neil was really quiet. I think he was just really freaked out by the whole thing. He looked like he was going to faint or something, 'cause he'd lost a lot of blood. No ambulance came, so they took a car and went off to the hospital.

Neil: Chrys was great—she kept on taking the piss, teasing me and telling jokes all the time, which is the best way to placate an Englishman in shock. She also went back to the hospital in the middle of the night to get me some painkillers. They gave me some nice drugs and about six local anesthetic injections in my tongue. I ended up with about twenty stitches, which took two hours. It hurt a lot.

It hasn't affected my relationship with Chrys too badly. However, cunnilingus is out of the question for a while, which may cause problems later on. As for the house, it's quite dull now that my searing wit has been curtailed. By the time I've written my witticisms down, they've lost their impact.

I got skinny. Now I have that Iggy Pop physique I always wanted. And I've got a glare that can kill at twenty paces.

STOLEN!

Jacinda: Lars's bike disappeared, and he didn't even notice for maybe four days. And he was like, "My bike has been stolen!" But there wasn't really anything anybody could do. We don't know who left the door open, and we don't know when it got stolen.

I'd already spoken to Lars about it one night, and I told him, "How awful, I'm sorry and upset for you," and everything. But I guess he thought, "Well, one day everybody says something and then it's forgotten about." He doesn't even think it was his fault, so I guess he's really pissed that nobody seemed to give a s**t that his expensive bike was gone. He doesn't have money to just go and get another one.

Lars: I would have expected everyone to say, "Hmm, when was the last time I saw the bike," or "How could it have happened?" I was sort of hoping my housemates would jump in and help me out, but everyone is probably so afraid that I blame them for leaving the door open that they're just not saying anything. And that really pisses me off. Some people are just so ignorant in this house.

Kat: I didn't know what to say when Lars started talking, because not only had no one told me about it, but I still can't get the exact date he realized it was gone. Mike said it was about two weeks ago, which was when I was in the States. So I don't know how I'm supposed to apologize for something I had nothing to do with. I guess I feel badly that his bike was taken, but I don't feel that he can be upset at me if he never told me. There's not a lot I can do.

I don't think Lars feels like the matter is settled. I plan to take him aside and ask him about it. He has said his piece, and we have kind of let it soak in, but now I'm going to go to him and say, "Listen, I just think that no one knows what to say."

Sharon: I came home and Jacinda walked in with a dog. Mike calls him Dookie, but his name is Legend. Mike's father is called Duke, so I guess that's where Dookie came from.

Legend

Neil: The dog can't get up or down the stairs, which is a constant source of amusement. If you want to get rid of it, just put it upstairs and it never comes down.

As far as I'm concerned, the dog is called F**k Off.

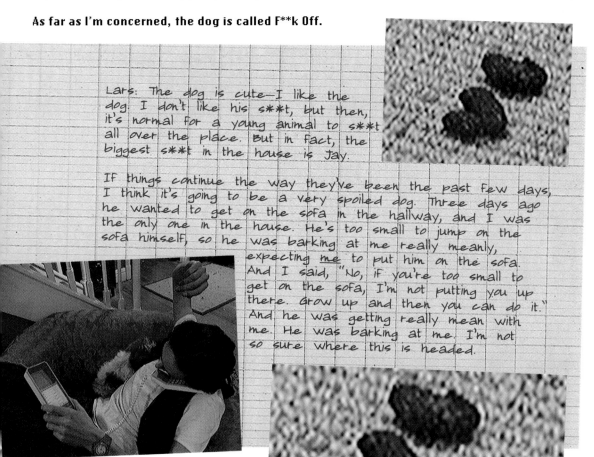

Lars: The dog is cute—I like the dog. I don't like his s**t, but then, it's normal for a young animal to s**t all over the place. But in fact, the biggest s**t in the house is Jay.

If things continue the way they've been the past few days, I think it's going to be a very spoiled dog. Three days ago he wanted to get on the sofa in the hallway, and I was the only one in the house. He's too small to jump on the sofa himself, so he was barking at me really meanly, expecting _me_ to put him on the sofa. And I said, "No, if you're too small to get on the sofa, I'm not putting you up there. Grow up and then you can do it." And he was getting really mean with me. He was barking at me. I'm not so sure where this is headed.

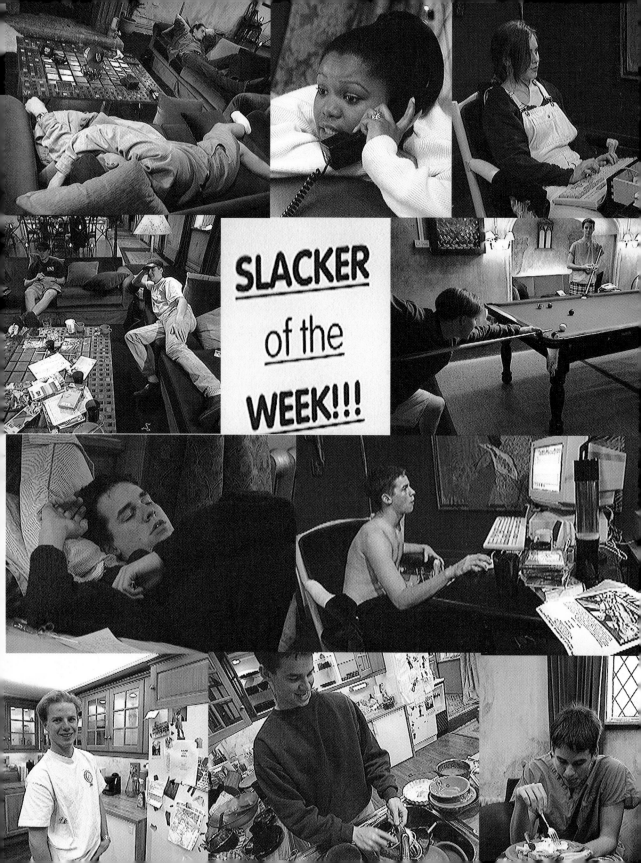

MARCH 26, 1995 (WEEK NINE)

Mike: A slacker is someone who is not doing anything, just hanging around slacking off, doing nothing, going nowhere, letting everyone else take care of him and his responsibilities.

I am the slacker judging committee. I decide all, am all, and do all. I write the rules and I post the awards. You could say that I'm Grand Master Slack.

Jay: In the house we have the slacker-of-the-week award. It's given to the person who isn't quite cleaning up enough or doing the job that they're supposed to. But basically Mike is the one who gives the award, so I think it's whoever Mike is pissed off at, 'cause <u>he</u> is a slacker, too.

Two times I was co-slacker of the week. I have yet to attain the status of slacker of the week, you know, outright. But I'm waiting for the day when it does happen. I'm working hard, and one day the slacker award will be mine and mine alone.

Jacinda: I asked Jay the other night, "Don't you get bored? Don't you hate not having a life?" And he's like, "No, I don't care. I'm happy." I'm like, okay, to each his own.

Neil: I don't think I have a fundamental objection to slackness in itself, but I literally would go mad if I was as slack as Jay.

The difference between Mike and Jay is that Mike at least is willing to go and try things, whereas Jay doesn't really have the inquisitive mind I expected from him. I haven't read his play, but I'd be more interested in seeing what Jay would write right now, rather than what he's written before. If I was stuck in a foreign town, in an alien environment, that would be the time when I would be writing stuff, that would be the time when I would be thinking about things in a different way. And I haven't seen him with a pen in his hand since we've been here.

Jay is young, and he seems to be resting on his laurels already, to a certain extent, with this play. I mean, it may well be a great play, but you need more than one work of art to be successful in this society. And it surprises me that he's not trying to create anything else while he's got this opportunity to hang out.

Kat: I always thought that Jay was a slacker, but now I want to take all that back, because he cleaned up for me one day, and when I came in everything was so nice and clean, and I was just so relieved. I stopped him and thanked him later, but I don't think he took me seriously, because it sounds so ridiculous: "Thank you for cleaning the kitchen. You have no idea how much it meant to me." But, God, I hate housework.

I want to make a list of the seven sick topics we all talk about. Like dog s**t, cleaning the house, sex, food, and language differences. I feel like that's all we ever talk about. And I mean, Jay wrote a play, and he's nineteen years old, and he made best playwright of the year, so there's got to be a lot to him, but I haven't found it yet. It seems like we've all reached this certain level with each other, and we're like, "Okay, I have an idea of who you are," and then we withdrew, because we all had our set roles. And it's so frustrating, 'cause it just makes the house so dull, and it could be such an incredible place.

UNDER THE MICROSCOPE

Kat: When people are speaking in the house, they're self-censoring. You're only going to expose so much of yourself before you're like, "All right, that's as much as I want people to see. This is as much of Kat as I'm willing to share and have criticized." Now, to really get to know me, you're going to have to see me make an ass of myself, stumble up the stairs, get too drunk once in a while, have a bad day, feel sorry for myself, be completely elated—all the vulnerable parts that I don't want criticized.

I don't like the fact that I'm incredibly moody at times. That's not something that I can always show in front of the camera, because I've been brought up not to show those emotions in public, that they've not socially acceptable. But when I do try, I open up too much and it comes across as really tinny and hollow, or I don't open up enough and it comes across as plasticine.

GIRLS' DAY OUT

Kat: Girls' day out was fun. I mean, we got separated, and we got hailed on, but it was still really fun. We got in trouble because we had Jacinda's dog, Legend, in the Tower of London. When we first went into the tower, there was a Beefeater who was just so enamored of the dog that he showed us the little pet graveyard. We must have talked to the guy for a good forty-five minutes. I didn't know that the Beefeaters actually live in the Tower of London. He was talking about how it's a great honor: You have to have served all these years and have been appointed by the queen. I had a better time talking to him than I did looking at the place, 'cause he knew so much about it.

So we walked all over the Tower of London, and I got lost, but we lost Sharon first, in the armory. And so I went back to look for her by myself, because Jacinda had already been kicked out—apparently you're not supposed to have dogs running around the Tower of London. I couldn't find Sharon, so I went and found Jacinda, and we put the dog in the backpack and waited 'til it fell asleep. Then we went back in to see the Crown Jewels, where we were chastised for walking on these escalator things that cruise past the jewels: we kept cruising past, and then running back and jumping on it to cruise past again. That was frowned upon, but it was such fun. We had a picnic by the Thames, and we had wine, and everything kept blowing away, but it was a lot of fun. It was incredible.

OUTWARD BOUND

Jay: The household had a change of pace the other day. We went on a little adventure with Outward Bound. It was interesting how each person reacted to being put

on the spot when it came time to do the trapeze course. I think Sharon did want to do the trapeze, but she wanted to be able to do it and not look foolish, and I think that was what was keeping her from it. Neil, I think, basically wasn't confident that he was going to be able to grab the thing, and he was scared of heights. It disappointed me that he didn't say, "I don't think I can make it, and I don't want to end up looking foolish." Instead, he said, "It doesn't look like my idea of fun."

Neil: It was pretty scary the way Sharon was goaded into doing the trapeze when she clearly wasn't comfortable. I found it quite disgusting that these people I know reasonably well could all gang up and force somebody into a situation she really didn't want to be in. Quite interesting from a psychological perspective, but I had a go at Sharon about it. I told her that she shouldn't give in to peer pressure like that. She's just a bit too weak. She's willing to be persuaded to do things that make her the center of attention. She's game, and she tries her best, but if I were stuck in the middle of nowhere with a toothpick and a can of water, she'd be the person I'd eat first.

Mike: Sharon, for some reason, is just so much fun to laugh at and to rail on, because she takes it well. First of all, she doesn't get mad or hurt. And secondly, she denies her discomfort, which makes it even funnier.

Kat: Jacinda likes provoking Sharon, and Sharon likes being provoked by Jacinda. I think that's the dynamic of their friendship. You would have known had Sharon really, really not wanted Jacinda to shake the ropes.

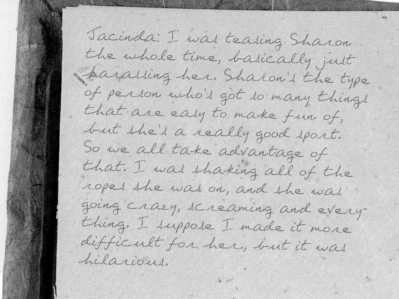

Jacinda: I was teasing Sharon the whole time, basically just harassing her. Sharon's the type of person who's got so many things that are easy to make fun of, but she's a really good sport. So we all take advantage of that. I was shaking all of the ropes she was on, and she was going crazy, screaming and everything. I suppose I made it more difficult for her, but it was hilarious.

Sharon: I think it was all done in jest, but my mother always says that there's truth in every joke. I know them all well enough to know that they wouldn't want to purposely hurt me, so if I ended up being hurt it would just be because they had gone overboard but weren't aware of that fact.

Kat basically said, "My, God, Sharon, I don't know how you put up with it. I couldn't possibly deal with everybody going after me the way they do with you." And I said to her, "Well, to be honest, it doesn't really get to me that much; it just rolls off. I don't really respond to it." But I wanted to say to her, "Then why do you take part, if you knew that you couldn't handle it yourself? You shouldn't really take part in this sort of thing, because you know you should treat others as you would want to be treated."

Lars: It's very hard to tell with Sharon. She doesn't ever seem to take offense at anything. You tease her, and she's laughing and giggling and this and that. So you really have to be careful not to go too far. Sometimes I don't know where that point is.

Lars: Mike, Sharon, and I had a little argument with Jacinda, where we were telling her that she's a bit disrespectful and egoistic. She basically told us that we didn't have any right to think that way, because we don't know her well enough.

We were trying to express that it's only a feeling we have, and everyone has the right to have feelings, but she didn't quite understand that. In fact, every time you talk or argue with Jacinda, you don't get anywhere. The only thing she seems to care about is winning the argument and not looking stupid afterward. I think discussions and arguments are also about learning or improving yourself. She doesn't seem to be interested in anything like that.

Jay: Some of the things Lars said about Jacinda not being able to accept being wrong, or to accept things being other than the way she's used to having them, are true. I've noticed that about her since the first week. I totally understand that it's because she's been out on her own for so long and making her own money and being really independent. Now she's suddenly in a situation where she has to make compromises.

Kat: Different people have different things going on. You can't expect everyone to rise to your level of protocol. And you can't say that the person's immature for not knowing exactly what your expectations of them are. It's called communication. It works on a very basic level.

Jacinda: I completely understand the point of having respect for other people's ways and beliefs, but you can't expect somebody to read your mind and know exactly what you want.

Jacinda: I thought of some funny things and started writing the stuff down, and then I kind of decided to organize it. Neil helped me get it all together on the computer and print out this newsletter. We wrote ridiculous articles about people in the house and their relation to different things, and we got some pretty nasty pictures, too.

For example, there was one article that made a correlation between Mike and his racing and Mike and his women. At that point, Mike couldn't race—he didn't have what he needed to race. Also, he didn't have what he needed to get the women that he wanted in London, so it was kind of both those things in one little story.

Another article was about Kat and all the sods she brought home, called "Kat and the Dweeb Olympics." I mean, we all tease Kat constantly about the guys she brings home, so it was basically about that.

And there was an article about Jay when he won the Slacker-of-the-Week award. Jay got a photo on page three as well—he was lucky. It was entitled "Jay Swallows His Pride." I meant the title to be a little deceiving, because it wasn't a very nice picture. I don't want to describe it.

Lars: It was hilarious. We all loved it. I mean, the page three picture was just the worst most of us have ever, ever seen. It was just so disgusting. People just couldn't believe that Neil owned pictures like that. And then all the rest of the stuff—taking the piss out of Mike and me was just so funny. We all just really loved it.

In one article, they were referring to me as the Queen of the Night—I think that was Neil's idea. I was the big advisor, the one who knows what's cool, knows where to go, and everything. And so they had Jay asking me, "I have a hard time being cool, Queen of the Night. What can you tell me?" Then the Queen of the Night says, "Well, basically you have to be like me, you have to dress like me, you should hang out with me a bit more. Then you will be cool. Just look in the mirror and say 'I'm cool' five times a day. And that's how you do it."

Jacinda: Do you know why I've decided I want to learn to fly? I just love being up there. It all looks like a fairyland from up there. And I always thought that up there you get the real picture of what we are. We're little specks, we're nothing. And everybody walks around with their own importance. In our society, everybody's trying so hard to be more important than the other person. And sometimes it's kind of funny to just sit back and watch it all.

Mike: I still can't picture Jacinda in the plane with the headphones on going, "Two-point-three quarter, this is one-nine-eight-seven-three." I think she'd be like, "Hi, I'm coming around now, and I'm going to land," and then, as she made her approach, saying, "nope, just kidding, I'm not landing," and doing a barrel roll or something. You know, I just can't see Jacinda taking it seriously. But obviously she is if she's gone this far.

JACINDA IN THE AIR

Mike: I went home to visit my parents. When I first arrived back in the States, I had a little layover in the New York airport, and while I was waiting, I started missing everybody in London already. I noticed that Americans were a little bit trashier and fatter than I had ever noticed before. Maybe it was just this airport, but as I was walking around, I saw <u>Ricki Lake</u> and <u>Jenny Jones</u> and all those talk shows on TV, and it just kind of shocked me. I was like, "This is where you live?" It was an eye-opener—my culture survives on watching trash.

In the UK, people are more independent. People don't bitch and cry as much, they don't sue each other every day, and they don't shoot each other every day. But in America it's just a way of life—people sue each other and shoot each other. That's not the right way to go about things.

I've always been strongly pro-American. And the instant I went back, I started looking at everything differently.

Kat: I talk a lot and I winge a lot about not being in a relationship, but I don't define myself by whether or not I'm in a relationship. That doesn't have anything to do with who I am as a person. I don't want to be defined by my relationships with men. So when I speak about how I haven't been with anyone in a while, or say "God, there's no men," or whatever, it's mostly just because everyone likes male attention. But it's not a necessary part of my life right now. I'm perfectly happy being single. I really like being by myself. I don't have the ties that relationships entail. Being careful about someone's very intimate feelings is a responsibility, and I'm glad that I don't have it right now. It's the time of my life when I should be a little self-centered.

I think that what I'm looking for is flirtation. Basically I feel that you get what you settle for, and if you're ready to settle for something that's not quite right for you, it's no good. I'd rather be alone than be with someone just to be with someone. I want to be equal with someone in a relationship. I think about the flirtations that I have had with people here, and none of them did me any good. It wasn't a healthy, constructive thing, it wasn't something that made us both feel good. It wasn't a good thing.

Neil: I have a few things I'd like to say. Let's talk about reality. It seems to me that the fundamental premise of this show is to capture reality. Given that premise—a false one, in my opinion—you have to construct a reality from the segments of life that you manage to record. I came into this scenario with the belief that it wouldn't affect my reality too much. I believed I could carry on more or less as normal. You would record my life, make your TV show, and we'd both leave happy. Unfortunately, that's not the case. The reality of this show is that it has undermined and destroyed the relationship I have with Chrys, who is probably the only person I've ever truly been in love with. You've destroyed it....I guess it's not wholly your fault—I should have been more prepared.

As it is, I spent the first few weeks being paranoid and confused. Due to the bizarre nature of this process, I found myself during those few weeks undergoing an encounter with somebody that I wouldn't normally pay much heed to. Now, taking that as a given, that there was some sort of encounter between me and Kat, I need to be sure that the reality you construct from beyond that point is gonna be roughly in line with the reality that I understand.

As I understand it, you're going to make some sort of episode about me and Kat. I accept that. And there's a certain level of trust that I've given to you. If it was only me, I wouldn't give a f**k, but as it is, this affects Chrys, who is someone I care about a lot. I accept that you are going to address the issue of me and Kat, but what I want *you* to accept is the fact that this was an anomaly in my life, and that, in the great scheme of things, it was trivial. What matters is that I don't wish for Chrys—or anyone else—to be affected by the representation of my errors in front of a hundred-twenty million people.

We've been in a relationship for a really long time. Things change once you overcome that initial euphoria of meeting someone and falling in love and having great sex. Things start going up and down quite dramatically. They certainly did for me and Chrys. And after five years, I've felt toward her, at one time or another, pretty much every emotion known to man. I have loved her and hated her, liked her and disliked her. I have felt incredible lust and utter repulsion. All sorts of dichotomous emotions. Pretty much everything except indifference. And the one thing that remains is that she is always significant—not that that's the best way to put it. But no matter what happens, she's always important to me. I can be screaming in her face and saying that I hate her, but it's still important that she's around and that I'm interacting with her, as long as I find her interesting and stimulating more than fifty percent of the time. Then it's worth putting up with a little s**t, and I suspect that she feels exactly the same way.

That's why the Kat thing wasn't such a big deal for us. I mean, yeah, obviously she was upset, but she knows and I know that, fundamentally, it's trivial. The fact that I got vaguely involved with someone like Kat is probably laughable to Chrys. In the great scheme of things, it doesn't really amount to much. If she did the same thing to me, I would be very upset, but I think that I understand her enough to ride out things like that.

JAY'S PLAY

MAY 7, 1995 (WEEK FIFTEEN)

Jay: *Bedroom* is the story of a kid who can't fall asleep. So he gets up and he decides to just act, to do a one-man show, because he can't fall asleep. And so he looks around his room and takes objects and just begins to tell stories. Gradually, in telling these stories, he comes across moments of truth. He talks about being seventeen and about what that's like. Then he tries to go back to sleep.

I like to think that at the end of the play a certain moment of honesty occurs, that if it catches people at the right time in their lives, they'll really appreciate it. That's what I'm most proud of, I suppose.

I really wish I had felt comfortable enough to perform my play earlier, because I think it's gonna change a lot of things around the house. I'm looking forward to seeing how my relationships with other people in the house change after they see my show, after they see what I really believe in.

Neil: It was surprisingly well written for a seventeen-year-old. And that was a pleasant surprise. On the other hand, it was quite teen-angsty, which I kind of expected, and that aspect of it I didn't really like that much.

Lars: It took a long time to get the crowd going at the party we had after Jay's play. No one danced when I started playing seventies classics, disco stuff. I even played the Beastie Boys and AC/DC and stuff like that. Neil's girlfriend, Chrys, was my dancing queen. She was dancing all night, and she was especially in love with all of my seventies and early-eighties stuff. But, the later it got, and the more drunk we all became, the more fun we had.

Neil: Once Lars stopped being so uptight about the kind of music he was playing, people enjoyed it more. Not to put him down as a DJ, but you have to gauge your audience, and I think the audience he had wasn't too into Handbag House.

Jacinda: I think Mike's kind of disappointed with how he feels he's being portrayed here. He even said, "All the guys back home are going to be so disappointed with me, 'cause I haven't scored and I haven't shown them I can get chicks here." I think he's a bit pissed about the whole thing. There's so much f**king sexual tension in our house. Maybe that's why he picked Hannah up at the post-play party.

Mike: This has been the driest period of my entire life. Fly me to the lake for one weekend, and then you can have as much fun with me as you want, 'cause I'll hook up with a bunch of girls. I've hooked up with three since I've been here. Let's go to the lake, and I'll show you guys a good time.

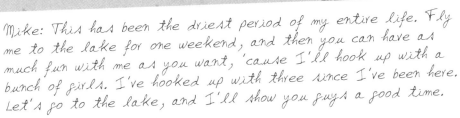

Hannah and I didn't have sex or anything. It was no big deal. It was just drunkenness. I think Sharon said it perfectly the next day: "It was just two drunk people having a good time." And that's all it was—no big deal. It was fun, it was great, I had a good time, she had a good time, and that was it.

Jay: So I do this play about not being able to fall asleep, and the next thing I know, there's this big old cover moving all around and these little noises and stuff. It doesn't take too much brains—if you sit through a play for an hour and a half about this kid not being able to sleep, and then you take a woman up into the room with that kid and make all types of noises until four in the morning, that it must be some kind of alcohol that's working on you. It's like, good for Mike, but after my play? I didn't get too much sleep.

Jacinda: I think Hannah must have no pride. She came over and got together with Mike, who was desperate for anything he could get, slept over in our house, and darted out in the morning with the speed of lightning. And then for a whole week Mike didn't call her. She called on Thursday or something, and I thought, Oh, my God, there's something wrong here.

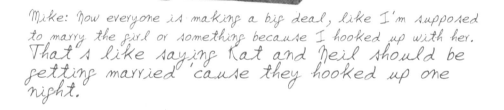

Mike: Now everyone is making a big deal, like I'm supposed to marry the girl or something because I hooked up with her. That's like saying Kat and Neil should be getting married 'cause they hooked up one night.

THE BLUES

Kat: I consider myself a fairly easygoing person. I don't think I raise a huge issue about things that aren't necessarily important. But once in a while I wish that my roommates would make a little room for me. Not to sound pathetic, but I am having problems with my moods right now. I'm going up, I'm going down, I'm going up, I'm going down.

I haven't been able to fence. That's something I do to help keep my head, myself, in order, and I need that as a person. I get kind of far out there if I don't have some sort of release. I think you can see the difference in me— I haven't fenced in two weeks, and I'm pretty wound up. There are times when I feel myself getting pent up or getting emotional, and I have two extreme reactions. One is that I get irritated and angry at everything. Or I get upset and weepy. It's so frustrating.

Kat: Neil's been in a real funk for the last few days; he's been pretty pissy. I went up last night and I'm like, hey, what's wrong? "I hate everybody." Oh, well, okay, I'll leave then. He's just been in a really bad mood. Part of it is that Chrys left—she's gonna be in Italy for ten days—and about the time she gets back, we leave for a vacation. So he knows that he's not gonna see her for close to three weeks, and it's gonna be rough. He's also just really burned out. He wants to go back to Oxford and be with his friends and do his degree. I think he's really ready for the simple life.

Jay: It seems kind of unfortunate that I haven't been able to handle this whole situation as easily as other people have. I have thought a couple times how wonderful it would be to show people that we aren't oblivious to the fact that we are getting our lives taped. The show's a huge deal. If you want to get to know me, the thing you don't do is stick your camera in my face. The reason I was here was to live my life and have these real relationships. I have failed in that way. I haven't been able to let go of my problems with the cameras, of not thinking about it, just trusting and giving in completely to the project. I feel like this whole *Real World* thing is beating the s**t out of me. The time I have been here has just been real tough on me. But never was there a single time that I thought that it'd conquer me.

Mike: I'm finding Jacinda more and more difficult to get along with. I don't trust the girl at all. I said from the beginning that I don't think she respects other people and other people's things, and the more I'm with her, the less I respect her. The more I'm with her, the less I trust her.

There's things you say to her when you're alone, like the time we went skating in the park, just the two of us. We sat by the fountains and had a good time, and we talked about a lot of interesting stuff. And she's like, "What do you think of Neil's girlfriend?" And I'm like, "She's nice, she's definitely not my type of girl, I couldn't go out with her, she's nowhere near what I would call my type of girl at all. She's interesting, but she's Neil's type of girl. I don't find her, you know, exciting at all."

At the time, Jacinda was like, "That's interesting, I agree with what you're saying." You know, just understanding what I had to say, like a good listener would. And then, when we get home and we're both in front of Neil, all of a sudden she's like, "So, Neil, Mike thinks that your girlfriend's a pile of trash." It's when she does stuff like that that I'm just like, well, wait a minute. Here I am trying to tell you something in confidence, and you totally change everything and make it sound awful.

I think she requires a lot of attention. And she seems to go out and find it, too. The reason she bought the dog, I think, was to get attention. The pierced tongue, the way she walks down the street and hits everybody, this is to draw attention to herself. Maybe she gets so much attention in modeling that when she comes to be with us, we don't give her enough attention, 'cause we don't find her any different. So maybe she has to go out and get it other ways. I think that if she were to just settle down a little bit, she could be such a great person.

Jacinda: Sharon is full of these guards and defenses. Today, even when there was nobody around, I asked her about some guy that I thought she liked, and she's like "No, no, no, I don't like him." And then we were completely alone, and she's like, "Well, I kind of like him, but I just don't want to talk about it." It's really taboo; she won't talk about guys. When you're really alone, she'll let down her guard, and you can really get to know her. So one-on-one, or in quiet situations, I like her and really enjoy her company, but when she's in a big group or when she's got all her defenses up, it can be really aggravating.

Lars: I think we are all aware that we're getting toward the end of this. A couple weeks ago I couldn't take it anymore. I was really annoyed with my housemates, and I just couldn't stand the whole thing. Things were just too complicated and too immature. But now that we're getting close to the end, I think we're all trying to pull our acts together. We're sort of realizing, Hmm, this person has this fault, and that person has that fault, but deep inside, he's quite a nice guy, quite a nice girl. So for the last couple of days, I've been getting along better with everyone in the house.

Jacinda: Everybody can be so disgusting; the conversation can sink down so low. Last night was a perfect example. Mike and Neil and Lars were talking to Sharon in <u>quite</u> explicit terms, asking Sharon how many men she had been with and what she'd done with them.

Mike is the king of talking about women like that. He calls women "bitches" and "whores" and says, "Smoke my pole." Mike can be so disgusting and filthy when he's talking about women.

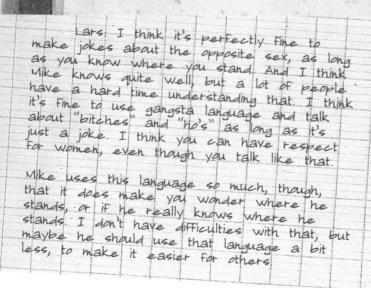

Lars: I think it's perfectly fine to make jokes about the opposite sex, as long as you know where you stand. And I think Mike knows quite well, but a lot of people have a hard time understanding that. I think it's fine to use gangsta language and talk about "bitches" and "ho's" as long as it's just a joke. I think you can have respect for women, even though you talk like that.

Mike uses this language so much, though, that it does make you wonder where he stands, or if he really knows where he stands. I don't have difficulties with that, but maybe he should use that language a bit less, to make it easier for others.

Kat: In some ways, I would say, I am a hard-core feminist. I wouldn't speak about my boyfriend in a disrespectful manner, even in a joking sense, because there's a grain of truth in every joke—there's a reason why it's funny. So I just wouldn't want to be spoken of like that. I don't think it's respectful. But Mike always asks, "Is it more respectful to actually say it, or to do it?"

Mike: I got in a conversation with Neil about using the word "bitch." He was trying to call me immoral because I called women "bitch," and I said, "Well, Neil, you've cheated on your girlfriend so many times. You tell me what is more disrespectful—to call a woman a bitch or to cheat on her?" I mean, I've never cheated on a girlfriend, and Neil does it as often as he can. It's funny that I'm supposed to be the bad guy.

Neil: Mike is all talk and no trousers. That boy, he likes to think that he can get women whenever he wants and seduce them and discard them willy-nilly, whereas in fact he's a sad sop who's gonna sit around and speak nicely to them and when the time is right, maybe just lean forward and kiss them gently, which is completely at odds with what he likes to project. I just think that's funny.

I don't think he is genuinely that misogynous. But he is comfortable joking about it, and as far as I'm concerned, that's where the rock starts really. If you can joke about disrespecting someone, then it's only a short step to actually doing it. It's something that doesn't aid the women's movement much, when he laughingly talks about them as bitches behind their backs. You're talking about fifty-one percent of the population, who have enough s**t as it is without people like Mike wandering around calling them bitches.

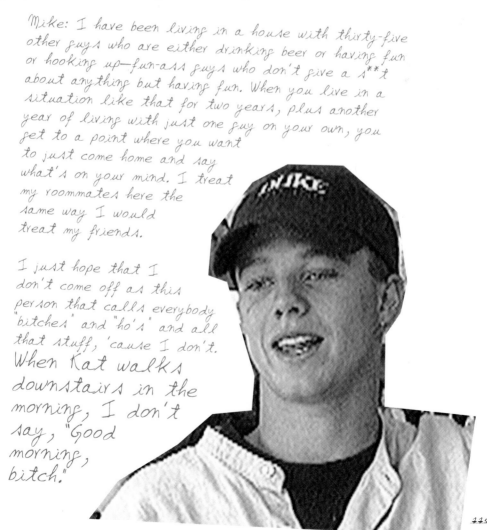

Mike: I have been living in a house with thirty-five other guys who are either drinking beer or having fun or hooking up—fun-ass guys who don't give a s**t about anything but having fun. When you live in a situation like that for two years, plus another year of living with just one guy on your own, you get to a point where you want to just come home and say what's on your mind. I treat my roommates here the same way I would treat my friends.

I just hope that I don't come off as this person that calls everybody "bitches" and "ho's" and all that stuff, 'cause I don't. When Kat walks downstairs in the morning, I don't say, "Good morning, bitch."

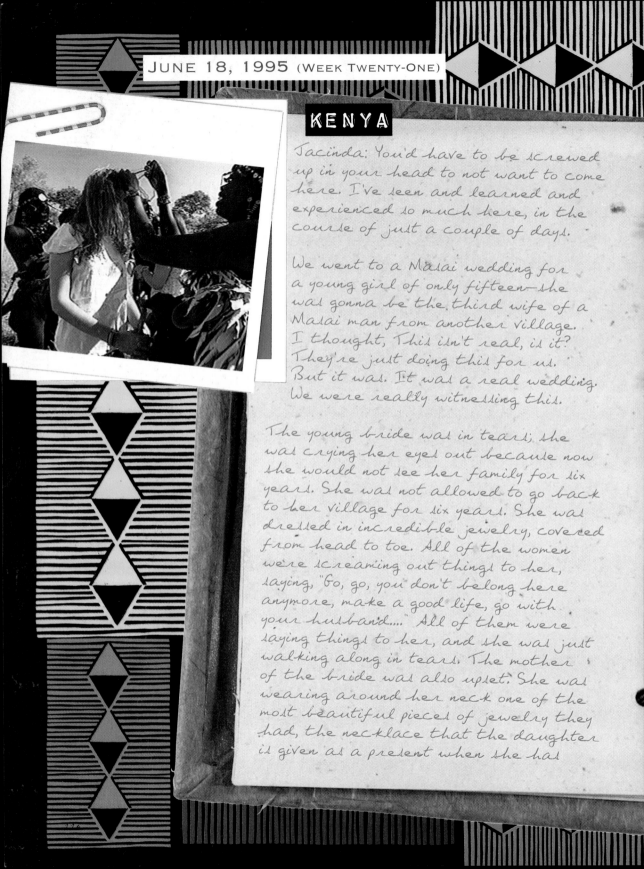

KENYA

Jacinda: You'd have to be screwed up in your head to not want to come here. I've seen and learned and experienced so much here, in the course of just a couple of days.

We went to a Masai wedding for a young girl of only fifteen—she was gonna be the third wife of a Masai man from another village. I thought, This isn't real, is it? They're just doing this for us. But it was. It was a real wedding. We were really witnessing this.

The young bride was in tears; she was crying her eyes out because now she would not see her family for six years. She was not allowed to go back to her village for six years. She was dressed in incredible jewelry, covered from head to toe. All of the women were screaming out things to her, saying, "Go, go, you don't belong here anymore, make a good life, go with your husband...." All of them were saying things to her, and she was just walking along in tears. The mother of the bride was also upset. She was wearing around her neck one of the most beautiful pieces of jewelry they had, the necklace that the daughter is given as a present when she has

her circumcision. And the mother was just in tears.

After we witnessed the wedding, we went into the house of the mother of the bride. For me, that was a really incredible thing. I was sitting down with her baby, who was just a tiny baby, and she was sitting there crying and crying and crying. And she came and sat down next to me and just put her arms around me, and I gave her the only piece of jewelry I had on, a silver bracelet. I gave it to her, and out of her own ear, she took one of the earrings that they wear up high in their ears and gave it to me. And it was just incredible to be sitting there, on her bed with her, on such an important day in her life.

I was just in tears about the whole thing. And it wasn't so much sad or happy, it was just--I just couldn't believe that I was there. It was just so overwhelming.

Jay: Dixon [one of our guides, a Masai who had also been to university] took us back to his village, because we wanted to buy some jewelry, and it was strange, because the first time, when we went to experience the wedding, we were welcomed. But the second time, they wanted something from us, and the balance had totally shifted. We wanted to buy their jewelry, but it was so anxious; they wanted to sell these things so bad. It was frustrating. I mean, they couldn't understand or accept when I ran out of money. We had to take refuge in the cars.

NICK

Sharon: My father was actually a Kikuyu, which is one of the principal tribes of Kenya. I was very interested to see if I could trace my line, or just find out more about the Kikuyu, because I don't know all that much. I've learned a lot more about Masai culture, because obviously we're in the Masai Mara, not the Kikuyu land. But the two peoples are not that dissimilar, and I knew a fair amount about the Masai before I came here, through documentaries and things like that. I find them to be an amazing, amazing people. Very beautiful.

I remember that Jacinda and I both made a comment to the effect that there are certain moments in your life when everything is just as you would want it to be, and you wouldn't change a thing if you had the opportunity. This is one of those moments.

DIXON

Neil: We had a conversation about trying to explain where we were from and where Jacinda was from. And it turns out that the Masai concept of the world starts and ends where the sun rises and the sun falls. That's the world. So if you try and explain that Australia is on the other side of this big round ball spinning in space, they have no concept at all. And Jacinda said, "If you dug a hole straight down, and went right through the earth, you'd come out the other side, and you'd be more or less in Australia." And they turned around and laughed and said that was stupid. Nobody lives in the ground. Every single fundamental concept of time and space that they use is completely different from mine. And it's just fascinating and incredible that this can still occur. I've taken for granted that everyone sees the world the way I, through my Western eyes, see it.

But there's also the downside: For all the awe and wonder that you see in this culture, barbaric and horrific things are going on. I was very shocked and upset to discover that they're still practicing female circumcision around here, and our other guide, Nick, was saying, "Yeah, that's something you can't even talk about."

That stirs up a whole lot of emotions. How do you feel about that? You're happy to let them live their life, and you don't want to corrupt them by bringing too much Western culture, yet when you see something so barbaric going on right in front of your face, you want to change it. But the desire to change certain aspects of their lives and not others leads into really sticky territory. It's shocking to know that all the women around us in that village had been through something horrific. It just made me uncomfortable.

Lars: The Masai people have a very simple life. They basically have everything they need. Their lifestyle might seem cruel to us, but they are fine the way they live. Unlike us, they respect their environment. They are one with nature and one with the environment. It's impressive to see people living off the land and with the land, not leaving any garbage, not polluting or destroying in any way. That's very, very impressive.

Mike: The difference is that when you go to McDonald's, you're given a burger, but when you have dinner with a Masai warrior, you see a goat walking around—your dinner was recently alive, and you actually see the difference between life and death.

FINAL THOUGHTS

Lars: I've never in my life been as lazy as in the last five months. I find it quite hard to understand why I was like that. I had so many goals, so many things I wanted to do, and not much came out of that, not much happened.

I was just going to say that I've become more tolerant toward things, but I'm not quite sure if that's the right word. It's just that things bother me less now than they did about half a year ago. I mean, stepping into dog s**t twice a day is a thing I would not have accepted about three or four months ago.

Mike: I think this whole experience has changed me. I had no intention of ever going to London. I had no intention of leaving the United States. I was happy there, I had everything there, and everything was comfortable to me. I could jump in my car, drive down the highway, drive wherever I wanted, and it would be Americans that I could deal with, American money. It was all set, you know; I didn't have to worry about it.

And I was very resistant to any change. But I went in with an open mind and accepted the change, and now, going home in a week, I look forward to traveling again and seeing parts of the world that I've never seen. The nicest thing anyone has said to me in a long time was something Lars told me the other night. It really almost brought a tear to my eye. He said that he respected me the most because although I came in very structured and organized, I still came in with an open mind, and that I have probably changed the most of anybody here.

Neil: The people I'm closest to, who've been observing me over this period, have noticed that I've become more tolerant. Which in itself is not a bad thing, but I think a lot of my wit came from being outright obnoxious to people, which is something I've stopped doing since being surrounded by people who get easily hurt by things you say. I find I have to temper what I say, and I do that automatically now. So I haven't got the option of being as up-front and nasty as I used to be. I guess in the great scheme of things it means that when I deal with other people, I'll be nicer to them, but in the environment I was previously in, it means I'll now be somewhat weaker.

Jay: I think the best thing is that last night we had a conversation around the table, and for the first time, I felt like these people understand quite a bit about me, and I understand a lot about them. It doesn't bother me that I didn't accomplish some of the things I set out to do. Rather, I see now that I didn't know what it was that I had to work on or what it was that I had to learn.

Kat: I don't think I'll miss being followed by a camera crew. Or having to page someone to tell them that I'm going to buy tampons, Coke, and Cheese Doodles at Tescos in five minutes. I don't think I'll miss that. No offense—I'm sure they won't miss my calling all the time, either.

Jacinda:
I'm just here to say farewell,
But no time to let all our heads swell.
Just here to say it straight,
before the [boom] goes down on Powis Gate.
We'll miss you—nah, probably not.
I know I won't miss Sharon's rock.
Poor old Sharon. She was just too slow.
And I know I won't miss Mike's horny glow.
And as for Kat's, well, trail of loser men,
there must have been f**king loads of them.
And Mike tried and tried to get laid.
By any girl, Mike was willing to be played.
But he really didn't get an English f**k.
In fact, even with Americans, Mike had no luck.
And as for our tongueless rock star, Neil,
burst in his pants to get a feel,
within a week he tried to jump Kat's bones,
I think Kat sensed the undertones.
So those two weren't meant to be,
A five-year relationship is something you just don't flee.
So good ol' Neil, our faithful Mister Cool.
But Neil's been played, he's just Lars's fool.
And there's our good old correct, straight,
  old-fashioned Jay,
tap, tap, tap in his old PC way.
So I guess that's it, that's us,
dog, cat, woman, and man.
Have we forgotten Lars again?
Yup, we have a tendency to do
that sometimes.
I'll gladly leave Lars alone
with his technochimes.
But that's it, that's all I can
think of. I'm here alone.
I'm just hanging to go home.
So I'll just leave this place
And go float somewhere in outer space.

PARTING IMAGES

Jacinda:

Sharon—one of the funniest things I guess would have to have been the high-ropes course at Ullswater. That was definitely in true form.

Jay—going to buy lingerie. I mean that was just so funny.

Mike—I guess Mike's little whisper in my ear at the party was funny. I guess I'll always remember that.

Kat—all our forever-long discussions in bed.

Lars—I'll remember his mannerisms, you know, the way he holds his cigarette, his eyes, his whole demeanor.

Neil—his desire to be gross and disgusting and tough and mean, when in fact he's this huge softy who gets upset about things and takes things to heart. I guess I'm talking about that huge gap in how he's pretending to be and how he really is.

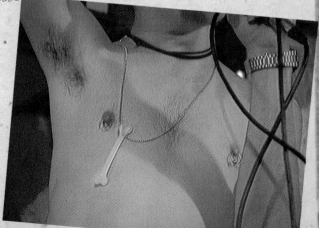

Lars:
Neil—the main picture I'll have is of Neil dressed in black, preferably leather pants, on-stage. But the stronger picture I'll have is of Neil at the computer, sitting there quietly looking at the monitor.

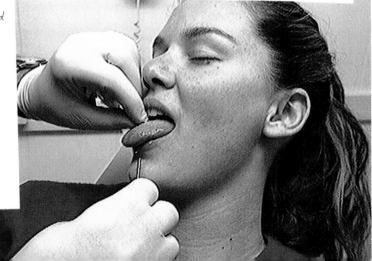

Jay—the picture of Jay will be me waking up and going to his room to see if he's awake yet so I can crank up my stereo, and then realizing, no, he's not awake yet. So Jay in bed is the main picture I'll have.

Mike—I think I'll have three snapshots of Mike. One will be him playing Monopoly and becoming ridiculously competitive about a stupid game. Two will be Mike using dirty language and being a f**king sexist. And the third picture will be Mike laughing and having a good time and making jokes and being happy.

Jacinda—"How's my boy, how's my boy, how's my boy?!!!!"

Kat—I'll have a picture of Kat sitting somewhere quiet, smiling.

Sharon—sitting at her table, eating off a very pretty plate with little vegetables and a little sandwich, talking very fast and very loud, and not saying anything.

Mike:
Jay—all I have is this mental image of him smiling, because he's usually smiling.

Neil—him and his nipple ring and his blond hair and his perplexed look. You know, his thinking look.

Lars—I see him with a headphone on one ear, some silver shirt, some see-through shoes. That smile-look, with the headphone on his ear.

Kat—some goofy red hat and a pair of overalls.

Jacinda—do I have to remember Jacinda? No, I'm just kidding. With a big pole through her tongue, probably, and just wild, rambunctious, out of control, in her big dress.

Neil:

Jay—it saddens me that he hasn't done more. I was really expecting him to be sort of enthusiastic about the experience he was having, whereas he just seems to be a bit of a slacker. But you know, he's the one I know the least about, so I don't have that much to say.

Lars—Lars lived up to the German stereotype that I had—his self-confidence and his manners, both of which could be interpreted as arrogance. It's not something that I have a problem with. I have a lot of very obnoxious and arrogant friends.

Sharon—I seem to remember around the middle period saying that I thought Sharon was a useless human being. I'll amend that: I think that currently she is useless, but she may yet serve some purpose to somebody.

Jacinda—if she had direction, she'd be a very dangerous girl.

Mike—he came here as the Mr. Clean-cut American Frat Boy. And he's leaving slightly softened at the edges. He now realizes that the whole world doesn't revolve around him and his American ways.

Kat—I don't think there was much potential ever. Knowing what I now know about her, I think it was a very bad move to get involved. But also I think it's good that we are in this situation, because were we not being filmed, chances are that I would have dropped her harder than I did and taken her farther than she wanted to go.

Sharon:

Mike—I'm gonna remember Mike curling up on all the sofas and chairs in the house. He's such a napper.

Jay—I'm gonna remember Jay sipping coke and eating pizza, 'cause that's when Jay's happiest. I want to remember Jay when he has his little spontaneous moments, his moments of comic genius or brilliance or schizy fun.

*Neil—I'm going to remember Neil onstage with his exploding penis, saying, "I dedicate all my songs to ass*****s." That's how I'm going to remember Neil.*

Lars—I'm going to remember Lars in the morning in the bathroom, with his mousse and his wax, looking at his eyes just so. He literally stands there like the Fonz.

Kat—I am going to remember Kat stretching. She's got this really feline stretch, and she is just totally herself. That's the essence of her. When she's stretching and she's purring away somewhere.... That's how I'm gonna remember her. She's my little sprite.

Jacinda—I'm gonna remember Jacie jumping and giggling and being all mischievous. Collecting dog turds with a big smile on her face and poking them in people's faces.

Kat:

Lars—Lars hauling my kitten around, she's on his shoulder, he's turning around and kissing her.

Jacinda—with Legend, "How's my boy, how's my boy, how's my boy?"

Sharon—the day that she had someone in her room, and the guitar was playing and she was singing. Jacinda and I pushed open the shutters and we were just both, like...it was so Sharon, you know. That was more Sharon than anything I had seen.

Mike—Mike gets this look on his face when he thinks you really caught him on something, and he gets all shy. It's a really sweet expression. like if you're talking about a girl or something, and you'll say, "Oh, but you like her, don't you?" And he'll turn bright red, and he'll look down, because he doesn't want to say, "Oh, yeah, I do."

Neil—I think of him singing, and then I think of him lying on the bed and saying to the cat, "You're the most beautiful cat in the world, and I love you." Probably 'cause there were just so many conflicting images.

Jay—playing pool, being like, "Hey, Kat, what's up?" like I got up for a glass of water at four in the morning and he's hanging out, just wanting to know how things are. "Do you want to watch _Harold and Maude_ with me?" That was very Jay.

VIA AIR MAIL

SAN FRANCISCO

JUDD

FIRST IMPRESSIONS

JUDD: MEETING RACHEL WAS LIKE ONE BIG BLIND DATE. I WAS SITTING THERE NOT KNOWING EXACTLY WHO I WAS GOING TO MEET, CONCERNED ABOUT HOW I LOOKED, BECAUSE SHE'S MEETING ME FOR THE FIRST TIME, AND ALL THAT. ACTUALLY, I PRETTY MUCH EXPECTED THAT A PRETTY WOMAN WAS GOING TO WALK OFF THIS PLANE. THAT WAS MY HUNCH. AND SURE ENOUGH, THERE SHE WAS.

Cory: I think Pedro is nervous about telling the guys. He's said that so many times, he'll tell a guy he's gay and they instantly react like he wants to get down their pants. And it's just another misconception.

— CORY

Mohammed: I think everything that Cory comes into contact with is totally exciting and new for her. She gets so into the moment, you know, so that it's just like, "Ohmigod! Hi, you guys!!!" And she just keeps going, and stuff. Most other people, if they were as excited about everything as Cory is, man, you would just want to, like, haul off and hit them on something. But she's a cool person, and that's just how she is. She's excited about everything, and everything is new.

JUDD: I WAS VERY CONSCIOUS OF MY FIRST IMPRESSIONS, AND I DIDN'T WANT TO START STEREOTYPING. BUT I KNEW I WOULD; IT'S JUST A MATTER OF HOW I DEAL WITH IT. AND IN HINDSIGHT, THAT'S WHAT I WAS DOING. PAM COMES THROUGH THE DOOR, AND I'M THINKING, OKAY, ASIAN GIRL. THEN MOHAMMED CAME IN, AND I'M SAYING, OKAY, AFRICAN-AMERICAN GUY. I WAS A LITTLE UPSET WITH MYSELF THAT I WAS DOING THAT. BUT IT WAS GONE AFTER TEN MINUTES, AFTER I GOT THE NAMES AND WHO THEY WERE AND WHAT THEY WERE ABOUT.

PAM

Pam: My biggest fear about moving to the house is that something really bad—medically—is going to happen, and I as the medical student would have to run in there and save them, and I won't know what to do. And I'll look like a total idiot.

Cory: Pam says she always notices people's veins. So, I don't know, I guess it's just a different perspective, but it's great. I'm a little grossed out by that kind of stuff, but that's okay.

Mohammed: It was a hectic move. I had a headache. I was fasting, too, which made things kind of complicated. It's my first day of Ramadan, which is a Muslim holiday, and so I couldn't eat or drink anything during the day, and I had this pounding headache that was just killing me.

MOHAMMED

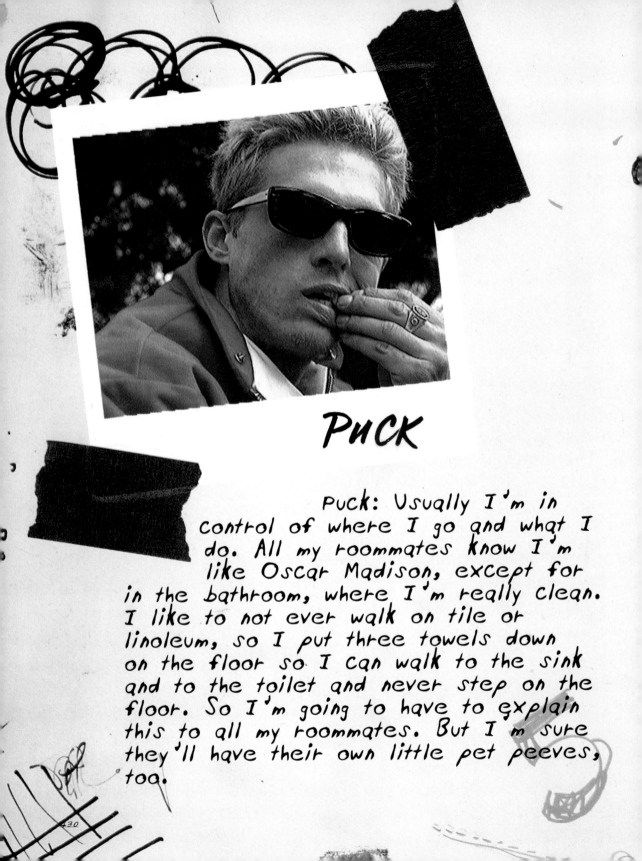

PUCK

PUCK: Usually I'm in control of where I go and what I do. All my roommates know I'm like Oscar Madison, except for in the bathroom, where I'm really clean. I like to not ever walk on tile or linoleum, so I put three towels down on the floor so I can walk to the sink and to the toilet and never step on the floor. So I'm going to have to explain this to all my roommates. But I'm sure they'll have their own little pet peeves, too.

Pedro: When I met Puck, I had some problems with him. And it was basically about his hygiene, or lack of hygiene. It was about his manners, his personality as a whole. And I reacted very negatively to it. I did tell him how I felt about his hygiene. And he pretty much said that he didn't care about that.

PEDRO

Mohammed: I know people who are like Puck, and he's a ham, you know. He's a cool guy and he has a good heart, so it's cool, but I felt like he was overdoing his sensationalism so that everybody would just categorize him as so crazy that he's cool.

JUDD: HE'S FUN. I THINK PUCK AND I ARE GOING TO GET ALONG REAL WELL.

RACHEL

Rachel: The only thing that really bothered me about Pam is that she's so damn P.C. Like on the first night, when we had the prayer, I felt that her response was really uncalled-for. I mean, all Puck said was, "Let's pray together."

JUDD: PUCK AND RACHEL ARE SO UPSET THAT PAM DIDN'T WANT TO HOLD HANDS AND SAY A PRAYER THE FIRST NIGHT WE WERE HERE. NOW, I KIND OF GAVE IN TO IT BECAUSE I WAS CURIOUS, I WANTED TO SEE WHAT WAS GOING TO HAPPEN. BUT PAM BALKED. I ASSUME HER REASON WAS THAT IT FELT SILLY. IT FELT SILLY TO ME, TOO. I'M NOT TRYING TO BELITTLE ANYONE'S RELIGION, BUT IT'S JUST NOT SOMETHING I DO. AND I GUESS SHE FELT THE SAME WAY.

I AGREED WITH PAM ENTIRELY. I DON'T THINK IT WAS NECESSARILY THE PLACE. WE'VE ALL JUST MET, AND WE DON'T KNOW WHAT EACH OTHER'S VIEWS ARE, AND IT'S EASIER NOT TO HAVE A PRAYER, TO DO SOMETHING KIND OF NON-SECTARIAN, THAN IT IS TO DRAG PEOPLE IN. WE CAN ALL TOAST, BUT WE CAN'T ALL PRAY.

IT'S NOT YOUR PLACE TO DRAG SOMEONE ELSE INTO SOMETHING. IT'S NOT YOUR PLACE TO PUSH YOUR BELIEFS ON SOMEBODY ELSE. IT WAS JUST AS EASY TO SAY A TOAST. WE DON'T HAVE TO BRING GOD INTO IT—THERE IS NO REASON TO. SOME PEOPLE DON'T BELIEVE IN HIM. BUT WE ALL BASICALLY BELIEVED IN EACH OTHER. THAT'S EASY.

AND PUCK AND RACHEL, WHO I REALLY DO CARE ABOUT AFTER SUCH A SHORT TIME, COULDN'T SEE PAST THAT. INSTEAD OF RESPECTING THE FACT THAT PAM DIDN'T WANT TO DO THIS, THEY THOUGHT SHE SHOULD CONCEDE, THAT SHE SHOULD JUST GIVE IN FOR THE SAKE OF OUR FIRST NIGHT TOGETHER.

GRACE

Pam: I come from a religious family, and I'm actually not a completely unreligious person. I have struggled with my religious beliefs. But what I was reacting to at the time was the fact that we were all just sitting down at the table, and Puck was trying to take control of the situation; I felt that he just wanted control.

For me, religion is still something I haven't resolved; I still don't really know where I stand on it. I've gone from one extreme to the other, everything from joining an evangelical Christian fellowship group and converting people in the mall for a weekend, to just being like, "I can't have anything to do with organized religion." But I'm still open to hearing what people have to say about their experience of it, because. . . .it's important.

JUDD: JUDAISM IS INTERESTING. IT REALLY BRINGS US TOGETHER, UNIFIES US. YOU CAN GET A GROUP OF FOUR OR FIVE JEWS WHO REALLY HATE EACH OTHER, PUT THEM IN A ROOM, AND THEN PUT AN ANTI–SEMITE IN THERE. YOU WON'T FIND FOUR OR FIVE PEOPLE CLOSER THAN THOSE JEWS AT THAT MOMENT. THEY MIGHT HATE EACH OTHER, BUT BEING JEWISH BREAKS DOWN EVERYTHING ELSE.

Mohammed: There are many religions in the house. My religion is Islam, and I'm a Muslim. I think a lot of people confuse the two. Muslim means one who believes in God. Islam means a religious way of life. I'm someone who believes in God and who's trying to follow a religious way of life. I'm trying to keep my head on in this world, trying to return to God all the time. Religion means returning to God, and I'm always trying to think about God, always trying to pray for other people.

233

Pam: I had a running joke with Pedro about being a control freak. Pedro tells me I'm a control freak. I think Pedro's a control freak.

I definitely like to be in control. I think that's partially why I'm in medicine: It gives me a lot of information, and information is power. With Pedro, you have to give him a lot of choices. If you give him a choice, he'll be nice. But if you tell him he <u>has</u> to do something, he'll say, "No, I <u>don't</u> have to."

Right now I like Pedro the best. I really respect him. Plus, his junior high school scrapbook is a lot like my own scrapbook from that time.

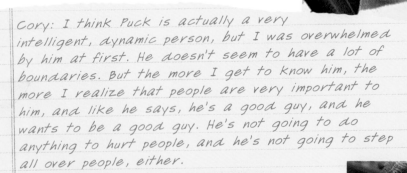

Cory: I think Puck is actually a very intelligent, dynamic person, but I was overwhelmed by him at first. He doesn't seem to have a lot of boundaries. But the more I get to know him, the more I realize that people are very important to him, and like he says, he's a good guy, and he wants to be a good guy. He's not going to do anything to hurt people, and he's not going to step all over people, either.

PUCK: If Cory opens up and quits being sheltered, it's going to make her a better person. She'll learn from other people's trips. And that's what I think life is about. You run into different people, and you take what you want and get rid of the rest—it's your choice. Every person has some aspect to them that I find interesting, including Cory.

Pedro, what do I think of Pedro? I think Pedro's gay.

Rachel: I like Cory. She's a very sweet girl. Maybe too sweet, too eager to be nice to everybody. But hopefully that will change. I'm looking forward to seeing her be less of a yes-girl. I think she's nervous, and she's the youngest one, which may have something to do with it. But I can see that we're going to be great friends. 'Cause you can't really be mad at her; she's just too nice.

Cory: Hopefully, by the end of all this, I'll be able to talk to a camera staring at me and not feel so silly.

FEBRUARY 13, 1994

(WEEK THREE)

DEALING WITH PUCK

PUCK: The house is kind of weird. It's like <u>Poltergeist</u>, or something. It pulls something weird out of you, and it throws it out there in the middle of the floor for everybody to kind of check out. And I'm good with it now, but, I mean, the first couple weeks I was just losing my mind.

Rachel: me and Puck got in our hugest fight during this big bicycle event in the city called Critical mass. In the beginning, he said, "we'll go halfway across the bridge if you think you can make it." I made it across the bridge, he came across and found me, and I'm thinking, "Cool, we're on our way home."

But Puck wanted to prove to his friends that he was the same old Puck he was before this project. So he insisted that we all go down farther, to the beach. We had no headlights at all. It was dark, there was no lighting on the path. It was bumpy and muddy. It started to rain. I said, "Puck, I think we should turn back." And his friends said, "yeah, let's turn back." And Puck's like, "Baaa, no, man, we gotta keep going. I'm still the Puck, man."

So one of his friends was like, "well, I'll go back with you if you want, Rachel," but I had just met him, so I didn't want to go back with some dude I didn't know.

well, we get halfway down, and I'm walking my bike, 'cause they all went ahead of me. And I get trapped in the mud. It's raining. And Puck comes back and goes, "what's wrong?" And I said, "Puck, it's really pissing me off that you don't realize that I'm cold. This is a twenty-two-mile bike ride you're taking me on, and it's my first bike ride in the city." There I was, going on three-and-a-half hours, rainy, cold, tired. my back and shoulders were killing me.

And his reaction, which I thought should have been, "Sorry, we can turn back now," was instead, "Dammit!" And he threw his bike down. And he goes, "I guess I won't get to go to the beach." And I was just like, "what an ass."

So then we went down to the beach. we were fighting, and I told him that I thought he was only doing this because of his friends, that he's twenty-five and still cares what his friends think about him, and all kinds of s**t. I was really mean. Then he told me a whole bunch of mean things, and then we went home.

JUDD: ABOUT TWO DAYS AGO, PUCK GOT A PACKAGE FROM A FRIEND WITH A BUNCH OF CLOTHES IN IT, INCLUDING A SHIRT WITH "IN GOD WE TRUST" WRITTEN ACROSS THE BACK AND FOUR GUNS ARRANGED IN A SWASTIKA. SO I SAID, "DO YOU HAVE TO WEAR THAT, PUCK?" AND HE SAID, REAL QUICK, "SWASTIKA, IT'S NOT JUST A NAZI SYMBOL. YOU JUST SEE IT AS A NAZI SYMBOL. IT COMES FROM THE INDIANS." AND THIS WHOLE LINE OF BULL.

WHAT I WANTED TO ASK HIM WAS, AS A FRIEND, TO STOP WEARING IT, THAT IT OFFENDED AND HURT ME. BUT HE KEPT SAYING, "DON'T TELL ME WHAT TO DO." I SAID, "I'M NOT TELLING YOU WHAT TO DO. I'M ASKING YOU AS A FRIEND TO NOT WEAR THAT." HE'S ARGUING THAT IT'S NOT A SWASTIKA. IT'S JUST GUNS. I KNOW HE'S WRONG. IT'S A SWASTIKA. WE ALL CAN SEE THAT. HE'S WEARING A SWASTIKA ON HIS BACK.

IT PROBABLY ENRAGES ME MORE BECAUSE I KNOW HE'S NOT A RACIST. IF HE WAS A RACIST, WE'D HAVE SOMETHING TO FIGHT ABOUT. BUT HE'S NOT. HE'S JUST OFFENDING FOR THE SAKE OF OFFENDING. HE'S JUST FIGHTING FOR THE SAKE OF FIGHTING.

I SEE IT AS A BETRAYAL OF TRUST. HE'S STILL MY FRIEND, BUT IT'S GOING TO BE DIFFERENT NOW. I DON'T KNOW IF ANY- ONE ELSE IS GOING TO SEE IT, BUT THERE WAS A CHUNK OF GOODWILL THERE BEFORE, AND NOW IT'S GONE.

Mohammed: This is just my opinion, but I think Puck is pretty dependent on alcohol, which comes into the picture a lot. He's always drinking something, you know, and that really changes how you are. I've talked to Puck on a few occasions when he was sober, and he was really cool; And there's actually a side of him that's sweet and warm and loving. But often it's covered up, in part by the alco- hol and in part by his persona.

STIRRINGS

JUDD: WE'RE GOING TO START EATING EACH OTHER SOON. I CAN FEEL IT. WE'RE ALL CRAMMED IN HERE, THE WALLS ARE CLOSING IN, WE'RE GOING TO START EATING EACH OTHER. HOPEFULLY WE'LL EAT PUCK FIRST, BUT I DON'T THINK SO; HE SMELLS REAL BAD. IF I WAS A RAT IN THE SAME BOX WITH PUCK, AND THE REST OF US WERE GOING TO EAT ONE OF US, I DON'T THINK PUCK WOULD BE THE FIRST, 'CAUSE HE JUST STINKS. IT WOULD PROBABLY BE RACHEL, 'CAUSE SHE'S THE LITTLEST. I REALLY LOVE PAM. SHE'S GREAT. I WAS RIGHT. I KNEW I WOULD BECOME VERY CLOSE WITH PAM, AND THAT IT WOULDN'T TAKE VERY MUCH— WE HAVE A LOT IN COMMON, AND WE THINK THE SAME THINGS. THAT WAS MY HUNCH. IT WAS JUST A MATTER OF US BREAKING DOWN THAT WALL AND BECOMING FRIENDS, AND NOW WE ARE.

Rachel: If you're looking for marriage, Judd is the perfect guy.

Mohammed: I wrote this poem about two nights ago, for Stephanie, my homie stromie girlfriend. And I like it a lot; it's kind of cool.

It goes: "You beautiful woman, open me up. You make me wet and sticky and flowing, the space between my thighs and ears. You beautiful woman, open me up. I am spongy in your warmth, gooey in your arms, comfortable around your thrust, feeling you painlessly hitting the edges, gracefully expanding my curves, making rainbow sparks with your friction. You beautiful woman, open me up to elaborate visions, papaya and azure and jade and opal prayers from the dreams of prophets. You beautiful woman, open me up."

That's it.

Stephanie

Pam: I think Judd is a good listener. But a pretty reluctant talker. I feel like I have the urge to really draw Judd out a little bit. I like him a lot. We had some bonding, and he's very sweet and he's very perceptive, and I think he's one of those people who appears really nice and is not going to say anything if you're not going to ask him, unless he's really, really moved to, but generally he's going to be pretty mellow. When he goes and sits down and draws his cartoons, that's when all his evil stuff comes out.

Pam: I hope Pedro doesn't get sick But I suppose that's the reality of it. I mean, it's like, "Hi, I'm Pedro. I have HIV, I'm intelligent, smart, cute, and you like me, and it's a terrible tragedy, but I'm also going to get sick and I'm going to die and you're going to see it happen."

I don't think that he's going to die in the next month, but he could potentially get really sick and look really gnarly. And it's going to be really hard. I suppose I'm the only one right now who's really focused on it, because I've seen it happen before. I certainly don't want to think about it. But I'm thinking about it anyway. I'm very worried.

JUDD: YOU KNOW, WHEN YOU HEAR YOU'RE GOING TO BE LIVING WITH SOMEONE WHO'S HIV-POSITIVE, YOU THINK OF A VIRUS WITH TWO LEGS, NOT A WHOLE PERSON. BUT ONCE I MET PEDRO, IT WAS ENTIRELY DIFFERENT. HE TALKS ABOUT IT OPENLY, HE DISCUSSES IT. HE'S ACTUALLY AN EXPERT ON THE SUBJECT. HE'S MORE CAREFUL THAN WE ARE. HE'S THINKING ABOUT IT MORE THAN WE ARE, AND HE'S LOOKING OUT FOR US.

Cory: It scared me, but then after that I was fine with it. After I'd talked to him for a while, his face replaced the disease.

Pam: I got to talk to Mohammed a lot this week, and we had a really long talk about spirituality and this psychic experience that he had. Of the people who practice religion actively in this house, I respect Mohammed the most. Primarily because he gets up and meditates and prays at four o'clock in the morning when there's nobody there to see him doing it. I think there's a place for community and religion, but it somehow just strikes me as more valid if nobody is there saying, "Hey, you're praying, that's really cool." Because if you pray at four o'clock in the morning, nobody knows, and to me that seems like he must be doing it for personal reasons. And that strikes me as more valid. So Mohammed's spirituality, his practice of religion, is something I respect.

Mohammed: Me and my best friend Will, one time we were over in Oakland at this talent show. We were, like, sixteen years old. And we were rapping. We had matching uniforms and everything. We had judges that had these sullen faces, and we started to perform, and from the minute we started to perform, I felt myself coming out of my body. I looked down, and I could see myself performing, and it was like slow motion. The music was playing, and the people in the audience started getting up and jumping on their seats, and the judges woke up and started clapping with us and totally getting into the music, and I could look down and see myself—I saw myself performing. I knew the words were coming out, but I wasn't saying them, really. It was incredible.

And then once the music stopped, I went back into my body. And I didn't know if Will had felt it. And I was like, "Man, did you feel that?" And he was like, "Oh man, it was magic." And I said, "But dude, did you feel it?" He was like, "Dude, I was out of my body." And I was like, "Me too." And we were like trippin', and we just smiled. I just smiled the whole day 'cause it felt so good. And we won, so it was cool.

FEBRUARY 27, 1994 (WEEK FIVE)

Cory: I haven't had sex yet. But that doesn't mean that I don't want to; I just want to meet the right guy. I don't want to have sex with just anyone who comes along. But I think it will be totally cool when I finally do meet the right guy and when I do get to be that intimate with someone. I wish that he'd hurry up and come along, because I'm sick of waiting. I don't want to have sex with someone just to have sex; I want to really, really care about this guy. I can't wait for that to happen.

JUDD: CORY SEEMS TO BE EAGERLY
ANTICIPATING HER FIRST TIME. AND AS WELL
SHE SHOULD, 'CAUSE IT'S A WONDERFUL
THING.

MY FIRST TIME? MY FIRST TIME WASN'T
ALL THAT EXCITING—BUT OF COURSE, AT THE
SAME TIME, IT WAS. IT WAS KIND OF RUN-
OF-THE-MILL. I'VE HEARD A LOT OF RIDICULOUS STORIES, BUT IN
MY CASE IT WAS MORE ALONG THE LINES OF: I HAD A LONG-TERM
GIRLFRIEND, WE WERE VERY MUCH IN LOVE, AND WE DECIDED WE
WERE GOING TO COMMIT TO THAT. HER PARENTS WERE AWAY FOR THE
WEEKEND, AND, YOU KNOW, WE HAD SEX. THERE WERE FIREWORKS,
BUT IN OUR OWN WAY. IT WAS NOT THIS RIDICULOUS BACK-OF-THE-
CAR, GOT-CAUGHT-DOING-THIS THING. IT WAS GLORIOUS, BUT NOT
ALL THAT INTERESTING AS AN ANECDOTE. MY FIRST TIME, THAT IS.

Cory: I guess Pam was handing out condoms and tampons
and things to people on the street who couldn't afford
them, and she brought a dental dam back for Rachel
and me. I had no idea what it was. I think she brought
it back as a joke, 'cause she figured Rachel and I
probably wouldn't use them. But Puck weaseled them out
of us and gave them to his friends, 'cause he figured
they'd probably get better use that way than sitting
in my little box for posterity.

Dental dams aren't for dentistry. Dental dams are
protection for sex. And I don't really need that, since
I'm not sexually active. But yeah, I think Puck's friends
will probably get better use out of the dental dams
than me and Rachel would.

But I can get them from Pam if I ever need them.

Cory: Basically, Puck will go out with any girl he thinks he can get what he wants from. And that's one thing about him that really hurts me, 'cause I see him taking possession of women and not really giving very much respect back to them. And it frustrates me when girls give in, and have one-night stands with him, because he comes back and he brags about how this person was so lucky that they had "the Puck." He obviously doesn't know much about these girls he's having sex with. He said he hired a prostitute just to laugh at her for an hour. And I feel that, because I'm a woman, he doesn't respect me as much as he does the guys in the house. I like Puck a lot, and I think he's fun, but I just see him treating women a lot differently. Even the way he talks to his mom. He tells his mom what to do. His mom doesn't tell him what to do.

PUCK: I'm probably the biggest ass**** in the house by far— you know, as far as how somebody else would perceive me. If you don't know me that good, well, I seem like kind of an ass****. But that's kind of a screening process for me. I don't want to know people close-up who aren't able to stand up for something, man.

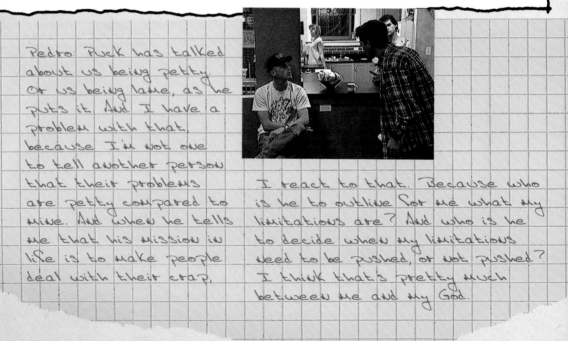

PUCK: I am hard to live with, I'll admit that. But that's why I live by myself. When I was, like, twenty-one I just took off and got my own house, and I would let people live in my house. I paid the rent, and then I collected from them. And that's easier for me, because then they can't really dictate what I do.

JUDD: USUALLY THE WAY I DEAL WITH PUCK IS THROUGH HUMOR. IT'S EASIER FOR ME TO GET MY POINT ACROSS SOMETIMES. I MEAN, IT MIGHT BE PASSIVE-AGGRESSIVE BEHAVIOR, BUT I FIND IT EASIER TO GET IT ACROSS WITH HUMOR. AND I KNOW PUCK APPRECIATES IT IN THAT MANNER. IT'S, KIND OF, WELL, IT'S KIND OF LIKE APPROACHING HIM WITH A WHITE FLAG SOMETIMES.

Pedro: Puck has talked about us being petty or us being lame, as he puts it. And I have a problem with that, because I'm not one to tell another person that their problems are petty compared to mine. And when he tells me that his mission in life is to make people deal with their crap, I react to that. Because who is he to outline for me what my limitations are? And who is he to decide when my limitations need to be pushed, or not pushed? I think that's pretty much between me and my God.

PUCK: When I smooched Rachel it was just kind of a, you know, spin-the-bottle type thing. You know, you're a kid, you're young, you spin the bottle, it points at the other girl, and you kiss her. That's my view. And for all of the sex that Rachel hasn't had, she really is good at mind-f**king. She's educated. So watch out.

Rachel: Puck and I were in a fight in front of everybody, and he started railing on me, and I called him an ass****. Twice. And he said, "That's two. If you call me that one more time, I'm going to bring the dogs out."

And what he meant by that was the fact that me and Puck had made out, or whatever, a couple times. I had told him that wasn't something I wanted announced. It wasn't anybody's business. And he has promised me that it was something that would be between us, that would be no big deal.

When I was actually standing up to him in front of his friends, when we were in this argument and I wasn't backing down, the only thing he could do was hold this over my head. And it pissed me off, because if we were really friends, as he claims we were, then why was he holding that over my head?

So I'm like, "Forget it; bring the dogs out." And I called him an ass**** again. And then he said, "Well, I'm sporting a hickey on my neck, and it's from you." And nobody was astonished. But it was just the fact that...he lied. He basically lied to me when he said it was just between us. So that was the beginning of the end, I guess. I tried to forgive him. A couple days later, we tried to talk and work it out, but I just was realizing what a hypocrite he was, and his words are so empty half the time that I just didn't want to deal any more.

Puck: I think she's real cool. She's cute, but not the girl for me.

Cory: I was never surprised by the fact that Puck and Rachel kissed. I could see how that could happen, and I don't think that either one of them has a reason to be embarrassed. They really did share something special, in its own way.

But now I think Rachel's feeling like Puck was very manipulative in the relationship, telling her what to do. And maybe in the end Puck didn't really want to know her as she was—maybe he just kind of wanted to see if he could make her over, tell her what to do and shape her himself.

THE BIG MEETING

Pedro: I have a lot of s*** happening in my life that I have no control over. I cannot control AIDS, I cannot control what is happening in my body, I cannot control people's attitudes toward my sexuality or toward my accent, or toward me. But I can certainly control living with Puck. So I did just that. I told the group that it was him, or it was me. I had the power to do something about it, and I did it. I don't regret the decision that I made.

Part of being an adult is accepting consequences. Accepting the choices you make. And Puck has to learn how to do that. He wants to blame everything on everybody else. And that's not the way it is.

Pam: When Pedro said he was leaving, I thought a lot about leaving myself. I wonder if it crossed everyone's mind. The one person I thought I'd really miss was Judd. I think it's because...I feel like we've connected. And if I were to leave the house tonight, I would miss Judd the most. That's the part that surprises me.

Mohammed: By the end, the only person who wanted to talk to Puck was Cory. And he was just like, "Shut up, little girl. You just shut up." And he was just throwing that back at her, to Cory, who is the person on the planet that if you were hurt or you were the underdog or something you would most want around. She's the person who would always come to you and try to find some good in you, no matter where you were at. And he shut her down. And once Cory shuts up, there's no one else out there. Everyone else has some beyond wanting to help you by that time.

And so by that time, I just felt a lot of...not even pity. He had really just gone beyond that. I felt like there wasn't really too much anyone could do to help the situation out at that time.

Mohammed: The reason I no longer wanted to live with Puck was, like, his attitude toward women. I don't really feel comfortable around someone who's—I won't even say sexist, because I feel like all men are sexist. But someone who's a misogynist, and who wasn't willing to change his ways at all.

'Cause I know my mom is going to watch the show, and my sisters, and other women I know, and they're going to go, "Mom, you didn't ever get on that guy for all that stuff he said. You talk all this stuff about trying to build equality between men and women, and between the races, and yet you have this guy on the show that you didn't even confront."

Puck said, "You guys haven't been through all the s**t I've been through; that's why my outer shell is so hard." And I'm like, "What do you know about what all the people in this house have been through? You haven't even taken the time to talk to each person individually and see some of the things that they've gone through in their lives." I felt it was another example of Puck saying, "Me me me me me, I've been through so much stuff, I deserve your attention because I've been hurt so much, that's why I'm this way, and—" Come on.

I think it's really an excuse. Man, I've got friends who've been strung out on heroin, crack, been in jail, some back to jail, come out, and then, decided that, hey, they're going to change, and all of a sudden they change their lives around and they work and they become somebody who's cool, or superdeep, or whatever. I don't think it's a barometer to say, "Well, I've been through so much stuff."

Pedro: Puck is always saying, "Life is hard, deal with it." And he basically looked at us and said, "Well, that's the way the Puck is. Deal with it." So we dealt with it. We threw him out. Now you deal with it. You made your decisions, be a man. And instead, he acts like a little kid and starts crying and saying, "I'm a human being, I have feelings, too." No s***! That's what we've been trying to tell you all night long. We know you have feelings. We know you're a human, that there's a civilized person somewhere in there. And we just want to see him more. But at one point he said, "I don't want to be civilized." So fine, then I won't treat you in a civilized way.

PUCK FOR GOD?

Pam: Dealing with Puck really reminds me of some psychiatric patients that I've dealt with. I think Puck has narcissistic personality disorder, and that's not to make light of his feelings. It's just my way of understanding the way he acts. That's part of the reason why I refuse to clash with him head-to-head, because I know it doesn't work. And I know that if you insult somebody who's predisposed to acting that way, they're going to rage back at you.

Narcissistic personality disorder is a character disorder, as opposed to a clinical depression or a psychosis, or a more transient psychiatric state. It is indicative of a pattern of behavior, and it's defined by nine characteristics that are sort of classic for people with this disorder and how they relate to other people. And I think, after that night, that Puck scored nine out of nine in the way he deals with people.

It's most strongly defined by how someone behaves when their self-esteem is insulted. And when Puck came back to basically scream at everyone in the house and insult them and make them feel as bad as he possibly could—that's classic behavior for someone with narcissistic personality disorder, to react with that kind of rage. And narcissistic people notoriously have little or no empathy for other people. They're very self-involved and really can't ever feel for the other person. They are only in touch with the way that _they_ feel. And I think that, time and time again, Puck showed that he's very good at expressing the way that _he_ feels, but he almost never took the time to think about how _other_ people in the house felt.

Rachel: At one point when he was crying, Puck actually said, "I had a plan for each of you." He had devised a plan for each of us to be incorporated into his life. And...if that doesn't explain to you how Puck felt about why he was here, about how lucky he felt we were to be with him—as opposed to maybe how lucky he was to be with us—I mean, it was all about Puck.... It was about Puck devising individual plans to fit each of us into his life. It really was probably one of the most revealing statements that the Puckster has ever said. It really does show what a God complex he had.

Puck: Pam approached me a few days before the meeting and said, "What do you think, Puck? You want to work with this, or do you not want to work with this?" And I said, "Yes, Pam, you're handling me correctly right now, and I do want to change enough to work it out with you guys. And let all the other room-mates take witness right now to the fact that you're handling me right. And this is the right way to handle Puck. You approach me and you ask me—you don't s***t on me—and we work something out." That's how it works.

151

JUDD: THIS IS AN OPEN LETTER TO PUCK:

DEAR PUCK,
I DON'T KNOW IF YOU'LL EVER READ THIS, OR SEE THIS, BUT MAYBE I'M JUST WRITING THIS FOR ME. I DON'T KNOW. I JUST WANTED TO TRY AND CLARIFY THINGS IF I COULD. ABOUT YOU AND US AND WHY WE ASKED YOU TO LEAVE.

TO BEGIN, THIS WHOLE THING WASN'T ABOUT YOU AS MUCH AS IT WAS ABOUT US. IT WASN'T SO MUCH THAT YOU COULDN'T LIVE WITH US, IT'S THAT WE COULDN'T LIVE WITH YOU. PUCK, I KNOW YOU WEREN'T TRYING TO BE ANYTHING BUT WHO YOU ARE. BUT THAT'S THE PROBLEM. WHO YOU ARE GOT IN THE WAY OF WHO WE ARE. WE COULDN'T EXPRESS OURSELVES WHEN YOU WERE EXPRESSING YOURSELF.

ON THE OTHER SIDE, YOU SHOULD HAVE SEEN THIS COMING. YOU SHOULDN'T BE SO SURPRISED WHEN THINGS LIKE THIS HAPPEN. WHEN YOU LIVE IN THE MANNER THAT YOU DO, WHEN YOU TRY TO BE BLUNT, SHOOT FROM THE HIP, CONFRONT, FIGHT, ARGUE, STIR THE WATERS, GET IN PEOPLE'S FACES—WHEN YOU DO THAT, YOU'LL GET BURNED. YOU'RE GOING TO LOSE FRIENDS, YOU'RE GOING TO LOSE JOBS, AND PEOPLE ARE GOING TO ASK YOU TO LEAVE. YOU KNOW THIS. IT'S NO SURPRISE. I DON'T HAVE TO TELL YOU THIS; YOU KNOW HOW YOU LIVE. YOU LIVE HARD. BUT NOT EVERYONE DOES.

AND YOU KNOW, PUCK, I DON'T WANT TO USE A CLICHÉ, BUT WHEN YOU ROCK THE BOAT ALL THE TIME, LIKE YOU DO, IT'S GONNA TIP, AND YOU'RE GONNA WIND UP IN THE WATER. AT THE SAME TIME, THE WORLD NEEDS PEOPLE LIKE YOU. IT NEEDS TROUBLEMAKERS, IT NEEDS ANARCHISTS, IT NEEDS PEOPLE WHO JUST REFUSE TO PLAY BY THE RULES. BUT THIS HOUSE ISN'T THE WORLD. IT'S JUST SEVEN PEOPLE TRYING TO LIVE THEIR LIVES. TOGETHER.

SO, PUCK, RAGE ON. FIGHT THE GOOD FIGHT, BE TRUE TO YOURSELF. I STILL CONSIDER YOU A FRIEND, THOUGH I KNOW IT'S NOT MUTUAL RIGHT NOW. AND IF WE CAN'T EVER GET BACK TO BEING FRIENDS, THEN I'LL SEE YOU IN THE NEXT LIFE. GOOD LUCK, PUCK. I MEAN THAT, GOOD LUCK.

Rachel: I can't say enough how much my relationship with Puck completely colored my relationships with everybody else. He had such strong opinions about everybody else, and for some reason, as much as I like to think of myself as a strong woman, and as much as I verbally stood up to him, I was very passive about my opinion formations in that I was taking what he was saying about all the other roommates and making those my opinions. And I don't blame him for that. That was my fault.

Over the course of the week, I've gone to random places and run into people out on the town who know all about what's happened. I've had people tell me stupid things, like that our ratings are gonna go down, or that we were jealous of Puck. I mean, I'm sick of it. Life goes on. And I am sorry...I am so much happier without him here.

PUCK: I definitely got something out of all of them. You know, whether it was learning about how people can say one thing and mean something else, or how a twenty-two-year-old virgin perceives life. And it was cool. I wish I could have got more. But I didn't. So I can't live in regret, you know. I got what I got. I'm okay with it.

PEACE

Mohammed: Pam and Cory both came to me at separate times and said, "I'm really happy that we made this decision, because it feels so much better here in the house now, so much more peaceful."

I started to clean my room, and then I started to clean up a lot of the stuff that was left there, like the debris from him, and I realized that it was the first time that the room had actually, like, really been clean. The house started to actually feel really peaceful, and it was a trip. Because I don't think the house has ever felt peaceful since I've been there, until that day after Puck left. And that's how I feel now. I feel really at peace. And I'm hopeful to see what relationships will develop with people now that Puck's not here.

Rachel: It feels now like I wish it had felt two months ago.

Pedro: One of the nights that I was having a fight with Sean, I went upstairs and had a conversation with Mohammed about it, and it was really neat, because he was telling me about his relationship with Stephanie, and about the same thing happening, and about trying to figure out, you know, the power struggle, the structure in the relationship. So it was really nice, 'cause I pretty much had never talked about those things with Mohammed.

I really like Rachel. I have some big issues with her, but I really like her as a person, and I think, to me, personally it's a growing experience. Because for the first time I'm really getting close to—or getting to know—somebody who not only has different views than me but opposing views. And that's really interesting to me. It's sort of a challenge to get to know them and to have a relationship with them.

Mohammed: Pedro and I have talked about some really deep things. And the other day I actually wrote a poem about it. I think I'm going to tell him one day. I saw him one time when he got really upset. That time with Puck, and then earlier on, when we had that first meeting about Puck. I was watching him, and he actually became a spirit. It was a trip to me, because I had never seen the spirit of a man who knew he was going to die. And it's....it's a very powerful thing to me.

154

Mohammed: This week, March 28th, I became twenty-four years old. It's great. I think a lot of people trip on getting older, but for me, getting old is cool. Everyone else is like, "Ah, I'm getting old. Oh, my God, I'm going to die." I don't even look at birthdays as a date as much as like a time period, you know? This is around the time when I was born, or when my spirit chose to come through my mom and dad. And it's just sort of a remembrance of that spirit.

It's also a weird time, because right now I kind of feel like, in a lot of ways, I'm connected to a physical world. And as I get older, I think I'll find more joy in actually spending a lot more time in the spiritual world. I look forward to that. I think that's going to be an even better time in my life. So getting older is cool to me. I don't feel any changes, though. I don't feel any different from when I was twenty-three.

JUDD: MOHAMMED'S BIRTHDAY PARTY WAS AMAZING. IT WAS A REALLY WARM AND WONDERFUL EXPERIENCE. EVERYBODY THERE WAS ENJOYING EACH OTHER'S COMPANY. THERE WAS A LOT OF LAUGHTER, PEOPLE CUTTING ON EACH OTHER, BUT IT WAS REALLY A CELEBRATION.

THE THING THAT REALLY GOT TO ME WAS WHEN MOHAMMED'S FAMILY SAT HIM IN THE MIDDLE OF THE ROOM. IT WAS A FAMILY THING. IT WAS A TRADITION THAT...IT'S NOT ONLY A BIRTHDAY. THEY CALL IT LIFE DAY. AND ON LIFE DAY YOU SIT IN THE MIDDLE, AND YOUR FAMILY GOES AROUND YOU IN A CIRCLE AND TELLS YOU HOW THEY FEEL ABOUT YOU. EITHER THEY TELL AN EXPERIENCE THEY HAD WITH HIM OR THEY TELL HOW MUCH THEY CARE ABOUT HIM. AND THEY CAN TELL MOHAMMED DIRECTLY OR THEY CAN SPEAK TO EVERYBODY AS A GROUP. IT'S WONDERFUL. YOU COULD CALL IT JUST A BIG EGO TRIP, BUT IT'S A LOT MORE THAN THAT. IT WAS VERY ENDEARING. AND I GOT MY TWO CENTS IN THERE, TOO, AND THAT FELT GOOD. AND WHAT WAS NICE ABOUT IT WAS THAT NO ONE WAS CUTTING ON ANYONE ELSE. WHAT EVERYONE HAD TO SAY WAS LEGITIMATE IN EVERYONE ELSE'S EYES. IT WAS WHAT THEY WANTED TO SAY TO MOHAMMED. THERE WAS NO SNICKERING; THERE WAS NO MAKING FUN.

SKI TRIP

Pam: Cory was the best skier. But I'd have to say that Mohammed and Judd were working a good Cypress Hill, hip-hop-skier thing. They were very fashionable, Judd especially, in those royal purples—it was quite stunning.

He and Mohammed went and obtained the winter wear from somewhere on the Haight before we left. So those two were stylin'. The rest of us were in our rental bibs, looking a little chunky. A little chunky and junky.

JUDD: MOHAMMED PICKED MY JACKET OUT FOR ME, AND SAID, "I THINK THIS WILL FIT YOU, MAN. I THINK YOU CAN WEAR THIS." "I CAN? IT'S ALL PURPLE AND EVERYTHING." "NO, PUT IT ON. AH, YOU LOOK GREAT." "DO I?" "SURE, YOU CAN WEAR THIS." "ALL RIGHT, IF YOU SAY SO." A BIG PURPLE GRAPE SKIING DOWN THE MOUNTAIN.

JO'S ARRIVAL

Jo: They all seem so happy that I'm here, and it's just so nice to feel so welcome, and I really don't feel like I'm the odd one out. And no, I don't want to rock the boat, because that's not in my personality, and I'm not interested in causing arguments or fights. And how can I fight with people that I like so much? It's impossible.

I married somebody who I really fell in love with. Didn't know him for very long. Absolutely thought it would work. Got married. And it didn't work out. We weren't very compatible. After a while, we found out that he tried to take my independence away—and I'm a very independent person, otherwise I wouldn't be here in America—and so he fell in love with someone who wasn't really me, because I wasn't independent when I met him.

I don't regret getting married, because I had a really wonderful time with my husband. But I felt like he took away a lot of my identity.

JO

. And I think that now I'm regaining it. And through that experience with him I've become a better person, because I learned so much about how people react to one another in a relationship, and what kind of things can go wrong. So I wouldn't be so ready to jump into another relationship like that, a serious relationship, again.

APRIL 10, 1994 (WEEK ELEVEN)

Jo: Rachel—I've really been having a lot of fun with her. Not that I don't with everyone else. But she does bring a lot of bubbly fun into the house. She's very concerned about the way you look, and things like that. Which is fun. I like to spend hours getting dressed and doing my hair and things like that with her. Because she makes it fun.

I have a different kind of time with Cory. When we are out, we're outside, doing something. Which of course I'm all for. I love that. The Tahoe trip that I took with Cory was so fun. We just had the greatest time. And I think she was really, really amazed by all that she got to experience in the very short time that we were there. It was great watching her. Her face was lit up the whole time. She had a big smile on her face.

Probably the highlight of the week was Pedro's presentation on HIV and AIDS. I felt myself getting very emotional and choked up, but yet sensed this incredible bravery coming from these two speakers. I'd love to go again. I have many questions I want to ask Pedro. But I want to wait until the time's right for me to ask them, for him. I want to be sitting with him having a conversation.

I got to spend some time with Pam, and I'm really glad I did. Because I hear that moments are precious with Pam, and she doesn't have a lot of time. She's very busy with school. She's very caring about everybody in the house. She's kind of like the mother hen, or she would be if she had more time to spend with everyone.

There are certain times, like right now, that I start to feel a little down, and I need a hug. And this morning, I just went up to Mo, and I said "I really feel like a cuddle." And we cuddled, and I felt totally comfortable doing that. And I'm really comfortable with everyone here. I feel like I'm gonna have some really good friends at the end of this.

Pedro: You know, one of the wonderful things about my family is that when I think of my family I don't just think of brothers and sisters and my dad, I think of aunts and cousins who are really so close to me and who give me so much support.

Whenever the whole family gets together, we always do a lot of stuff as one big group. But at some point we always go into little groups and just talk. Usually some of the men go outside and they smoke and drink their beers and just talk about work or whatever. And usually the women go to another corner and they just sit around and gossip and do whatever they do.

The wonderful thing about being a gay man is that you can do whichever you want. If I want to go with the men and talk, I can do that. If I want to go with the women and gossip and talk about all their men and talk about how cute somebody is, I can do that, too. That's one of the wonderful things about being a gay man.

CONFRONTING HIV

Mohammed's sister was in the house, baking a cake for Mohammed, and I just started talking about Sean, and Mohammed's sister turned around and said, "Can I ask you a personal question?" And I said, "Sure." And she says, "Do you guys have sex?" And I said, "Of course!" And then she said, "Well, how come? I mean, you're HIV-positive." And I said, "Well, it so happens that Sean is HIV-positive, too, but even before that I was in a relationship for three years with somebody who is still negative."

We just had this whole conversation about HIV and AIDS in this country. And she wants to know where HIV and AIDS came from, and behind that there's a belief that it's man-made, that the government made it, that they screwed up somewhere and are not taking responsibility for it. And I really have a problem with those theories. I really don't believe them. I believe that HIV is a virus, it's a natural thing, like any other natural thing. Where did HIV come from? Well, where did trees come from? Or, chicken pox, or any other virus or bacteria? It was just here. Something changed and now it's affecting us, but it's always been here.

But at one point in the conversation I realized that she was not going to change my beliefs and I was not going to change hers, so I kind of just changed the conversation and moved on.

I think a lot of people want to blame somebody else for their problems. They don't want to take responsibility for their actions. So it's easier to blame the government, or the educational system, or society, or to say "Oh, it's a punishment from God." And in that way they're blaming a third party and they're not taking responsibility for their own actions. The bottom line is that HIV is a virus that can be prevented if you take personal responsibility. We know how HIV is transmitted, and we know how to prevent it, so it's just about taking responsibility for your actions and your body.

Pam: I feel like Pedro's this time bomb planted among us, and the time bomb is ticking and I'm this bomb expert. Not even an expert—I just know something about bombs. And I don't know enough to defuse the bomb and fix it, and maybe it's a bomb that nobody can fix. But I hear it ticking, and I try to ignore that because it's a drag to have someone around all the time who's like, "Hey, that bomb is ticking; something bad is going to happen." And I try to go on without thinking about it too much, but I think about it a lot.

AIDS is still affecting poor sectors of the population, and more and more women, and people who don't have a lot of power in our society.

Mohammed: I think that seeing Midnight Voices on stage helps people to see where we're coming from. It can sell us in terms of having them know us a little bit better and understand us. A lot of people hear our music and go, "You guys are talking about so much stuff; I don't get it. It's so eclectic. I don't know whether to call it hip-hop, or alternative. I don't know what I can call it."

And then they see the live show, and the theatrics and everything come together, and they go, "Oh, I didn't know what to call it before, but I know now that it's just Midnight Voices, and I understand what that is." I mean, I think it's the same confusion that came about when Public Enemy first came out. People would write about it, and they didn't know what to call it, cause there wasn't such a thing as militant rap yet. And then all of a sudden they said, "Okay, this is militant rap." And then Arrested Development came out, and they didn't know what to call that. They didn't know what to call De La Soul, or whatever.

JUDD: PLAYING THE FILLMORE'S A PRETTY BIG DEAL. EVERYONE HAS PLAYED THERE, FROM THE GRATEFUL DEAD TO THE B-52's. JAZZ ARTISTS, ROCK 'N' ROLL. AND LENNY BRUCE, A PERSONAL FAVORITE OF MINE.

THE FILLMORE IS A VERY, VERY IMPORTANT PLACE IN ROCK HISTORY. AND FOR MIDNIGHT VOICES TO PLAY THERE WAS A VERY BIG DEAL. IT WAS AN INTERESTING GIG AS WELL. THEY WERE OPENING FOR MICHELLE SHOCKED, WHICH IS NOT NECESSARILY WHAT ONE WOULD PRESUME THEIR TARGET AUDIENCE TO BE. BUT BASICALLY THE PEOPLE WHO COME TO MICHELLE SHOCKED ARE A LOT OF, WELL, POLITICALLY CORRECT FOLK FANS— NOT THE TYPE OF PEOPLE WHO USUALLY CRAM INTO THE UPPER ROOM OR THE KENNEL CLUB TO SEE MIDNIGHT VOICES. BUT I TOLD MO BEFORE THE SHOW THAT THEY'RE JUST GOING TO EAT IT UP. WHICH THEY DID.

AT FIRST I HEARD RUMBLING BEFORE THEY WENT ON. YOU KNOW, "WHO'S THIS RAP GROUP OPENING MICHELLE'S SHOW?" AND THEN I HEARD SOME STUFF, LIKE, "I HEAR THEY HAVE SORT OF A SPIRITUAL THING GOING ON; THEY HAVE A LOT OF PEOPLE ONSTAGE—IT'S KIND OF A PERFORMANCE-ART THING AS WELL AS MUSIC." AND THAT WAS SORT OF IT. AND THEN THEY CAME OUT, AND, BY THE SECOND SONG, THE PLACE WAS GOING CRAZY. AS CRAZY AS A BUNCH OF, YOU KNOW, WHITE POLITICALLY CORRECT FOLK FANS CAN GET AS THEY'RE TRYING TO DO—VERY POORLY— THE HOMIE STROMIE.

I THINK ONE OF THE IDEAS THAT BILL GRAHAM HAD WITH THE FILLMORE WAS TO TAKE SMALL, EVEN LOCAL, TALENT AND GIVE THEM A SHOT AT THE BIG TIME. SO, YOU KNOW, GIVING MIDNIGHT VOICES A SHOT UP THERE IS SOMETHING THAT I'M SURE HE HAD IN MIND.

Pam: I think Mo has a really wonderful presence on stage. I think that you want to look at him, and that's nice. And as a rapper, he's very natural; he's very inventive and fun. And, I mean, Mo raps in the shower, in his room, standing around the house, and I'm always a bit flabbergasted that he's able to do that, because it's a sort of mind-mouth connection that I don't have. As a vocalist, I mean, in terms of pure singing, Mo isn't so impressive. I don't think that Mo has a golden throat, per se. But I think he's a very talented rapper.

161

MAY 8, 1994 (WEEK FIFTEEN)

Pam: There is no money in medicine anymore. Anyone who says you're going into medicine for the money is screwed in the head, because basically there is no money in medicine anymore—not that it's a bad profession, but it's not going to be as highly paid. And, you know, I'm going into medicine for the power, for the information, for the respect, not for the money. And I know it's a stable field. People are always going to get sick, and so you're always going to have work. But if you want to make money, go into business or banking or something instead of staying in school for an extra decade of your life. Gotta do it for another reason.

Cory: I just want to say that Pam is incredible. And she has so much to do all the time. Today she came home and was just—I mean, I think that she tries really hard not to show her emotions and not to show how stressed-out she really is. And, like, today she just came home and was in tears. I didn't know what to do. She's worried about her patients at the hospital. She's worried about school.

Pam: I had this one experience in the ER, when I was on OB-GYN. It's my first rotation, so I've only seen women patients. I've done a lot of pelvic exams, and I was getting good at it. I was working with this resident, and we went down to the ER, four o'clock in the morning, and she said, "Come with me to see this patient." And when we walked in, there was this six-foot-five man standing on top of the gurney, towering over us, totally naked, with this huge penis, whacking off. I was impressed, I have to say. That's my most striking memory of the ER. It hasn't happened since then. Obviously this wasn't our patient. It definitely was not a GYN problem.

They don't tell you in medical school that you should have a certain relationship with a patient. It's implied that your relationship is fairly professional, and the point of the relationship is the patient's health. It's not to make me feel good, and not even necessarily to make the patient feel better, but to keep the patient well. So sometimes I say something to the patient that doesn't make her feel good or doesn't make me feel good. But it's for her own good medically. Most of the time I try to be fairly connected. I have the best days when I have actually had time to talk to the patients and feel like I was able to help them in some way, even if I didn't do much more than listen to them or get them a glass of water or something. Sometimes in the hospital it seems like those things are small, but they make a difference.

MAY 22, 1994 (WEEK SEVENTEEN)

Rachel: It's kind of cool, because I always have, like, these perceptions about my body and how I should look. And a lot of them are based on what the Caucasian ideal of a woman is. And obviously, as anybody who's seen my body would know, I don't really meet those standards very well. I've had a lot of trouble dealing with that, especially since my sister does meet those standards. She's very thin and has boyish hips and is really small-framed, and that's just the way she is. So I've had to deal with this problem always.

But hanging out with mo and throwing those views about myself out at him is very therapeutic. Because mo will come back at me with the fact that African-American men tend to not find the skinny, ultrathin ideal of a woman very attractive. They just don't. They like fuller-figured women. So whenever I feel fat, I'll talk to mo, and he'll be like, "No, I don't think you look fat. You don't want to be that skinny—you just need to tone up, girl. Let's go work out." So he's really made me feel a lot better about myself physically. I need to be reminded that there isn't just one ideal of a woman. And granted, I'm not going to be attractive to, whatever, 85, 90 percent of white men who like very thin women. But there's a whole other group of people who might find my body attractive, and knowing that, I feel more comfortable with who I am.

Jo: I constantly struggle with the way I look. But it's not an obsessive thing with me. I was dieting for years. I'd never do that again, because it doesn't work. Dieting doesn't work. I just lead a very healthy, active lifestyle. And that's the only way to truly feel confident about yourself, and to look good.

Cory: When I was in seventh grade, I moved to a new town. I was a gymnast, and that's basically all I did. Outside of that, I didn't have many friends. I was really shy. So then, in my junior year of high school, I quit gymnastics because it was just too time-consuming and I wasn't ever going to be good enough to go to the Olympics. But when I quit I did gain weight and I was a little bit pudgy.

And then the summer before my senior year of high school I decided that I was going to go on a diet and lose some weight. And the difference in the way people responded to me and treated me was incredible.

All of a sudden I had all these people calling me, talking to me, guys becoming interested in me. All of a sudden, losing weight wasn't just something that was healthy, it was something that I had to do in order to maintain friendships, in order to maintain this attention that I was getting, and it became a really obsessive thing for me. I always thought about food, I always thought about exercise. I couldn't eat pizza without crying myself to sleep. It was ridiculous.

It's taken me a long time to realize that the people you're going to feel most comfortable with are those people that accept you and love you for who you are.

That sounds pretty generic, but it's true, and the friendships I've maintained in high school haven't been the ones with the people who came up to me senior year and all of a sudden were talking to me and noticing me. The friendships I've maintained are the ones that I had all along, the ones that helped me through change and loved me no matter what I was doing or what I looked like.

Women's obsession with their body weight, and their desire to become thinner, will push them to amazing limits. I don't know what's causing it, but I'm really frustrated with it. I watch a lot of incredibly beautiful, firm, talented people enslave themselves to this worry and let fear of their body weight and fear of inadequacy take over their lives.

And that's what it does. It takes over their lives. It enslaves them, to the point where one girl told me she'd rather be lying in a hospital bed than living her life—it would be so much simpler. She'd rather be committed to a hospital for anorexia than actually have to fight anorexia every single day in real life. Because there's so much pain involved, and so much fear. And I don't know how it gets ingrained in these kids' heads, but it's there, and it needs to go.

JUDD: CORY HAS A PERSONAL AGENDA THAT MEANS A LOT TO HER. SHE'S REALLY CONCERNED WITH THE MEDIA'S PORTRAYAL OF WOMEN, AND THE NEED FOR THE MEDIA TO HAVE WOMEN THAT ARE THIN AND BEAUTIFUL. YOUR FASHION MODELS. EVERYONE YOU SEE IN THE MAGAZINES. ALL THESE TINY WAISTS, BIG BREASTS, ALL THAT. AND I KNOW THAT SHE REALLY DETESTS THAT.

AND THAT'S ONE THING. THE OTHER THING IS THAT SHE'S STILL CONCERNED WITH HOW SHE LOOKS, AND SHE ALMOST WANTS TO BE THIN AND BEAUTIFUL AND FEED INTO THAT STEREOTYPE. AND IT BOTHERS HER THAT SHE THINKS THOSE THINGS. SHE KNOWS IT'S WRONG, AND IT MAKES HER CRAZY.

FOLKS DON'T GIVE CORY ENOUGH CREDIT FOR KNOWING WHAT'S GOING ON, BUT IT'S A VERY DIFFICULT THING TO ADMIT SOME-THING ALONG THOSE LINES, TO SEE THAT YOU HAVE A PROBLEM. SHE SEES A PROBLEM GOING ON IN THE COUNTRY, AND SHE ALSO AGREES THAT SHE HAS THIS PROBLEM. AND SHE DOESN'T KNOW NECESSARILY HOW TO SHAKE IT. SHE EVENTUALLY WILL. SHE'S GOT A LOT OF TIME. AND SEEING THE PROBLEM NOW WHEN SHE'S A YOUNG WOMAN, IS A LOT EASIER THAN SEEING IT WHEN SHE'S OLDER.

JUNE 5, 1994 (WEEK NINETEEN)

Rachel: I think it's obvious that there's sexual tension between Pam and Judd. I don't think anything would really ever come of it, but they do spend a lot of time together. We always invite him out to do stuff, and he's always like, "no." But then Pam will ask, and he'll go. So it's kind of obvious that if Judd had his way, they would be together.

JUNE 19, 1994

(WEEK TWENTY-ONE)

FINAL THOUGHTS

Mohammed: I think we all came into the house as titles. And then we became people. And that conversion was really cool. Like when Judd went from Jewish cartoonist to this guy who makes cartoons and is pretty cool and knows all the trivia about every TV show that's on the air, and knows as much Richard Pryor as I do. Stuff like that. That transition, all those transitions were cool.

Jo: Cory's an adventurer. And I think that if she can really pull this whole thing off afterward, and really make a stand for who she wants to be, she's going to be having a lot of fun. I think that she's going to go through lots of different channels and paths in her life.

JUDD: CORY WOULD SURPRISE ME ALL THE TIME. AS WELL AS AGGRAVATE ME. SHE MAKES ME CRAZY HALF THE TIME, AND THE REST OF THE TIME, SHE'S CHEERING ME UP.

Rachel: I like Cory. She has allowed me to see a lot of things about myself that I don't know I would have discovered without Cory pointing them out to me. The problem, though, is that she doesn't do anything about her own life. She sees what she does, and she sees how she feels, and she doesn't like it, but she's too weak to change it.

JUDD: JO IS A FUNNY, PRETTY, ENGAGING PERSON. I STILL DON'T REALLY KNOW JO. AND I THINK A COUPLE OF US FEEL THAT WAY. JO CAME ALONG WHEN THIS BOAT WAS ALREADY SAILING PRETTY FAST, THEN JUST BECAME ANOTHER ONE OF THE PASSENGERS.

Pam: I suppose I wonder a little bit what Jo would have been like if Rachel hadn't been here.

Mohammed: I don't know what's going to happen to Jo. I think she's going to spend about a year and a half or two years trying to find someplace where she really fits in. It's probably going to take her that amount of time to get over her ex-husband and finally become herself again.

Jo: Well, I'd like to hope for Judd that he's the budding cartoonist star that he wants to be. And I'm sure he will become a star 'cause his stuff's very good. But I hope he learns that work is not everything, that, if it doesn't happen, it doesn't happen. That there are a lot of other opportunities in life, and that being a cartoonist is not the only one. But I hope he makes it.

Mohammed: I think Judd's going to go down to L.A. and put on the Hollywood uniform and pretty much do the whole thing. Cause he seems like he could do that. He could be that stressed-out. I mean, he already is, you know.

Rachel: I'm really starting to like Pam a lot. She's the most honest. She really does ask about you. She really does care about what's going on with you, and she'll take the time. I really have come to like her a lot as a person.

Cory: I can't decide if Pam will end up really becoming a doctor or not. She's great. She's such a compassionate person, and she's so smart, and I know she'd be an incredible doctor. I think she'd be happy being a doctor, but I don't know. I could see her doing something else kind of crazier and more on the edge as well.

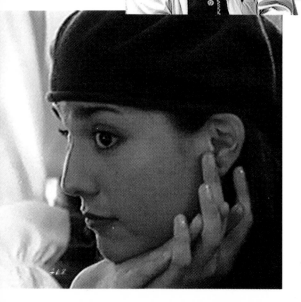

Jo: I hope Rachel never changes. Even though she's the little Republican conservative, I hope she never changes that rebel side of herself. And I don't think she will. If she can pull it off through the rest of her life, I think she's going to have a lot of fun.

Cory: Rachel loves the cameras and the attention. So I think that either she'll be a really famous politician, or she'll be an actress on a Spanish-speaking television channel or something like that.

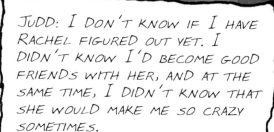

JUDD: I DON'T KNOW IF I HAVE RACHEL FIGURED OUT YET. I DIDN'T KNOW I'D BECOME GOOD FRIENDS WITH HER, AND AT THE SAME TIME, I DIDN'T KNOW THAT SHE WOULD MAKE ME SO CRAZY SOMETIMES.

Jo: I'm not sure that Mo is going to do this music thing for the rest of his life. But I think he's always going to have something that he's really passionate about, and I think that he's always going to be able to be very good at what he's doing.

JUDD: MOHAMMED SURPRISED ME, BECAUSE I DIDN'T THINK HE WOULD BE SO FUNNY, ENGAGING, GREGARIOUS. I THOUGHT HE'D BE MORE SERIOUS. BUT MOHAMMED CAN GET DOWNRIGHT GOOFY. I THINK MOHAMMED AND MIDNIGHT VOICES ARE GOING TO BE ELSEWHERE ON THIS CHANNEL AT SOME POINT.

Cory: I think that Mohammed is going to make it in his music. I think that he'll end up going far with that, and earn money doing it. I don't see him staying with Stephanie. I don't know when he'll get married. Probably not for a while.

Jo: I hope that Pedro finds something else in his life that he can be passionate about, apart from being an AIDS educator and a gay activist. I think he's very good at what he does. He makes an excellent stand, and he's obviously very educated. But I think there comes a time when you have to say, is there anything else that I'm doing? And, I hope that some day he finds something else that he can be as passionate about.

JUDD: WHEN I MET PEDRO, HE SEEMED LIKE A REALLY NICE GUY. BUT I DIDN'T REALIZE THAT HE'D BECOME ONE OF MY CLOSEST FRIENDS.

Rachel: Puck and Pedro are the same. They are both used to a lot of attention, and they both like to be the center of attention, and that was why they clashed.

Mohammed: I think Pedro is just going to spend his time loving life. Which is cool. I think a lot of people would love to be in his shoes, to be with someone that you love and just spend time. And it's going to be great now, 'cause it's going to be private time.

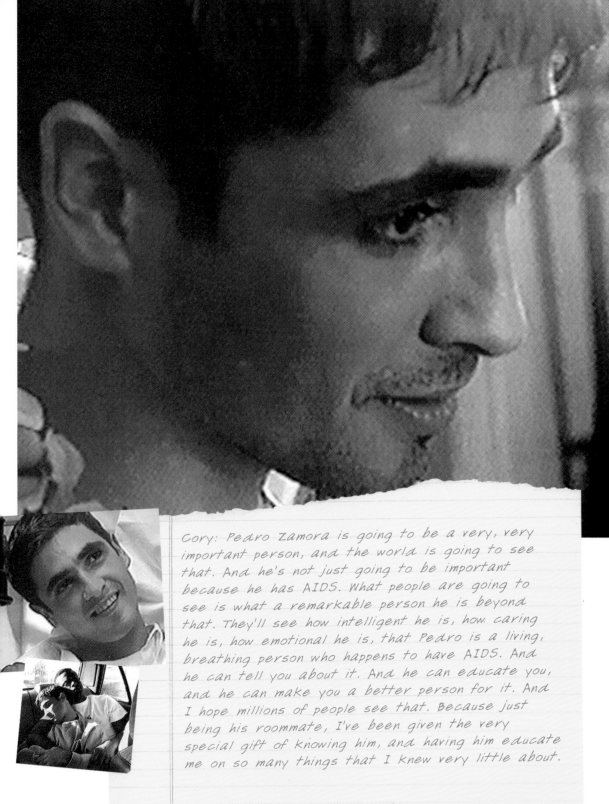

Cory: Pedro Zamora is going to be a very, very important person, and the world is going to see that. And he's not just going to be important because he has AIDS. What people are going to see is what a remarkable person he is beyond that. They'll see how intelligent he is, how caring he is, how emotional he is, that Pedro is a living, breathing person who happens to have AIDS. And he can tell you about it. And he can educate you, and he can make you a better person for it. And I hope millions of people see that. Because just being his roommate, I've been given the very special gift of knowing him, and having him educate me on so many things that I knew very little about.

171

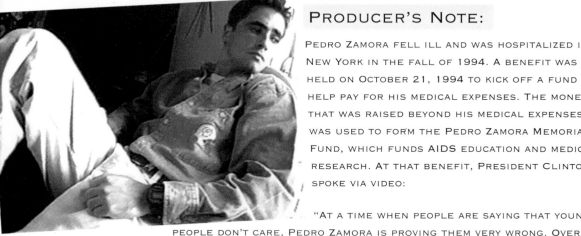

PRODUCER'S NOTE:

PEDRO ZAMORA FELL ILL AND WAS HOSPITALIZED IN NEW YORK IN THE FALL OF 1994. A BENEFIT WAS HELD ON OCTOBER 21, 1994 TO KICK OFF A FUND TO HELP PAY FOR HIS MEDICAL EXPENSES. THE MONEY THAT WAS RAISED BEYOND HIS MEDICAL EXPENSES WAS USED TO FORM THE PEDRO ZAMORA MEMORIAL FUND, WHICH FUNDS AIDS EDUCATION AND MEDICAL RESEARCH. AT THAT BENEFIT, PRESIDENT CLINTON SPOKE VIA VIDEO:

"AT A TIME WHEN PEOPLE ARE SAYING THAT YOUNG PEOPLE DON'T CARE, PEDRO ZAMORA IS PROVING THEM VERY WRONG. OVER THE PAST FEW YEARS, PEDRO BECAME A MEMBER OF ALL OF OUR FAMILIES. NOW, NO ONE IN AMERICA CAN SAY THEY'VE NEVER KNOWN SOMEONE WHO'S LIVING WITH AIDS. THE CHALLENGE TO EACH OF US IS TO DO SOMETHING ABOUT IT, AND TO CONTINUE PEDRO'S FIGHT. PEDRO, ALL OF US ARE VERY PROUD OF YOU."

PEDRO'S CONDITION CONTINUED TO DETERIORATE. WITH HIS FRIENDS AND FAMILY AROUND HIM, PEDRO ZAMORA DIED OF COMPLICATIONS FROM THE AIDS VIRUS ON NOVEMBER 11, 1994.

Sean Sasser, Pedro's partner: Being on The Real World was a big deal. I think it was an especially big deal for someone living with AIDS to expose himself. For me, it was different, I was part of him, we were a couple. And I took a lot of strength and courage from his bravery to step out front. I think that's what people should remember about Pedro: his courage and his honesty.

Pam: Pedro Zamora could have been my colleague. Or he could have been my brother, or my best friend, or he could have been me. We knew that every day he faced death, and uncertainty, and sickness, but he always reminded us that he was living with AIDS.

JUDD: WHAT PEDRO DID WAS RAISE AWARENESS. AND THAT'S WHERE IT HAS TO START. PICK YOURSELVES UP AND DO SOMETHING. WHATEVER IT IS. THERE'S A CLINIC IN EVERY TOWN. THERE ARE PEOPLE WITH AIDS IN EVERY CITY. GO FIND THEM OUT AND JUST DO SOMETHING.

FOR MORE INFORMATION ABOUT THE PEDRO ZAMORA FOUNDATION, WHICH, IN PART, PROVIDES A FELLOWSHIP PROGRAM TO TRAIN FOUR YOUNG VOLUNTEERS EACH YEAR TO EDUCATE OTHER KIDS; ENCOURAGES POLITICIANS TO SUPPORT UNCENSORED AIDS EDUCATION PROGRAMS; AND HELPS COMMUNITIES TO PLAN AND IMPLEMENT HIV PREVENTION PROGRAMS, CALL OR WRITE:

THE PEDRO ZAMORA FOUNDATION
AIDS ACTION COUNCIL
1875 N. CONNECTICUT AVENUE
WASHINGTON, D.C. 20009
(800) 790-2332

LOS ANGELES

INTRODUCTIONS

AARON

Aaron: This is definitely gonna be the experience of a lifetime. It's such a twisted, psycho experiment. You could see someone after all this was over, and they'd know all these deep and dark little things about you. But I guess we're kinda like the sacrificial lambs to this whole project.

I don't know how well I'll fit in. I'm different than lots of people my age. I don't believe in premarital sex. I thought I was going to have sex at a young age, but I'm glad I caught myself, because I'd have been making a big mistake. It's something that I want to save for my wife; it's my gift to my wife when I get married. I don't whack off at all, I swear to God. That's the first thing people say: "Are you gay, or do you just whack off a lot?" No. I don't do either at all.

Beth S.: I was having some really twisted dreams before I moved in here. I was having dreams that either I was gonna be the one that stuck out, the big psychopath, or that everyone was out to kill me. I had this one dream that, for some reason, everyone in the crew kept getting their heads chopped off.

DAVID

BETH S.

David: I dropped out of school when I was fourteen 'cause I ran away from home. I had to get a job, and then I found comedy. I started doin' comedy, and comedy helped me get back in high school. Comedy helped me accomplish a lot of things that otherwise, I think, I might not have done.

174

Dominic: In Ireland, all we ever saw of Americans was bright-green pants, polyester, white golf caps, and plaid shirts. You know, big fat Americans walking up and down tourist streets in Dublin with lots of money and cameras, saying how cute and quaint things were. Your typical stereotype of tourists. And you get the impression going to America that they're all going to be stupid, and that you are just going to rule this land, you know? Then you get off the plane, and it takes you about two minutes to realize that it ain't that way at all.

DOMINIC

Irene: I've been divorced since 1989. Getting married again was the last thing I was looking for, but once I'd been married and divorced, I knew what I was looking for and could shop around.

Tim asked me to marry him two days after my birthday. He took me down to a Chinese restaurant. He had been acting really nervous the whole day—I thought he was pissed off at me or something. When the waitress brought out the fortune cookies, he did a little switcheroo. He had taken out the fortune that was inside and replaced it with one that he'd had his mom White-Out and type over earlier that said, "Irene, will you marry me?" So he put that one back in. When I opened the fortune cookie, my heart started pounding really fast. And he goes,

"Are you going to answer me?" And I said, "I don't know, is this for real?" Then I started sweating a lot. And he goes, "Well?" And I go, "Well, okay, I guess so."

IRENE—

JON

Jon: I guess I'm naïve in that I haven't experienced everything there is to experience, but I really feel like I have the key to life as far as my belief in Jesus Christ.

I've never, ever had a single drug in my body. Never had a drop of alcohol. And you know what? I'm not even sure that those things are wrong, scripturally, in the Bible. But what I do know is that the world perceives it to be against the Christian religion. So no matter if it's wrong or not, if people who know what I stand for see me drinking, they're going to think, He's full of it—I'm not listening to anything he says.

I'm a firm believer that if you don't believe the basic principles of Christianity, then you're lost. But I don't believe that if you don't worship exactly the way I do that you're doomed, 'cause there's several denominations in the Christian religion.

I might have blinders on, but that's just so I don't get thrown off course, 'cause I wouldn't want anything to change me. This is the way I am; this is the way I'm gonna be forever. And if I have blinders on, that's just to keep me from changin'. If I'm narrow-minded, then I'm narrow-minded—that's who Jon is, Jon's narrow-minded.

Tami: California's nice. I've been here for six years. Sometimes the people are absolute jerks. Everybody's into this glamour-high-society thing. And I'm not about that. I just wanna get back to New York and meet some people that are like me, some real people that are down-to-earth. I mean, I have days when I just wear sweats, days when I wear a hat. I like to just chill on occasion, and these people always have to be lookin' like they just came off the <u>Soul</u> <u>Train</u> line.

TAMI

EARLY IMPRESSIONS

Aaron: Talkin' to David, I realize that I really admire that he does his own thing. He doesn't try to be someone that he's not. I mean, you look at his comedy, and then you look at him off-camera, and he's exactly the same way. He's his own person.

Beth S.: David's funny. I mean, he's funny. He really is hilarious. I mean, the camera-men can't stop laughing half the time when David talks.

Irene: My first impression of David was that he sort of scared me. I guess I fear that his comic side might come out and embarrass me for saying something, so I try to say the right things around him. And so far it's been okay. I've been safe with him.

Tami: David seems like a cool person. He's definitely a comedian. He seems like a person that I'll be able to talk to about my guy problems and that'll be able to talk to me about his girl problems. I think it's gonna turn out to be like a brother-and-sister-type relationship.

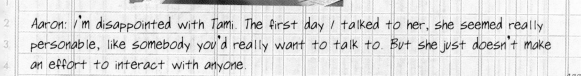

Aaron: I'm disappointed with Tami. The first day I talked to her, she seemed really personable, like somebody you'd really want to talk to. But she just doesn't make an effort to interact with anyone.

Jon: I'm a country boy from Kentucky and Tami's a black girl from L.A. I'm supposed to be prejudiced against her. I think it bothers her that I'm not, and she's trying to create that.

Irene: My first impression of Tami was bossy, bossy, bossy. She's going to let you know what she's thinking.

David: Jon—the first thing, what did I see? A tall, white cowboy hat with an ol' silver belt buckle with the words "Jon" and a picture of a cross and some poor cow being lacerated by a little man on top of it. I walk up the stairs, and Jon says, "Howdy," and I say, well, okay, this guy must be a redneck.

Irene: I felt sorry for him, because it looked like he did not fit in. I mean, he probably wears his cowboy hat to bed.

Dom: I spent a week on the road with Jon, and we got along, we became friends. But we discovered certain differences: I smoke a lot, and he's allergic to nicotine; I like to drink, and he doesn't; he doesn't believe in sex before marriage, and I believe in lots of it.

Aaron: Jon makes these blanket statements, and I don't know where the hell he gets them from. I mean, it must be, like, some esoteric Kentucky literature that he's been reading on the side. He brings up these points that I think are completely half-assed. And I question that, because if I don't agree with something, I'll always challenge it.

David: Dominic is on a vibe all his own. He's from another planet.

Beth S.: I think that, all in all, Dominic is a very fair person, but if he's not happy about something, he will just slam on you.

Tami: Dominic is the beer-drinkin', happy, comical side of the bunch. He's the man with the one-liners.

Tami: Aaron is very carefree and big-hearted. He has the greatest personality, and he always wants to debate an issue, no matter what it is. I mean, it could be washing the dishes—he'll debate why you put the soap on the dishrag and then wash the dishes instead of filling the sink with water, putting soap in the water, and washing the dishes. We call him Spock 'cause he's always debating something.

David: Aaron is cool, 'cause Aaron likes to analyze things a lot. He never lets a subject go or enjoys it without questioning it. Aaron's a very hard person to make a fool out of, 'cause he's so analytical. And I didn't expect that from a guy who likes to surf. Aaron proved that stereotype wrong.

Dom: Aaron likes to pick political conversations from nowhere. I mean, it's amazing. "How you doin' today, Aaron?" "Pretty good. What do you think about abortion?" I mean, that's the way he is. He's into this debate stuff.

David: I think everybody's getting attached to the cat now, so actually the question is, "How are Beth and her cat?"

Dom: I came in last night, and Beth comes over, sits on my lap, puts her arm around me, and tells me, "We're distant. We should talk. We'll spend more time with each other." Bulls**t. Don't sit in my lap and put your arm around me.

Beth S: I really like Irene. I think that she and I connect the best out of the bunch. I don't know if it's because we're the oldest in the group or what, but she's just really nice, and we get along really well. She's kind of like the mom of the house.

Aaron: If Irene isn't your ally, there's something wrong with you. She's the most respectful person, as far as other people's things go. There's no way you could get in a confrontation with Irene unless it was your fault.

David: We took Jon to The Mayan. I've been there before, and it's, like, a strictly hip-hop, deep-underground-type club. Jon went into the club actin' like it didn't faze him. You know, he was dancin', and people's walkin' up to him and sayin', "Hey, what's up, cowboy?" And he'd say something like, "Word to your mommy." I thought that he would get hit or something, 'cause you don't talk about somebody's mother in that type of establishment. It was a good time, but I just wanted to get outta there, quick, fast, and hurry—you know, before something happened.

Jon: I think I was the only white guy in the place, and dressed the way I was, that's what made it so fun. It was so odd that I was there. We were fightin' our way through the crowd, and this big huge black guy with this sock hat that they wear all the time comes up to me and says something like, "Well, yee-haw, pardner!" And I was like, hmmm. . . . So I said, "Well, word to your momma!" And that's when I think Tami left me alone. But she did come back for me.

Tami: Jon is definitely a character. He tries to fit in in any situation. And seeing him dance out there was quite embarrassing, actually. Pretty much everybody at the Mayan knows me, and I was just totally embarrassed. Jon was out there—he was doing the funky chicken!

TENSIONS RISE

Aaron: The issue started when Jon and David were arguing about cleaning up and everybody doing their part. From my perspective, they were both getting on each other's backs. Jon was being his usual smart-ass self, and David was just kind of bossing him around. So they started to get in a verbal confrontation, and they started getting in each other's faces. One pushed the other, and they started strangling each other. It was great. It was ridiculous.

David:
I'm not normally a violent guy, I swear I'm not. It's just that, when I get disrespected, or when you put your hands on me, you know.... I was in a very edgy mood that day, and I cleaned the house and Jon was just eating stuff, and he didn't put his dishes away or clean 'em. I was like, "Jon, can you please come here and clean your dishes?"—'cause we have a little ant problem. He's like, "Ah'm gonna get it when Ah'm gonna get it. And not a second sooner." So I was like, "Jon, you're makin' the front of the house look like some sh**. Why won't you come out here and clean

it?" "Look here, boy, you are too little and too skinny to be bossin' somebody around." I forget the word that triggered me, that made me run over there and push him and choke him like that, but he just really pissed me off, and I

He said the funniest line. He stands up and goes,
"You have crossed the line, son!"
And it just made me laugh, 'cause he was serious about that line. You know, it's like a <u>Dukes of Hazzard</u> line. I was lookin' for Boss Hogg or something. But I'm not gonna choke him anymore.

Aaron: After that Jon incident, I should have talked to David more about how it's just stupid to get that upset about something like that, to be that aggressive. I should have pulled him aside initially and said, "Just be a little more smart about the jokes you're making, because they're gonna hurt someone's feelings and you're gonna hit a soft spot, you know?"

Beth S.: I'm really starting to see David's true colors. At times, he's very superficial and fake. And I don't like that at all. I think that's a really ugly part of David.

We got in a fight because Irene and Tami and I were upset that we're always the ones cleaning up the kitchen. And so he totally turned the whole thing around, saying that the reason that we're neat and they're not is because our rooms are bigger. What does that have to do with our kitchen? And I—ooh, I could've strangled him. I felt like killing him. He turned everything around on me and started taking these low shots at me, saying that I should go upstairs and pop all the zits on my face—like I've got fifty thousand zits on my face—because I need to get laid and I couldn't get a guy if I wanted to. So, whatever. If he wants to go around and say all these things about me, that's fine. That's the only way that he knows how to fight. But I'm not going to stoop to his level.

Irene: Half the time I don't like David. He's got an attitude problem. He's the type of person that has to be right all the time—he can never be wrong, he can never say something nice about somebody, he has a dirty mouth. And his humor's not funny anymore—he doesn't have to be dirty, he doesn't have to be mean. I think he just brings out the worst in a lot of people, and that's why everybody's fighting here.

Jon: David's loud, he's obnoxious, he's rude, he's profane, he's constantly showing off—whether it's in front of other people, his girlfriends, the cameras. He says some thing to girls that are just unbelievable. And then he thinks it's funny. He thinks it's all a joke. Well, it's not a joke, and he's making enemies real fast. Hopefully he'll get the hint and take a hike. I don't know. Still, I think that it's all that rap music he listens to. Because you don't see people who listen to country music running around that way.

Tami: It was a joke at first. David co[me]
running by and snatches the covers [off]
of me—knocks me over. I'm trying to [hold]
on to the covers, but he finally gets [the]
covers off of me. Beth jumps on top [of]
me to cover me up, and I guess Jon [got]
the covers back from David and thre[w]
them on top of us so that we could c[over]
up. But David snatched them off agai[n,]
so finally I just got up and ran into [the]
bathroom. I got really, really pissed, [and]
I wanted to lash out and get him ba[ck]
for what he did. I wanted to kill hi[m.]

David: So I was pulling the blanket, and she was
laughin', everybody was laughin', and I kept pullin'.
I got it off of her somehow, and Beth came runnin'
and jumped on top of Tami. They got the blanket
back, and then I pulled it off 'em, and when I got
it completely off, I ran into the other room. All
of a sudden I hear a lot of commotion goin' on. I
still think, we're playin', that somebody's lookin'
for me, like it's a hide-and-go-seek game. But
evidently Tami had thrown my boots in the toilet.
They found me and started kickin' me, and I came
out like, "Yo, don't kick me. What's goin' on?"
     After that it just escalated. One thing led
to another, and it seemed like Beth kept instigating
it. She kept putting more hot air into the balloon,
making Tami madder and madder. I felt like, okay,
she was embarrassed. I didn't think she ordinarily
would have acted like that if Beth hadn't kept
instigating it.
     So one thing led to another, and I was
like, "Okay, I'm sorry, blah, blah, blah." And
she's like, "No, you motherf**ker, you violated
me," sayin' this, that, and the other, and I was
like, "What do you want me to do? Want me to
drop my pants?" I was just talkin'. "Okay, here
you go, I'm dropping my pants. Are we even?"

Jon: Beth says, "How can you say she wanted it? She was screaming at the top of her lungs. That's something a rapist would say." And then David was like, "A rapist? How can you call me a rapist?!" Now this is just my opinion, but I think it was very extreme of her to bring up rape, because it was nothing like that.

Beth S: Yeah, I did use the word rape. The reason I used the word is because he was saying that even though Tami was saying, no, she didn't mind what he was doing. I knew I couldn't live with David anymore after that night.

David: What scared me was when Beth said the word rape. Beth was clearly overreacting. You know, "You violated her privacy. It's just like rape. You don't know when to stop." That freaked me out, because the word rape,—women shouldn't play with that word.

Tami: I heard a couple of the comments Beth made about how it was like rape, and all this other stuff, and I actually didn't feel like that. I was humiliated and embarrassed, but I didn't feel like it was a rape situation.

Irene: We had two days before we talked to David, and during those two days I did a lot of thinking. I talked to the girls at the house, and they had the same feelings that I did. At first I thought I was wrong for wanting him to leave, but they had the same feelings and the same thoughts, so I knew I wasn't crazy, and I knew I wasn't being selfish. So that's the conclusion we came to, to ask him to leave—because we did feel that he was a threat.

David: I didn't mean to hurt nobody. The girls, they have their power, you know. They say, "We feel uncomfortable," so I gotta go. So I got the short end of the stick. I'm tired of Irene callin' me names, tellin' me I'm an ass****, I'm wrong, I'm dangerous. Just goes to show you, man, women can cry rape and cry sexual harassment, and the guys automatically look like the bad guy.

Tami: Everyone should be granted a second chance, and though I probably would not have forgotten what he did, I would have been able to put my feelings aside and just stay away from him and hope that he stayed away from me. But he's gotten into conflicts with everybody. I think that he was just a time bomb waiting to go off. So at the end of it all, I thought I was making the right decision.

185

Aaron: As far as us having the right to choose who our roommate was, me and Dominic said this virtually at the same time: "What right do I have to pick someone?" I'm not gonna play God and act like I'm better and say to someone, "Well, you're worthy of living here with us." Because look at us—I mean, we're like the mutated Brady Bunch. So I guess you just want another mutant.

GLEN

Dominic: After David moved out of the house, we had to find a new roommate. We had only known Glen for forty-five minutes before we asked him to move in. He and I have had some words, already. I felt that he was accusing me of performing for the camera, which insults the hell out of me. We tried to explain to him that this wasn't a show but a living arrangement that we've all gotta get on with. He seems to veer off on the fact that this is a TV show.

GLEN: I'll just do anything I want, and nobody's gonna tell me what to do. I'm gonna use whatever I have inside of me, whatever's in my heart. I'm gonna let it out, and people can react whichever way they want. This is something I believe in; it's a part of my philosophy: I can say one thing, and then tomorrow I can totally change my mind. That sort of throws people off right there.

I get bored with people, I get bored with things. I think maybe it's because I hate myself. I generally hate the concept of being a human being. I'd rather not be a human being. I think I'd wanna be a dog. No, I'd rather have no material essence. I am insecure, and I hate the way I talk. Maybe by exposing my insecurities to every damn person on this earth, I'm gonna have to deal with them.

I'm kind of wary about Dom right now. I don't know if it's because he acts so smart, but he's just so sure of himself. I didn't care for him that much. I just tend to stay away from anybody who thinks they're always right.

Jon: I think Glen's a great guy, but I think he doesn't know how to react to moving into a new situation. I think he's goin' about it the wrong way. He's kinda tryin' to come in and play catch-up, like he's missed out on something before, like he needs to be in the spotlight. I think that's makin' him some enemies.

Dom: This is not a plea for sympathy, charity, attention—I'm not good at receiving that—but there's something that's happening to me.... Recently, I was home for Christmas, and this was the first time my family had been together in seven years. Since I left Ireland, my father has become gravely ill. For a long time we didn't realize it. In fact, he'd been to lots of doctors, done lots of tests, and they all came back negative, and when I got home for Christmas, he was sittin' there, feelin' depressed, feelin' sorry for himself. And we were like, "Come on, get your sh** together, get up, make the most out of life." And I actually sat down and had a real go with him.

So I came back to America from Christmas, and I was back in the country two days when he collapsed and was rushed into the hospital. And for the past month they've been tryin' to find out what's wrong with him. He's been in the hospital since the day after New Year's.

Everything else just seems so trivial. It's, like, all of a sudden a certain real-ization smacks you in the face like a punching bag. You feel helpless being so far away, and yet, if I was there, I wouldn't be helpful at all. He would think, Why suddenly have you come home? Is there something I don't know? Is this a last-visit type of deal?"

MARCH 21, 1993 (WEEK NINE)

Tami: When I found out that I was pregnant, I first had to decide how I was gonna tell my mom. Secondly, I had to decide if it was something that I wanted to carry through or not, and thirdly, I had to tell my boyfriend that I was pregnant, and then deal with all of his stuff.

Telling my mom was the hardest thing for me to do. She was really not happy about it, 'cause it brings back a lot of memories for her. My boyfriend is not happy with the fact that I want to have an abortion, 'cause he wants me to have the child, so I'm dealing with that. It was definitely a hard decision to make.

I wanted to tell everybody in the house that I was pregnant, because we all have to live together and I don't feel that we should have any secrets or that any one person should feel uncomfortable about sharing something with the others, so I decided to get the group together and let everybody know at the same time. From previous conversations with Aaron and Jon, I knew that they're totally against abortion. I also decided to do it in a group setting so that if they had any opinions or anything as far as this issue was concerned, they could express them in front of everyone, not later, when I would be taking that type of criticism alone.

Aaron: I think having this happen to someone you live with brings the issue very close to home. And it's extremely difficult to deal with. I mean, if there's anything I could do for Tami to make her reconsider, then I would. But it's her decision, and that's her right as a person.

Jon: Tami and I differ very much. She knows how I feel about abortion. We don't really agree, but I think there's a certain amount of respect we have for each other. In no way, shape, or form do I think abortion's an easy thing to do, so I think that instead of judging Tami and telling her how wrong she is, it'd be better to show her the love that God has put in my life. If I show that through being a friend to her through it all, maybe then she'll see that the God I serve is a forgiving and loving God.

Dom: I back her all the way in her decision.

Tami: I had complications with the abortion. I had to go back and have the whole procedure done over again, and that was not an easy thing to do. That made it even more trying. If you're ever in the predicament where you have to make a choice between having an abortion and having a baby, and you decide to have an abortion, make it the last time you have to make that decision. Do the right thing and practice safer sex after that. Because this was exceptionally hard for me—I'm just glad it's over.

Irene: I think this has changed my view of Tami just slightly, the way she's treating it as no big deal. It should be a big deal. I don't respect her any less or any more for it, but I think that if she showed just a little bit more compassion, I would understand her decision more and maybe I'd feel for her more.

APRIL 4, 1993 (WEEK ELEVEN)

Irene: I'm leaving to get married. I'm gonna miss everybody to death. I'm not gonna miss the cameras, the lights—just the whole setup. I'm gonna miss all the guys here; they are just wonderful people.

This has been quite an experience, and I am never gonna forget it. I don't think you can explain the feelings you get while you're here, the basic feelings of frustration, fear—there's just something inside that you can never really explain.

There were times when I was mad that I did this, because it hurt Tim. I love him so much, and the last thing I wanted to do was hurt him, but I think it was something I had to do and had to experience for myself. I'm glad that I did.

Jon: My parents were both Christians, both grew up in Christian homes. It obviously played a big role in their life, and they decided to raise their children that way. We were more or less forced to go to church when we were little, and when I was eight years old, I decided to accept Jesus Christ as my savior. So I made the decision to live my life as a Christian at a very young age.

Then, as I got older, it started getting harder to be such a good little boy. But one thing about me is that once I've made a decision, I wanna stick to it. So I started gettin' involved in church. I really kind of strived to live it out, and got involved in the youth group, which really helped me, because when we'd have struggles, we'd help each other out, and we'd get through it. I guess I had the reputation in high school of bein' a goody two shoes: "Oh, he's that Jesus freak. He doesn't drink, he doesn't do anything. Nice guy, just kind of boring. You don't wanna have anything to do with him."

In this house, I'm always in an argument with somebody about something. When we were all in the Winnebago, I had arguments with Dominic and I had arguments with Tami—Tami and Dominic never argued, just me. Then I had my run-in with David. And I have my problems with Aaron. So I'm starting to think that maybe I'm not the easiest person to get along with. Maybe _I'm_ the jerk. I don't know.

Aaron: I think Jon doesn't want it to look like the country boy's comin' to the city and fallin' in love with the city, so he's doing everything to separate himself from adapting whatsoever to the California lifestyle, even though it might be fun to try something new, dress different, you know. I think he doesn't want it perceived like, "Jon's changed." He wants it to be "Jon stayed the same exact person." Well, I hope _I_ change, because I'm here to change and be exposed to different things. I think he's so hardheaded about that.

GLEN: WHEN BETH A. FIRST CAME IN TO REPLACE IRENE, I WAS FEELING INTIMIDATED BY HER. SHE CAME IN WITH FORCE. WHEREAS I DIDN'T WANNA SEEM PUSHY AT ALL WHEN I FIRST CAME INTO THE HOUSE, SHE JUST SEEMED TO SWARM RIGHT IN AND CONQUER HER GROUND.

Aaron: Beth A.'s really outgoing. She seems like someone who's got a lot of energy, enjoys going out, enjoys meeting people. She seems extremely personable.

Beth A.: I don't think that it was difficult for me to come into a situation where people had already bonded, because I'm really easygoing and able to just fit in with people.

I am extremely religious. I think a big reason that I'm religious is because I'm six-years sober, and when I decided to get my life together, I asked for God's help. I'm hoping that this will give me the opportunity, since I'm not working as much, to be able to go back to church.

Before I stopped drinking I was an insane nut. Then when I stopped, I got my life back. I mean, there's not a whole lot to tell—I think everybody knows the story of the person who drank too much and sat in their own puddle of tears and didn't have anything to grasp on to. For me, I had a really hard upbringing in a lot of ways and had a lot of anger, and there was violence in my life. I chose to drink and do drugs to numb that out until I was ready to deal with it. Now I cope.

I haven't really thought about what image I want to create, though I realize that in a sense I am the token lesbian. But first and foremost, I am me. Being a lesbian is just one preference in my life. I don't like to categorize myself, to have a label. You know, some nights I have makeup and nail polish and minidresses, and then other days I'm in sweats and jeans and boots, so my image is my mood.

BETH A.

191

Beth S.: Aaron says that he's this virgin and that he has no girlfriends, but he's got all these girls calling him, and he goes out with all these girls. He says, "Well, you know, I'd really appreciate it if you didn't talk about these girls while we're around the camera." Why? Because maybe they'll find out about each other? I don't think he's as innocent as he's playing it.

Aaron: As far as dating, I kind of went nuts my first year at school. I'd just broken up with my girlfriend of three years, and you get to this new environment with a lot of women around, and you kinda go nuts. So, yeah, for a while I was a definite cheeseball. Right now I don't have a girlfriend, so I've been dating a few people and having a great time. I'd rather date someone who's quality than just go out with someone who's good-looking. I've been a cheeseball, but you get bored of just dating and scammin' with people. It just becomes a joke.

HOME Dominic: I really don't like to compare my family. All families are different. I mean, I've said to myself, "God, is my family crazy?" But you know, my mom once said to me, "There'll always be someone better off than you, and there'll always be someone worse off than you." I think it's a great thing you can apply to anything. There's always gonna be a family that you look at and say, "Couldn't my family be a bit more like that?" Then you see another family, and it's like, "Thank God my family isn't like that." I think every family has its little abnormalities.

My trip to Ireland was a great, great trip, my best time home. But now I'm home in Los Angeles, as opposed to home in Dublin. And though I'm always happy to be in L.A., I have a real content feeling this time. I'm relieved and content.

I'm not very interested in mortality and what happens after life. Have I sat down and thought about what it would be like if my father died? Or if my mother died?—God forbid. No, never. You'd think I would have, but no. I don't know how I can put this into words, but it's like bein' hit by a ton of bricks. I never thought for a second that I'd be without either of my parents. Then it suddenly dawned on me, I've been away from home for seven years, living this life, doing what I do to keep me happy and in the end make them proud.... Then all of a sudden, I'm close to losin' one, and it was like, there were emotions that I'd never felt before, never had to.

Aaron: I kinda miss my family a little bit, right now. I'm really close to my parents, and I'm just thinkin' about how much I miss my dog, my family...it's weird, 'cause I don't miss 'em so much when I'm living at school.

Beth S.: I really don't spend any time with my mom, because she's so busy. We didn't really have the typical mother-daughter relationship, that whole nurturing thing, going on. I think now I can kind of forgive her for all the things that I went through growing up, because now I understand. She went through a lot growing up, escaping from Poland and everything. And she didn't have the greatest relationship with her own mother, and I don't think anybody really taught my mother how to express her feelings. She doesn't know any better. But she does the best thing she knows how to, and I can't really expect any more. But I love my mother very much, and I know that she loves me.

Beth A.: My whole dream in life is to someday be in the forest, to be in love, to have a child, to have a garden, to be self-sufficient. I love growing things, and I love eating food that I've grown. It's such a full circle, to eat in harmony with earth, to know that what you're eating doesn't harm you, doesn't harm anything it came from or anywhere it's going. It is completely balanced. Simply to be in your garden is one of the highest fulfillments to me in life. Just to sit in the soil, and mix your garden, and everything is growing out of your love. I guess the family in the home is the same thing. You're sitting in the midst of your environment, what you've created, what you are working towards, and what's growing around you—that's some life to me, that's my dream.

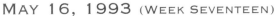

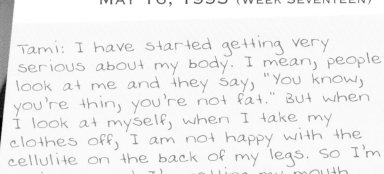

Tami: I have started getting very serious about my body. I mean, people look at me and they say, "You know, you're thin, you're not fat." But when I look at myself, when I take my clothes off, I am not happy with the cellulite on the back of my legs. So I'm doing more sit-ups, and I'm getting my mouth wired. Everyone thinks I'm crazy to do this, but I am getting my mouth wired for three weeks, and hopefully I'll lose some weight. I have a tendency to eat too much, and I did this before, when I was still modeling.

A friend of mine grossly described this to me: He says, "Tami, you need to carry wire cutters with you, because if you don't, and you have to throw up, you're gonna choke to death."

I had never thought about that. That had really not entered my mind. So, yes, I have my wire cutters ready. In case something like that should happen, I can cut them off.

My sex life is going to be great even if I have my mouth wired, because I won't have to do anything, and I can get everything done to me. But it doesn't matter, 'cause I haven't been getting any lately anyway, but if the situation should change, everything'll be done to me, and that will be great.

Aaron: I asked Tami about it, and she's a bit sensitive about getting her jaw wired shut. The whole principle behind dieting is that, obviously, it should be coupled with exercise. I think it's completely stupid, because basically what you're doing is starving yourself. Then your body goes into shock and wants to replenish all that is lost, so she's just gonna gain the weight right back. It just doesn't set a good example—if I was watchin' the show, and I had an eating disorder, it would give me a bad message.

Beth A.: I think if someone has to wire their mouth shut to stop themselves from eating, it shows all lack of control. That's the most demeaning thing a woman could do to herself. To keep her mouth shut—it's sad that in the nineties women feel they have to do that still.

Tami: Everybody in the house seems to think I'm crazy, that it's a waste of time, but I am not happy with my body, I'm not happy with myself. So I go through the necessary steps to make myself happy. To others, the steps may seem very drastic.

Jon: I'd never wire my mouth shut, 'cause I like for people to hear what I'm saying. I think that what I have to say is important, and I love food too much. Before I let it get to that point, I would probably quit eatin' so much.

Dominic: We made a ten-minute film about a spoiled little brat of a child who was left everything in her parents' will. Then her six or seven long-lost brothers and sisters attempt to murder the girl in order to get the house and all its worldly belongings. It was pretty much a verité kind of movie.

Best actor: I thought Aaron did a terrific job—a little too real, maybe—as a religious salesman. Beth S. put in a stunning performance, one of her best, as the Polish daughter who was left everything, but who has been selling her cat off to do Polish kitty commercials—typecasting, it's terrible. Glen, as the frustrated filmmaker hiding behind the couch upstairs, was wonderful. That was well scripted on our behalf. But I was really disappointed with my Elvis performance. I can do better. I am working on it. Our very good friend and security guard Brett donned his French maid's outfit to play Beth's French maid, but he was also one of the long-lost children that was left nothing in the will, and he killed everyone in the end.

Someone came up with the really original idea of calling it House Night. Someone suggested Venice Fiasco, but the title is actually a closely guarded secret.

I tried to become one with Elvis, but I don't think it was indicative of the best Elvis I can do. I did a really good one in Palm Springs about four years ago, around seven in the morning by a swimming pool. But I didn't have enough time to get into the role. I was kinda disappointed with my impersonation, to be honest.

Tami: Dominic played Elvis, and he was excellent. He had this really big belly, and he staggered on his words. You know, he did this "oooow, baby," type thing—it was great. But he got killed right off the bat, so we didn't get to see much of Elvis.

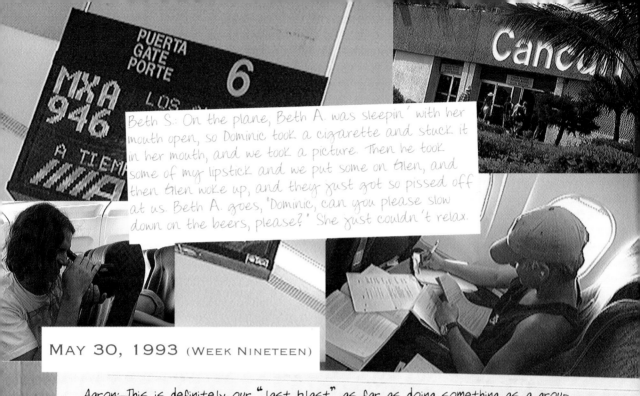

Beth S.: On the plane, Beth A. was sleepin' with her mouth open, so Dominic took a cigarette and stuck it in her mouth, and we took a picture. Then he took some of my lipstick and we put some on Glen, and then Glen woke up, and they just got so pissed off at us. Beth A. goes, "Dominic, can you please slow down on the beers, please?" She just couldn't relax.

MAY 30, 1993 (WEEK NINETEEN)

Aaron: This is definitely our "last blast" as far as doing something as a group.

Jon: We were all excited about gettin' there, and I guess that had something to do with it, but peanuts started hittin' me in the back of the head, and I turn around, and Dominic and Aaron have handfuls of peanuts, throwing 'em at everybody. So we had this big peanut war. Glen and Beth A. were like, "I'm just not gonna participate in this." But it's funny, because Glen was doing it, and then he looked over at Beth A., and she was like, "Ahhh," so Glen quit doin' it. He started pickin' 'em up and puttin' them in the ashtray.

COZUMEL

Glen: At one point during the plane ride, a bunch of idiots were throwing peanuts at my head, which I thought was very immature. I was basically embarrassed by everybody that I was traveling with except for Beth A.

Beth S.: We are like spoiled little brats on this island. We've been given everything, and we can't even get along. It's pathetic. After this is all over, everyone's gonna look back and just be like, "You know, I wish I wouldn't have acted like that," or "I should have done this," and it's gonna be too late.

Aaron: Beth A. and Glen have a really cool relationship. I think they're both very weird in different ways. They kind of feed off each other in their weirdness. I think they relate to each other because they're both very honest people.

Beth A.: I think the fact that Glen doesn't have to be concerned about sex with me makes him a little more comfortable with me as a woman. He can think of me like one of his sisters. We're affectionate, we're playful, we're friends. Doesn't have to be any deeper than that.

Dominic: Beth A. and Glen have discovered their weirdness together. They finally came out of the closet: Both of them are just whacked out of their minds. I mean, both of 'em are looking for women, so they've got that in common.

Tami: I think that they try to make their relationship as genuine as possible, but I personally feel that it's so fabricated. I think they just decided to be friends 'cause nobody was talking to either one of 'em. Now they get a lot of attention by being so weird together.
     Glen has two different personalities. When he's around the rest of us, he's a character. He's animated, he has fun, and he joins in on our games. But when Beth A.'s around, he becomes Mr. Politically Aware, don't pollute the environment, don't do this, don't do that—because she's that way.

GLEN: WE THOUGHT THAT WE WERE GOING TO BE JUDGES FOR A BIKINI CONTEST. THEN THE GIRLS JUST THREW ONE-PIECES AT US AND SAID WE WERE THE ONES THAT WERE GOING TO BE JUDGED—ALL OF US GUYS HAD TO DRESS UP AS "WOMEN." SO I JUST SAID, "WHAT THE HELL," AND WENT WITH IT AND HAD A GOOD TIME.

Dominic: I'll give you a summary of the evening real quick. Basically, I'd been drinkin' in the sun too much, had a couple beers at dinner. I could lie and say that I knew this was going on, but no, my body just decided, "Dom, it's time to rest now." I'd had a few beers, and it was time to lie down. It's quite simple; it's not that big a deal.

Basically, I've been collecting sand particles to see how deep I can embed them in my face. It's a project I've been working on with USC and UCLA. I get a grant every year to do it. So far I've got 'em an inch into my face, and my sponsors are real happy with the progress. Cozumel was just a side thing to the sand-particle-embedding-in-my-face project I've been working on for years.

JUNE 13, 1993 (WEEK TWENTY-ONE)

Beth S.: I just think it's too bad that everybody didn't really put one hundred percent into being roommates. Some people did, some people didn't, and that's too bad, because after it's over, it's over—you can't go back and say, "Cut! Go back! I wanna say this!" It's there, and we're gonna see it over and over and over and over again.

At this point I could really care less. I've always tried to get along with everybody—nobody could say that Beth didn't try and get along with everybody. Everybody's being petty about me, so I'm starting to get petty about everybody else, and it's just a vicious circle. It's like, why are we spending so much energy fighting when we could just get along?

Tami: Every time there is a confrontation, I always look like the bad guy, 'cause I'm the only one who speaks up for what I believe or who stresses my opinions and my concerns. I think that's the whole problem in the house, especially with Jon and Beth S., 'cause they don't know how to express themselves. They do very well when the person they're having a problem with isn't around, and they can actually open up and say what they think the problem is. But when that person's there, they can't actually say anything to that person—they walk away and back down from the situation. **It bothers me because I always look like the bad guy; I always look like the bitch.**

But that's something that they need to deal with—they really have to start speakin' up for themselves, 'cause if not, people are going to continue to walk over Beth S. and treat her like an idiot. As far as Jon is concerned, he's always gonna annoy people and be the butt of everybody's jokes, because he doesn't know how to express himself. He backs down and walks away from any form of confrontation, and **I don't think that's healthy.**

I think, just on the outside lookin' in, that Aaron has a real problem with how he's perceived. He doesn't want to ever look bad in front of anybody. We all probably have that little part—nobody wants to look bad in front of anybody else—but I think Aaron is just overdoing it. He wants to be Mr. "I know everything, I've done it all, I've been there, and if I don't know, I'll make you think I know, 'cause I know _you_ don't know." That's how Aaron is. **He's gonna be an excellent accountant. Excellent.**

THE TROLLS

Jon: Well, we came up with this little term for the people that actually capture this experience on tape. I guess it was actually a surfer-slang term—Aaron was the first one to come up with it. I think that, you know, we got these other people in the house that aren't our roommates, and they're not allowed to speak to us because if they become part of our lives, the experience would no longer be focused on just us.

So that made it hard, because we couldn't talk to these people we see every day, and obviously they had to work with us, had to put microphones on us, had to be there to get close-ups of us—so it wasn't people that we could ignore too easily. They were always hoppin' around the house, turnin' on lights and everything else, and then Aaron says, "You know, they're just trolling around, doin' this and that," so we came up with this name for 'em: the trolls.

And this being the last weekend, we thought, Well, rules are made to be broken. We've managed to obey them all the way up till now, but curiosity got the best of us, and we wanted to see what was behind that door we weren't allowed to open. So we just bombarded the troll bowl and saw everything that was back there. Actually, I feel sorry for 'em a little bit, 'cause it was really kind of small, and it was hard to get around back there and do all the very hard work they did.

Aaron: In order to show our appreciation for what we've been going through for the last five months, we thought it would be appropriate to take every single troll and toss him in the spa with a little bit of an appetizer to go with 'em.

So the first troll we tossed back there was the director. We kind of lured him in—he was a bit naïve. We said that we wanted to tell him how much we really appreciated everything he had done. He was a very understanding guy, very committed, works long hours, and we said, in all sincerity, "You know, we really appreciate what you've done" in order to get his attention away from Dominic, who went and got the cake. "Great experience, we appreciate you puttin' up with us. We know it's been very difficult." And then Dominic ran in and just drilled him with the cake, and we took him and tossed him in the spa.

We proceeded to do that to everybody, even the executive producers, and all the camera and sound trolls. It was kind of a bonding experience, 'cause we finally could just be wild and have a good time and mess around with everyone who was on the other side of the troll fence.

FINAL THOUGHTS

Jon: One day we're just gonna wake up and we won't be here anymore, and it's gonna seem like it was all a dream. Then it's gonna be on TV, and it's gonna be a very strange, odd feeling. The whole reality of it is really settin' in—those were television cameras, and this will be shown, and we'll relive these experiences we've had. People are gonna pass judgment on who I am as a person.

When I think of this whole experience, it's like a slide show. I picture us lowering Beth S. down the cliff on Outward Bound, I picture Irene's wedding, I picture posting Aaron's picture all over the wall, Dominic wheelin' his Harley into the livin' room, Glen baking lasagna. I remember how many times a day David played "Hip Hop Hooray."

GLEN: WELL, I'M STILL INSECURE, I STILL DON'T LIKE A LOT OF
THINGS I DO. IT WAS A TRUE TEST, AND I'M SURE I'M GONNA
LOOK BACK ON IT WHEN I GET OLDER. THE TOUGH THING IS GOING
TO BE RAISING KIDS—WHEN THEY SEE THE WAY I WAS IN FRONT OF
THE CAMERA AND WHAT I'VE DONE, THEY'LL BE TELLIN'
ME, "YOU SHOULDN'T HAVE DONE SOME OF THOSE THINGS."
I WAS YOUNG....

I'LL REMEMBER JON DRESSED UP AS A COWBOY WHENEVER
WE'D GO OUT, SINGING ALL THE TIME. DOMINIC JUST WAS
ALWAYS SO BUSY. LIKE, IF HE WASN'T
DOIN' A FILM, HE WAS HELPING
SOME BAND WITH MANAGEMENT.
HE'D STAY OUT EVERY NIGHT
UNTIL LIKE
THREE IN THE
MORNING, GET
UP THE NEXT
MORNING AT
SEVEN. I DON'T
KNOW HOW HE
DOES IT; HE'S JUST
UNSTOPPABLE.

AARON SEEMED TO
HAVE A GOOD TIME—VERY POLITICAL, EVEN
THOUGH HE SAYS HE'S NOT. BETH A. WORKS
HARD, BUT AT THE SAME TIME, SHE'S VERY
INVOLVED WITH THE UNDERGROUND SCENE,
WHICH I THINK'S COOL. BETH S. WAS
MISS HOLLYWOOD TO ME. WHEN I SAW HER AT
THE ROXY ONE NIGHT, SHE FIT SO WELL THERE. TAMI, I DON'T KNOW.
I NEVER GOT TO GO OUT WITH HER AND HER FRIENDS AT ALL. MAYBE
SHE THOUGHT I'D EMBARRASS HER TOO MUCH. BUT SHE DID SOME
CRAZY THINGS WHILE SHE WAS HERE, AND THAT SHOCKED ME. SO I
COULD SAY TAMI WAS A SHOCKER. IRENE WAS JUST A HARDWORKING
POLICE OFFICER, BUT VERY MOTHERLY AND VERY NURTURING.

Aaron: For me this would have been more of a personal fulfillment if I could have sat down more, just on a one-to-one level, with everyone and just talked about life without getting in debates. I think everyone, being very headstrong, was very much on the defense about opening up to other people. I can say that for myself, 'cause I have opened up to a couple of people, and they used that as ammunition against me. You tend to be far more introverted when people are like that.

Tami: Initially, coming into this experience, the one thing I wanted to do was a little self-improvement, to learn how others view me. Coming into a situation with six other people who know absolutely nothing about you and hearing what they think of you, and how they perceive you can really change you for the better. And that's exactly what's happened to me. Now I know that when I view myself as being aggressive and strong-minded and hardworking, people on the outside seem to think that I'm overbearing and overaggressive and sometimes offending. I'm learning now how to approach people in a more positive light and not be so strong and so straightforward. It's not going to happen overnight, but I do try to be more positive and more lighthearted with people.

If you're a soap opera fan, I think I was pretty close to Erica Kane, the character who causes a lot of confrontations in her household and is considered to be very moody and very bitchy, for lack of a better word.

Aaron played the Professor from Gilligan's Island. He knew everything. The professor could make a time bomb out of a tampon if he wanted to, and that was Aaron.

Jon reminded me of Screech from Saved by the Bell. He's like this character that came in and was really nerdy and set in his ways. He got into all the little things and liked to cause all this mischief. At the end everybody still loves Screech, just because he's Screech.

Beth S. was Marcia from the <u>Brady Bunch</u>. Marcia used to irritate me, because she was the oldest sister. She was the one sister that got into everything. She annoyed Greg, she annoyed Peter. She was the one sister that annoyed everybody.

Beth A. was like Susan Dey from the <u>Partridge Family</u>, because Susan was the one character out of all the kids in the <u>Partridge Family</u> that I hated. And I can only identify Beth A. with someone that I absolutely just do not like.

Glen could be Brutus from <u>Popeye</u>, because he likes to be in control. I think Glen has this tendency to pick on people that are smaller than him— like he used to intimidate Beth S. a lot. He lashed out at me. He was really obnoxious. So I'd make him Brutus from <u>Popeye</u>.

Dominic's a lot like Sid Vicious to me. There are a lot of things about Dominic, as far as his personal life is concerned, that remind me of Sid Vicious.

Beth S.: What people have to remember when they watch this is that we are all human, we all make mistakes, we all say things sometimes that we don't mean. I'm sure there's gonna be times when people are watching this and they're gonna think that I'm the biggest idiot in the world, or they're gonna question why I said something. I'm not perfect, and neither is anybody else in this house. All we can do is learn from our mistakes. Just because they have sixty hours of film on me or any of us doesn't mean that they know who we are.

Dom: We've got to return to some kind of normal living standards, and hopefully we won't wake up with nightmares, wondering where the cameras are, which has already happened to me once. This whole experience is weird, but you know what the strangest thing is? It's now become normal, you know what I mean? This is now the norm. It seems very natural to come home and have a camera waiting here.

Beth A.: The first week I was here I tried to see if anybody wanted to do stuff together. I felt it out. people don't want to. I said, "Fine." I'm not gonna force anybody to do anything they don't want to. That's not my job. It was a waste of my time.

NEW YORK

FIRST IMPRESSIONS

Kevin: Seven young people from various backgrounds come together to interact and learn and grow and share our different experiences and ideas and beliefs. That's *The Real World* to me.

Eric: Andre plays the guitar, but he doesn't like to say what kind of music he plays, because artists aren't supposed to do that. They are not supposed to label their music, or something. I'm not sure what he said.

ANDRE

Becky: When Andre walked in, he seemed like this really nice, quiet presence, but also not that quiet. You could tell right away that he was a musician.

Kevin: Andre seems kind of hesitant at times to express a view. He seems to be the kind of person that just doesn't want to talk about certain issues. You know, "I wish everything with an *ism* in it would just go away." I don't know if that's good or bad, but that's the impression I get from him.

Heather: I love Andre because he's like my rebel side. He doesn't care. He snores, he stays up late, he wakes up when he feels like waking up, he leaves when he wants....I like that.

Kevin: Becky is very straightforward. One thing that struck me was when she said she had no problems doing this show. No hesitations. Her friends were saying it might hurt her career, but she said, "You only live once." And I like that, because that's how I feel. You only live once, and why not do it?

Eric: Becky seemed to be very quiet at first, but she is starting to come out of her shell.

BECKY

Heather: Becky I can relate to, because she loves her music. And I don't care what she does from here on out, I will always respect her for that. She said something to me that really blew my mind as an artist: She doesn't care what she's gonna be or do in life, she will always write music. I personally thought that I was the only person that felt that way. My career might not always work out, I might be somewhere flipping hamburgers, but I will always pick up a pen and write a song. I don't care about the money; I don't care about the fame and television and videos; I just care about expressing myself, and that really comes across with her. I'll always respect her for that.

ERIC

Andre: Eric's the life of the party. Likes to be in the middle of everything. That's great.

Heather: I think Eric's totally different around his friends. Around people that he has to impress, he's more, "Hi, I'm Eric, I'm a model in New York." But I think around his friends he's like, "Yo, let's go to a party, let's crash, let's hang out, let's bug out." I like that, and I know that he works to balance out the two.

NORM: ERIC'S A VERY POSITIVE, ENERGETIC PERSON. HE SEEMS LIKE A VERY BUSY PERSON, SOMEONE THAT IS REALLY EXCITED ABOUT LIFE. I LOVE HIS EATING HABITS—I'M LOOKING TO ERIC FOR HEALTH INFLUENCE.

HEATHER

Andre: Heather talks about, you know, feeling like she's being watched in stores when she goes in, feeling that the store owners think that she's going to steal something, and I'm very acquainted with that emotion. I get the same treatment, you know, with the hair. I wear a long leather jacket and some- times people follow me around every- where, because they think I'm going to steal something, too.

Julie: Heather—she didn't grow up under the best of circumstances. I think a lot of people fall into their circumstances and let their circumstances kill them, but Heather hasn't done that. She's a good person, and it hasn't been easy for her to become that person.

Becky: Heather walked in, basically a bundle of energy. On the move, ready to go, she had her keys in her hand, she was like, "Man, I can't believe I'm here, but okay, I got to go to the hip-hop club. See ya later, bye!" She takes it all in stride. She's really energetic and funny, and real warm. I like her a lot. She's spunky.

Kevin: Heather and I, we are from the same hometown. So we have an immediate affinity. Also, we are both black. She's very articulate, very dogmatic. She seems to know what she wants to do with her rap career. She seems pretty together, you know?

Julie: Kevin, I mean, he is wonderful. I mean, he is an exceptional man, and I think he is stereotyped to death. He feels a lot of that—just getting to hear his poetry says a lot about that. Kevin's poem was so cool—you could just feel such pain, and you just kind of got caught up in the words. He can really write some moving stuff.

Becky: Kevin was very laid-back and completely mellow, kind of like the granddad of us all. He absorbs a lot, you can tell, and that would make sense, because he's a writer, so he has to look around and keep that inner eye. He's also very sweet, and not really into a lot of hubbub and pretentious stuff. He struck me very strongly, Kevin. He's quite intelligent.

KEVIN

Andre: Kevin's cool. Kevin, you know, he likes to make a joke out of most things. And that's

JULIE

Heather: Julie is very curious. She'll say whatever she's thinking, whether it makes sense or not, and I'm the same way. Actually, my beeper went off the first night, and she said, "Are you a drug dealer?" and everyone laughed, but I probably would have thought the same thing. I like her open attitude.

Becky: I instantly fell in love with Julie.

Eric: Julie is the sweetest. She has the cutest little accent. I don't know if she gets offended, but sometimes I make fun of her when she says something, and it is not because I am making fun of her. I want to have her accent, too. I love it.

Kevin: Julie really wants to learn. She asks a lot of questions, a lot of questions. She's real inquisitive.

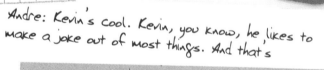

Norm: It makes me feel like I'm on vacation when I'm with Julie.

Julie: I think that Norm's just really caught up in so much stuff that he can't even enjoy anything. It would be different if he had just three jobs, but he's got, like, ten.

NORMAN

Eric: Norm is just a great person. He has a lot of feelings, and he is caring. He really enjoys himself, and he enjoys the people around him. I guess that makes him kind of special, because everybody likes Norm.

Kevin: Norman comes to you like a patriarch. He's a lot older. He's savvy—wow. Norman seems to be the most level-headed of the group. It was kind of symbolic that he was sitting at the head of the dinner table when we went out. He has the straight answers.

Andre: I've never experienced a dog that big before. It scares the hell out of me.

Eric: Smokey is exactly like the cat from Pet Sematary, exactly the same.

Becky: Smokey stands up to Gouda and bullies Gouda, even though Gouda's about twenty times the size of Smokey.

GOUDA AND SMOKEY

Kevin: I saw Gouda first, and I was like, "Oh, my God, there's a horse in here!" And Smokey jumps on me when I'm sleeping. But you have to adjust to different situations. So I just did.

MARCH 1, 1992 (WEEK THREE)

NORM: I KNOW I GET KINDA MOODY, AND IF I GET MOODY ENOUGH, I'M REALLY DRAMATIC AND I MIGHT LEAVE. BUT I'M HAVIN' A GOOD TIME. I'M GETTING TO KNOW SOME REALLY INCREDIBLE PEOPLE, SO I'M GOING TO STAY.

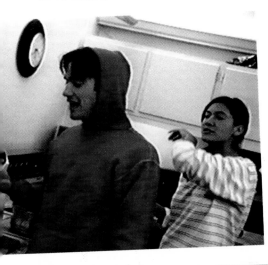

Heather: I don't even know the size of this dog. Just take six, seven people bending over, and that's the size of this dog Gouda. And I was so scared for my cat, because I just got her. But I let the cat down, and Gouda and the cat talked more than me and these other people.

Eric: Maybe it's conflict between me and my roommates or whatever, or maybe it's the line of work that I'm in. I think sometimes people take a different attitude toward actors and models, 'cause they think that they're a step away from everybody, and in reality we're no different than anybody else. We're human, too.

Heather: I think the major stress that's goin' on with some of the people here is that people are not being expressive enough. Eric is at the center of most problems around here because he complains the most and says the least. So I just constantly pick, pick, pick, say things to him just to let him know: "Hey, Eric, stop bein' like that. Stop holding your feelings in." It's almost a phoniness about him—he puts on a front, everything is fine, everything is cool, and that's not gonna work around here.

Becky: My love life goes in spurts. It's usually extremely active when I'm not busy, because I wanna meet as many people as possible when I go out. But I've been really busy, and when I'm really busy and focused and concentrated, I just don't have the time to look around.

I feel a little deprived. I feel deprived because I don't have the time right now, and I'm kind of figuring out how to approach this. I definitely want male company. That's a big thing in my life—I don't like going to sleep alone every night.

It's kinda fun to play a femme fatale to Eric and just kind of torture him a little bit. He deserves it. You know, if he's gonna walk around in his little Calvin Klein underwear all day long, he's gonna get tortured, and that's the end of that.

Eric: If I was financially secure, I would probably wanna spend the rest of my life with my ex-girlfriend Missy, but things are happening with me now, and I can't just put my life at a standstill, 'cause things are happening to me. I'm meeting interesting people, like Caron, the girl I met at the photo shoot, and I can't be a monk and just sit inside all week. You gotta do what you gotta do, y'know? You gotta please the women. That's my job.

THE HOUSE

Andre: My roommates are pigs, they're absolute pigs. I mean, I'm not a neat freak, but I'm not a slob.

Heather: As far as cleanin' up and cookin', I am not trying to do it. I don't offer, I don't make any suggestions to do it, because that's not me. I mean, even at home in my apartment it's a mess.

Julie: Heather's not gonna pick up a dish if it's hers, mine, anybody's. She's not going to. And everyone laughs, and she says, "Well, you can't make me, so I'm not gonna do it."

It just goes so much deeper, I think, with Heather—why is she like that? There's more to it. And the way she's always sayin' that she doesn't care, that's just not even true. She says that she doesn't care, but I'll talk to her, and I'll just slowly bring things up, and it turns out that she has been thinking about these things that she said she didn't care about—for days and days. There's a lot more to Heather than what she projects.

MARCH 29, 1992 (WEEK SEVEN)

Eric: As far as getting along with everybody, from what I can tell, I think I have a pretty good relationship with everybody. Except for one person. Becky is a bitch—y'know, straight out, and it's obvious. I just can't take that. You can be a bitch up to a point. I can respect when girls are bitches, especially when it comes to guys and stuff like that, because that's their security. You have to be careful. But all the time? I just can't take that.

I don't know how long her personality and her attitude have been like this, but is she ever gonna listen to me? I'm only twenty years old, she's twenty-five. I'm so immature compared to her. I mean, please, why would I wanna take time out to talk to her? She won't even give me the time of day. Forget it, I don't even wanna... I don't like her.

Eric: Last week we were all sitting home. Kevin was not here. And we sat around the table and we were just talkin'. So we came up with this brilliant idea to throw off the camera crew: We were gonna change our personalities for a week, and the camera crew was supposed to be like, "What the hell's goin' on?" But we couldn't do it, because there wasn't a time when we could plan our roles off-camera. So we decided that night we were gonna play the joke on Kevin, since Kevin wasn't here, and it worked.

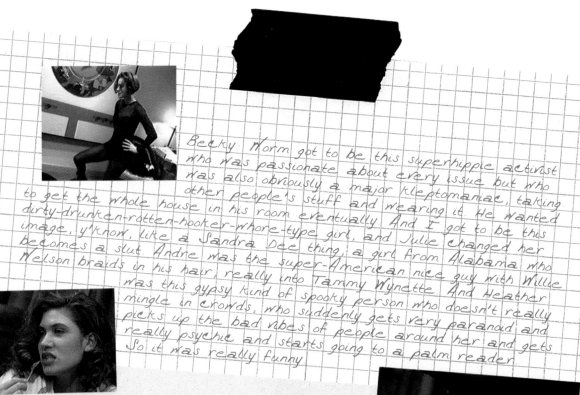

Becky: Norm got to be this superhippie activist who was passionate about every issue but who was also obviously a major kleptomaniac, taking other people's stuff and wearing it. He wanted to get the whole house in his room eventually. And I got to be this dirty-drunken-rotten-hooker-whore-type girl, and Julie changed her image, y'know, like a Sandra Dee thing, a girl from Alabama who becomes a slut. Andre was the super-American nice guy with Willie Nelson braids in his hair, really into Tammy Wynette. And Heather was this gypsy kind of spooky person who doesn't really mingle in crowds, who suddenly gets very paranoid and picks up the bad vibes of people around her and gets really psychic and starts going to a palm reader. So it was really funny.

Norm: I WAS TAKING THINGS RIGHT IN FRONT OF KEVIN. I TOOK POOL BALLS WHEN WE WERE PLAYING POOL, AND HE DIDN'T EVEN RECOGNIZE THAT I WAS TAKING THE BALLS OFF THE TABLE. SO MUCH WAS HAPPENING THAT EVENING—WE WERE HOPING THAT HE WOULD JUST RECOGNIZE THAT THIS HAD TO BE A JOKE, BECAUSE IT WAS JUST TOO INSANE, EVERYONE WAS GETTING A LITTLE TOO CRAZY. KEVIN WAS LIKE, "GOSH, I'VE BEEN AWAY FOR SOME TIME."

Kevin: All that was just real overwhelming to me. These personality changes—I just didn't understand what was going on. So I said to myself, "Man, I need to get out of here."

Eric: He finally came back, thank God, and we told him what was going on, and it was a surprise. April Fools'!.

Julie: I don't think anything could be more eloquent than how the whole joke got thrown right back in our faces. We had done all of this, and he didn't even get the joke. I thought that was just beautiful. It could not have been planned any better than that. And then the fact that Eric is flippin' out over it and sayin' how he feels so guilty and how we're so mean. You could totally see how he was feelin' guilty and was just scared to death, like we all were.

I think we proved a very strong and valid point. We've been living together for how many weeks? And in just these few hours we could flip him out that bad and he could question our personalities that much. I understand that he has to be away a lot, but Kevin should be here more.

FIGHTING WORDS

Becky: Kevin and I got into a discussion, and at the start of it we were agreeing on certain things. But then I said something to the effect that, innately, this is a great country. That doesn't mean it doesn't have its problems, and it doesn't mean it's not completely screwed up right now, but I think it has the potential to be a great country.

Kevin: If you say it's a great country, who are you talking about? Are you only talking about a small segment of people? Because you can just go outside and see the homeless man who sits outside the loft every night and know that for him, it's not really a great country, because he's homeless.

Heather: Kevin is not around much, as we all know, and Becky is very moody, which she admits. So I think that when Kevin is around, they just clash. There's been tons of arguments and little spats between Kevin and Becky that no one has really seen on camera. It's been terrible.

Kevin: I was just pissed off, y'know what I mean? I realize that I came down hard on her. But if you can't sit there and take fifteen minutes of debate, how can you be serious about changing this society? Her ancestors went through a lot more s**t in Germany. My ancestors went through a lot more s**t during slavery—and even now—than she went through in

Becky: I think Kevin thought that I was saying that this is a great country and there are no problems. He was thinking that I was being blind to things that are going on right now, and that's not true. I'm hip to a lotta things. I'm not the biggest activist in the world, and I'm not the most righteous person, but I certainly know the struggles in my own life, and I can feel for other people's struggles.

those fifteen minutes. If she can't take fifteen minutes of that, just, like, you're stupid.

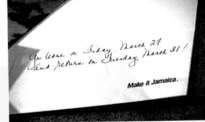

JAMAICA

Julie: Well, we knew we were gettin' a surprise— I'm thinkin' it's gonna be this big ol' package with something good. But instead it's an envelope, and I'm thinkin', There is nothing all three of us want that fits inside this envelope. So I'm disappointed and kinda confused. We read the letter, and the letter says, "We decided that you need a backdrop for romance." And we open up the envelope and find out we're goin' to Jamaica. We were really excited.

Andre: Did I say I had a good sex life? Well, I'm not going to Jamaica, so apparently I have a better sex life than them.

Heather: The whole idea of comin' down here was to meet guys. But it didn't work out. When I first got off the plane, I met a guy at the airport. I didn't like him because he gave his telephone number to Julie to give to me. And I don't like that. I'd rather a guy come up to me on his own. So afterward, he came up to me and introduced himself, but I wasn't gonna call him, 'cause he'd already made a bad first impression.

Julie: I think we were supposed to come down here to Jamaica 'cause we're desperate to meet men. So we come to Jamaica, and there's a bunch of loser birds flying all around these trees. This is a jungle full of desperate men, and I don't know what we were expecting. That there's gonna be Mr. Doctor/Lawyer sittin' around waitin' for us? No deal.

Becky: Heather, Julie, and I decided we were gonna check out the nude beach, so we went out, and it was great. I was dying to take off my bathing suit, 'cause it's so beautiful, and you don't feel like wearing a bathing suit. We went out there thinking it'd be really cool, respectful, nobody bothering anybody. So I go out there and I'm dancin' around nude and Heather was laughing her head off. Heather wouldn't take off her bathing suit. Julie took off her top, but the second Julie got in the water, she was just, like, bombarded by dirty old men. And I got on a fishing boat with this lady named Rosie who braids hair, and I got my hair corn-rowed, so I was sitting on the boat the whole time with Heather, and Julie got stuck in the water. She had to defend herself against all these weird guys, these eighty-year-old men.

I never feel self-conscious about being naked. When I was growing up I ran around naked all the time. Until it

was too freezing to be naked. I was naked all the time. There's nothing wrong with being naked—it has nothing to do with sex and stuff like that. I mean, it's just your body. You wanna be naked because it feels nice. You're skinny-dipping, and you're on the sand, and it feels great, you're like a kid again. I guess I'm an exhibitionist. Nothing wrong with that.

Julie: We're all in the water, and this older man who's been runnin' around nude—he looked like he was sixty—comes over and tells me, "You've got the best breasts out here. Do you mind if I touch them?" Well, yes, get away! I just wanna know if he was thinkin' I'd say, "Oh, sure, go right ahead, y'know, yeah." No! Get out, get lost. So he's like, "All my friends think so, too", and he's bringing them over. "Doesn't she have wonderful breasts. They're so taut—I think of Saran Wrap over a salad." What is he thinkin'? And then he's like, "We can go back to my room and talk more about your breasts." No, forget it. So I'm kinda skeptical about all this, people wantin' to touch my boobs. I'm gettin' outta the water, goin', "Forget it." Becky on the other hand is hightailin' it out to some boat, in the nude, climbin' up, moonin' the world, wantin' her hair braided.

Heather: Becky is a bit funnier to me now. I used to just look at her before and be like, "Why?" You know, about some of the things that she did and said. Now I just look at her and laugh. I guess because every time I see her, all I see is this naked girl doin' jumpin' jacks on the beach.

APRIL 12, 1992 (WEEK NINE)

ISSUES

NORM: ANY KIND OF SEXUAL TERM IS EXTREMELY CONFUSING TO ME. I'M JUST LIKE A YOUNG PUP TRYING TO GROW UP AND FIGURE IT OUT. I OFTEN USE THE TERM <u>GAY</u>, AND I OFTEN USE THE TERM <u>BISEXUAL</u>, ALTHOUGH A LOT OF MY FRIENDS IN THE GAY COMMUNITY BELIEVE THAT THERE IS REALLY NO SUCH THING AS BISEXUAL. THEY THINK IT'S A REALLY CLEAR-CUT SITUATION: ONCE YOU'VE SLEPT WITH A MAN, YOU'RE IMMEDIATELY GAY. AND I DON'T REALLY KNOW. I MEAN, I'VE HAD A LOT OF VERY OPEN AND HONEST RELATIONSHIPS WITH WOMEN. I HAVEN'T THROWN THEM OUT OF THE PICTURE. I MIGHT DEVELOP AND HAVE MORE HONEST RELATIONSHIPS WITH WOMEN. I MIGHT HAVE OPEN RELATIONSHIPS WITH MEN. I'M JUST MYSELF, AND I'M TRYING TO FIGURE THIS OUT. WHAT CAN I DO?

MY RECENT DATING WITH THIS GUY CHARLES IS KIND OF INTERESTING. I KNOW THAT HE IS TRYING TO WORK OUT THE GAY POLITICAL CLIMATE, TRYING TO FIGURE OUT WHAT IT IS. I SPOKE WITH HIM ON THE PHONE TODAY AND INVITED HIM TO COME WITH ME ON THE PRO-CHOICE MARCH, AND HE SAID THAT HE WAS GONNA GO WITH SOME OTHER PEOPLE. BUT HE WANTED TO KNOW IF I WAS GOING TO WEAR ANYTHING GAY. AND I SAID, "NO, I REALLY DON'T HAVE ANYTHING THAT SAYS 'GAY' ON IT." AND HE'S LIKE, "YOU SHOULD DEFINITELY HAVE A GAY SHIRT." AND I WAS LIKE, "THE ISSUE THAT I'M GOING DOWN THERE FOR DOESN'T HAVE ANYTHING TO DO WITH BEING GAY." IT'S REALLY IMPORTANT TO RECOGNIZE THAT GENDER POLITICS ARE KIND OF RETARDED.

Julie: Charles was at the march in Washington, and you could kinda tell that he had been waiting for us or somethin'. I wasn't excited to see him, because Charles is just a jerk. He is all screwed up. He's more interested in getting on camera and displaying his gayness than in who he is as a person. I have no problem with him being gay. I wish that he would get over the fact that he is. If he likes Norman, then he should like Norman. But don't have some screwed-up plan about it.

223

NORMAN: I LOVE MY FRIENDS IN THE HOUSE, BUT CHARLES WAS SOMEONE WHO FILLED A VOID IN ME THAT I NEED TO KNOW A LITTLE BIT MORE. HE'S BEEN THROUGH A LOT, AND HE'S VERY ESTABLISHED IN TRYING TO FIND OUT WHAT IT IS

TO BE A GAY MALE IN SOCIETY TODAY—YOU KNOW, WHERE DOES HE COME FROM, WHAT DOES IT MEAN? I AM KIND OF NEW TO THIS WHOLE WORLD AND ALL OF THE DIALOGUES THAT GO ALONG WITH IT. THAT WAS AN IMPORTANT PART— I WANTED TO GET TO KNOW SOMEONE THAT I COULD ASK QUESTIONS OF, WHO WAS SHARING THE SAME KIND OF EXPERIENCES AND FEELINGS. I WAS EXTREMELY TAKEN WITH CHARLES. I JUST THOUGHT HE WAS THE GREATEST THING SINCE WONDERBREAD.

I KNOW THAT WHEN I WAS GROWING UP, IT WAS KIND OF A DIFFICULT THING FOR ME, BECAUSE I WAS ACCUSED OF BEING GAY VERY EARLY ON IN SCHOOL, WHICH WAS A VERY DAMAGING EXPERIENCE. I FELT THAT I DIDN'T KNOW WHAT THAT WAS, BUT THAT IT WAS BAD—THAT GAY WAS BAD. I WOULD COME HOME AND I WOULD BE UPSET. SOMETIMES I WAS EXCLUDED FROM SPORTS TEAMS AT MY SCHOOL, EVEN THOUGH I WAS THE BEST RUNNER THAT TEAM COULDA EVER HAD. MIDDLE SCHOOL, WHAM, I WAS THROWN OFF THESE TEAMS, AND KIDS WOULD CHALLENGE ME OUT OF THE BLUE. THESE OLDER KIDS WOULD COME UP, KNOCK ME DOWN ON THE GROUND, AND SAY, "YOU FAGGOT, YOU FAG," THIS AND THAT, AND I WAS LIKE, WHAT THE HELL IS A FAGGOT? WHAT IS THIS? I WAS SCARED BY THIS. I THINK THAT I DEVELOPED A CERTAIN AMOUNT OF HOMOPHOBIA.

LATER I WENT TO THIS INTERLOCHEN SCHOOL, AND THERE WERE STUDENTS THERE THAT WERE OPENLY GAY, AND I WAS STUNNED. I WAS KINDA NERVOUS ABOUT THEM, AND I JUST AVOIDED THEM, 'CAUSE IT WAS A BAD THING IN MY MIND. BUT AFTER SPENDING SOME TIME AT THE SCHOOL, I GOT TO LEARN AND APPRECIATE SO MANY PEOPLE. I COULD UNDERSTAND THOSE PEOPLE.

AFTER I WAS IN THIS AUTO ACCIDENT, I STARTED TO LOCATE FEARS AND TRY TO CHALLENGE AND CONFRONT THEM AND ASK MYSELF, WHY AM I SO AFRAID OF BEING ATTRACTED TO SOMEONE OF MY OWN SEX? WHY SHOULD I BE AFRAID OF IT? WHY SHOULD I HAVE TO BE SO ANGRY ABOUT IT? WHY NOT TRY TO LEARN FROM FRIENDS WHO HAVE GONE THROUGH THIS? THOSE PEOPLE ARE OKAY. THEY'RE PRODUCTIVE. BEING GAY IS NOT BAD.

MELTDOWN

Kevin: I was on the telephone talking to someone at a record company about a job possibility, someone I was tryin' to get in touch with for a while, and Julie picked up the phone. I really don't remember verbatim what she said, but it was with this real testy attitude, and the guy on the phone was like, "Who's that?" A couple moments later I kinda got the vibe that he really wasn't interested in talking to me anymore, and the conversation fizzled out. So I was real pissed off, and I yelled at Julie—"Don't do that anymore. I really didn't appreciate what you did. Do you realize what you did?" Something to that effect. And she yelled back down, "Well, f**k you." We like started cursing, and it got into this full-blown argument, and I was just real pissed off about the whole thing. And I remember barging outta the house. I'm like, "Let me get the hell outta here. I can't take this." Because I felt like she didn't really understand the significance of the kinda lifestyle I have, in terms of always tryin' to get work as a writer. It got real ugly.

Julie: I think it's really obvious after living with Kevin that he has a lot of frustration inside, and I think it was obvious that it was gonna come out in some way, but I hoped that it was just gonna come out with his little fights, his little verbal fights with everyone. I've never doubted that he was capable of some physical violence, and that it wouldn't make a difference whether it was against a woman, that he would not take that into consideration. But I always kinda thought that it would be Becky and not me. So I was very surprised and hurt.

225

NORMAN: I REACHED HEATHER ON THE PHONE FROM WORK, AND SHE SOUNDED KIND OF ALARMED AND STRESSED, AND SHE BROKE INTO THE STORY VERY EMOTIONALLY. SHE WAS LIKE, "KEVIN WENT OFF ON JULIE AND WAS YELLIN' AT HER. THEY WERE TALKING ABOUT THE PHONE, AND THEN HE SPIT IN HER FACE AND THREW THIS CANDLESTICK." I'M HEARING THIS OVER THE PHONE, AND EVERYTHING IS SPINNING, I'M GOING, "WHAT THE HELL?" AND SO I WAS JUST LIKE, "GET JULIE ON THE PHONE, CAUSE JULIE IS MY BABY. I WANT TO KNOW WHAT IS GOING ON WITH MY BABY." SHE GETS ON THE PHONE, AND I'M LIKE, "DID THIS HAPPEN?" SHE'S LIKE, "UH-HUH." I'M LIKE, "AARGH!" I WAS SO ANGRY.

IT DOESN'T MAKE SENSE TO HER THAT HE WOULD DO THIS, BUT FROM WHAT I KNOW OF KEVIN, THIS MADE SENSE TO ME IN A KIND OF CRAZY WAY. I COULD SEE HOW THESE SITUATIONS DEVELOP, AND HOW THEN THEY JUST EXPLODE.

I GOT OFF THE PHONE, AND I WAS ALL WORKED UP, AND THEN THE MANAGER PULLED ME IN, AND HE WAS LIKE "NORM, WE HAVE TO LET YOU GO." I'M LIKE, "OH, GOOD, COULDN'T HAVE COME AT A BETTER TIME. MY CAR HAS BEEN TOWED AND I'VE GOT ALL THESE THINGS TO DO, AND NOW I DON'T EVEN HAVE A PART-TIME JOB." GREAT, REAL GREAT.

I WALKED IN THE DOOR, AND I'M LIKE, "KEVIN, DID YOU SPIT IN JULIE'S FACE? I DON'T WANNA GET INTO THIS AND THAT ISSUE, BECAUSE I DON'T

CARE—THOSE ARE ALL YOUR ISSUES, AND THAT'S FINE. I JUST WANNA KNOW TWO THINGS: DID YOU SPIT IN HER FACE, AND DID YOU THROW THIS CANDLE THING AT HER? THAT'S ALL I NEED TO KNOW." HE'S LIKE, "WHY DON'T YOU COME UP HERE, AND I'LL TELL YOU THE STORY."

AND KEVIN WAS DOING A VERY GOOD JOB AT SAYING NO, NO, NO, HE DIDN'T DO THAT, BUT THE THING IS THAT, IN THE PAST, KEVIN HAS NEGLECTED TO MENTION THINGS THAT HE HAS DONE. I MEAN, BECKY AND HIM WILL GET INTO A FIGHT, AND THEN THE NEXT MORNING HE'LL SAY THAT HE DIDN'T HAVE A FIGHT WITH BECKY, THAT HE DOESN'T KNOW WHAT I'M TALKING ABOUT, THAT HE DID-N'T DO THAT. SO HERE I AM, AND HE'S SAYING HE DIDN'T SPIT, HE DIDN'T THROW THESE THINGS, HE DIDN'T DO THIS STUFF, THAT ISN'T ME, NO WAY, THERE'S NO CAMERAS, AND I HAVE NOTHING ON HIM. HE TELLS ME I'M ACCUS-ING HIM, AND I'M WHITE. AND I WAS JUST LIKE, FINE, I'M GONNA DROP IT.

Kevin: In light of the Rodney King verdict being announced and my recent discussions with Norman and Andre, I was like, "Yo, Julie does not understand," and we got into this big argument in the middle of the street. The reason why I went outside with her like that was that I don't feel like havin' another third party interrupt what we're tryin' to talk about. But we got into this argument anyway outside. Next thing I know, there's a whole crowd around and we're, like, screaming at each other. It didn't help the situation at all.

But Julie didn't back down at all, I mean, she has a lot more courage than most people in the loft. I've had arguments with people and they just were like, "Lemme outta here," even if they were right. But she believed in what she was saying strongly, and she wasn't gonna back down. What else can I do but respect that?

Julie: I really like Kevin, and I could never deny that. I respect him a lot. I think he's really intelligent and has a lot of important things to say. That doesn't mean that I ever want to be alone with Kevin again in my life. I will never be comfortable. I don't really understand how I could be expected to be. But I do think I make a special effort to be around him and to make myself as comfortable as possible.

Andre: I think they just moved on. I don't think anything was really solved. I think Kevin just realized that he couldn't push Julie around. I thought she was fabulous.

KEVIN'S BIRTHDAY PARTY

Kevin: This was the first birthday party I have ever had in my life. It was also the biggest party I've ever had. I felt responsible for every single person that walked through that door. Like, my editor from *Rolling Stone* came with his friends, and I was like, man, I need to make sure they're cool. Then friends I had from college came, friends from my neighborhood came, and I just felt responsible for everyone. I don't know why I did, but I just lost the party mood after a while. Plus Eric was with his friends, and he was really buggin' out. He was drinkin' and the whole nine, and he was enjoying it, which I wish I would have done in retrospect, given all the stuff that happened that night. I don't know. I have the tendency to take too much on, to worry too much at times.

NORMAN: I DON'T KNOW IF KEVIN WAS ENJOYING HIS PARTY AT ALL—HE WAS WATCHING OVER EVERYTHING LIKE A MOTHER HEN. HE WAS MAKING SURE NO ONE WAS GONNA GET HURT, AND THAT EVERYTHING WAS IN CONTROL. POOR GUY— I DON'T THINK HE GOT TO ENJOY HIS OWN PARTY. ERIC, ON THE OTHER HAND, WELL, HE HIT THE BOTTLE, AND THAT BOY WAS WIGGLIN', WIGGLIN', WIGGLIN'. IT HAPPENED ALL EVENING LONG. JUST DRUNK AND WIGGLING. THAT WAS GOOD.

Heather: Eric was drunk. I told Eric, "You better never drink again, because you don't know how you was actin'." He was drinkin' soda, he ate pizza, all things that he was against. He just was doin' it. I think he ended up losin' his jacket, though, his five-hundred-dollar leather jacket, and his glasses—but he found the glasses. He never found the jacket. But Eric, he was yellin' out things and screamin' at people and sayin' F to cops. He was just outta control. But he was happy.

Julie: I had been anxious to get back to the loft to this huge party that was goin' on. I walk in the door, and the first thing I hear is, "Julie, you need to talk to Heather—she's gonna be arrested. She hit some girl." So, sad but true, I did not even question it. I just immediately find Heather. I'm tryin' to be really serious. Heather's gonna be arrested as far as I know. So I was like, "Heather, did you clock her?" And Heather's like, "Oh yeah, she went down." And I was just like, "Well, did she deserve it?" And Heather was like, "Definitely. She threw a cup in my face." And I knew we couldn't have that.

Heather: Okay, all right, now, we had everything goin', we just sittin' there pumpin' beer, rakin' in the dough, gettin' friendly with everybody—we had it goin'. This woman comes up, and she just grabs a cup. I was like, "Excuse me, we're not runnin' the game like this. You have to pay for a cup." She was like, "I'm not payin' for a cup." Then her friend came and grabbed the cup and gave it to her, so me and my girlfriend went over there and we were like, you know, "What's up? You can't do that— you have to pay for a cup." And she said, "How much is a cup, a quarter?" And I said, "No, it's three dollars." And she said, "You know what? You're a cheap bitch," and she took the cup and she just mushed the cup in my face. I was so shocked, so I just <u>boom</u>, <u>boom</u>, threw punches and hit her, and she went back, and somebody grabbed me. It was like, "Oh, it's a fight, it's a fight." And then my girlfriends saw me fightin', so they went over and they started hittin' on her and they punched her in the face, and she was just, "Aaahh, aaaah." I'm like, "I can't believe this woman hit me." So I got a bottle, and I hit her in the head with a bottle, but it missed, just the extra pieces came over her head. And I was like, "That's not good enough for her, she hit me in the face with a cup." So I grabbed another bottle and I broke it. I said, "I'm goin' cut her." I went over to try to get her, but by then Eric had me in this karate-man lock and I couldn't get out. I was like, "Just get her outta here, 'cause I wanna kill her."

She was threatenin' to call the cops. I told her, "Go ahead and call the cops." She's out in the hallway, and somebody's tellin' me she's bleedin' or somethin', I could care less. I really wanted to go back out in the hallway and get her again, so it didn't bother me. Finally, about a half-hour later, the cops came. And they got me, and we went downstairs and they put me in the cop car. They see all the cameras comin' downstairs, and the cops are like, "Well, who are you?" And I was like, "I'm Heather, who are you?" It was like, "Well, are you involved in a fight?" And I said, "Yeah, it was a fight." And they was like, "What are you talkin' about, what's goin' on? Is this part of the show, are you actin', is this part of your show?" And I said, "No, I can't explain what I'm doin' right now." And the cop said, "Well, you <u>have</u> to, 'cause I don't understand these cameras." I said, "Well, they're documenting a story of our real life, and it's for real. In real life, my roommates gave a party." And she said, "What roommates? Where they from?" And I said, "We just met." She said, "You live with six other people you just met, and the cameras are followin' you around, but you got into a fight for real?" And I said, "Yeah," and she was like, "Go away."

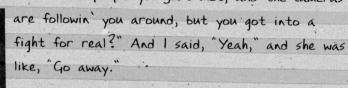

This cop started becomin' interested—"How did you get involved in this? Who's in charge?" And I said, "Some camera people. They pay the rent, we just live in there for free." She was just blown away. She started askin' me what time the show's comin' on, everything. She just couldn't believe what was takin' place. I gave her all my information. I told her I was a rapper, and she was like, "Oh, wow, I heard of them." She finally gave me the name and number of the other woman, and I couldn't believe that she was thirty-five years old and a writer for a magazine. I had heard that she was makin' threats to, like, dis me in a magazine. I was like, "I don't care if she disses me in a magazine. So what? Just spell my name right, and let everybody know you got beat up at our party," and that was it. It was just, it was so funny how it happened. It was crazy. We still laugh about that. They call me Slugger and all kinds of names around here now. So it's just crazy, real crazy.

FINAL THOUGHTS

Becky: I don't know how the show is gonna change me yet, 'cause I'm not out of it yet. I don't think I could go back and do it again. It's really kind of a once-in-a-lifetime thing. It takes a lotta energy, but it was great. I mean, it got a lot of things going for me musically, just because I want people to come see me play. So I played more and did more. I was more productive in these thirteen weeks than I've been in a long time. I have a tendency to kind of get lazy and drink a lot of red wine and not go anywhere for weeks on end. So I don't know how it's changed me yet, but I know it has.

234

Julie: _The Real World_ is my family. It means everything to me. This has been the best. It's been a life's experience packed into three months. You don't even hope for things this big. You learn things that you don't even wanna learn, you don't even wanna hear, and you don't even wanna see. And things that are good, like me and Heather's relationship. That's wonderful. We'll be friends till the day we die. We're inseparable. I think I have a great relationship with everybody on the show, and I love them all so much.

NORMAN: ONE THING I THINK I LEARNED WAS THAT I HAD THIS FEAR: I DON'T PLACE MY SEXUALITY OUT THERE. IN THE FIRST COUPLE OF WEEKS, I DIDN'T KNOW THE PEOPLE I WAS GONNA BE LIVING WITH, AND I WANTED TO GET TO KNOW THEM AND LET THEM FEEL COMFORTABLE WITH ME SO THAT I DIDN'T SEEM LIKE AN ALIEN TO THEM. I THINK I DEFINITELY WAS NEUROTIC ABOUT HOW TO BRING MY SEXUALITY UP TO SEVEN PEOPLE THAT I DIDN'T KNOW. WOULD THEY TREAT ME DIFFERENTLY? I LEARNED THAT THEY DIDN'T. I LEARNED THAT IT WAS MY OWN FEAR AND THAT NO ONE WOULD RUN AWAY. NO ONE STOPPED LISTENING TO ME. AND I THINK THAT WAS SOMETHING THAT GAVE ME STRENGTH.

Andre: I thought the name _The Real World_ was not particularly fitting for the project, but that's my opinion. If you wanted the real world, you could have set the cameras up in my house, because that's real. But on the other hand, I thought it was great, I thought it was a lot of fun. Getting to meet and know and, yes, understand these people was a great experience. Something I would have never expected.

Eric: You don't wanna talk to me about Becky. I got nothin' to say about Becky. Kevin, I still don't know what's goin' through his mind. He's got his views and points about things, and it just seems you're not gonna change them. I don't really know if he's learned or anything, 'cause you never really got a chance to talk to Kevin about anything, you just, like, hear his views all the time.

Kevin: I don't have any animosity toward Norman, I don't have any bitterness toward him, 'cause I think he's a very—he's a *done* human being, if I can use that term. I got a lotta respect for him. In spite of everything that's happened, in spite of that argument, I definitely could see myself being in touch with him.

Eric, we've definitely grown, we're friends. We're cool, we talk about a lotta different things. I think there's a mutual respect there.

There are two people that I don't feel so comfortable with, for different reasons.

Heather: Everything was cool. Everything was really cool. Probably the only thing I won't miss really is the neighbor, that lady next door. I won't miss her one bit.

Andre, probably because it took so long for us to ever communicate about anything. And even though we did have some discussions the last few weeks, I still don't—I'm still not sure where exactly he's coming from. I guess sometimes I feel, like, real suspicious of some of his motives.

I tried to explain to everybody why there's no sex in the apartment. It's because everybody is ugly, just like you don't think your brother or sister is cute. Who would sleep with Norman and Andre and Eric? Get away! I see you too much, stay away from me.

And with Becky, it's like I don't honestly have that much respect for Becky. It's not even because of that argument we had, but just because of a lotta things that happened afterward that I've observed that don't even have anything to do with me. I can't really see myself staying in contact with her.

NORMAN: FOR ME, ERIC HAS BEEN A COMPLETE PLEASURE TO HAVE AROUND, BECAUSE HE'S JUST SO INNOCENT AND SO MOLDABLE. HE'S DEFINITELY GONNA BE THE LOOKER OF THE SHOW: CUTE AND HE'S GOT THE DIMPLES AND EVERYONE'S SCREAMING AND YELLING AND WANTING TO RIP THE UNDERWEAR OFF THIS PERSON. AND YOU SHOULD—DON'T HESITATE. HE LIKES THAT. HE LIKES TO WALK AROUND IN HIS UNDERWEAR, AND HE LIKES TO HAVE FUN WITH HIMSELF. HE KNOWS HIMSELF AS THIS OBJECT. HE'S NO FOOL. HE KNOWS EXACTLY WHAT'S GOING ON. I THINK HE DEALS WITH ME ON A VERY COMICAL KIND OF LEVEL, BECAUSE HE KNOWS THAT I'M ATTRACTED TO MEN. WELL, EVERYONE SHOULD BE ATTRACTED TO ERIC—FORGET IT: DOGS, CATS, WOMEN, WHOEVER.

ANDRE'S MY FRIEND. HE IS GREAT. IT'S SO INTERESTING, BECAUSE WHEN I LOOK BACK, HE'S BEEN SUCH A GREAT SUPPORT FOR ME, FROM DAY ONE. I MEAN, HE GOES TO BARS THAT I GO TO, HE GOES AND MEETS MY FRIENDS THAT ARE OUTTA CONTROL. HE GOES TO MY ART OPENING, HE'LL COME OUT TO THE HOUSE, HE'S INTERESTED IN WHAT I HAVE TO SAY. THERE'S SOMETHING ABOUT THAT MICHIGAN BLOOD. WE HAVE THAT MICHIGAN BONDING.

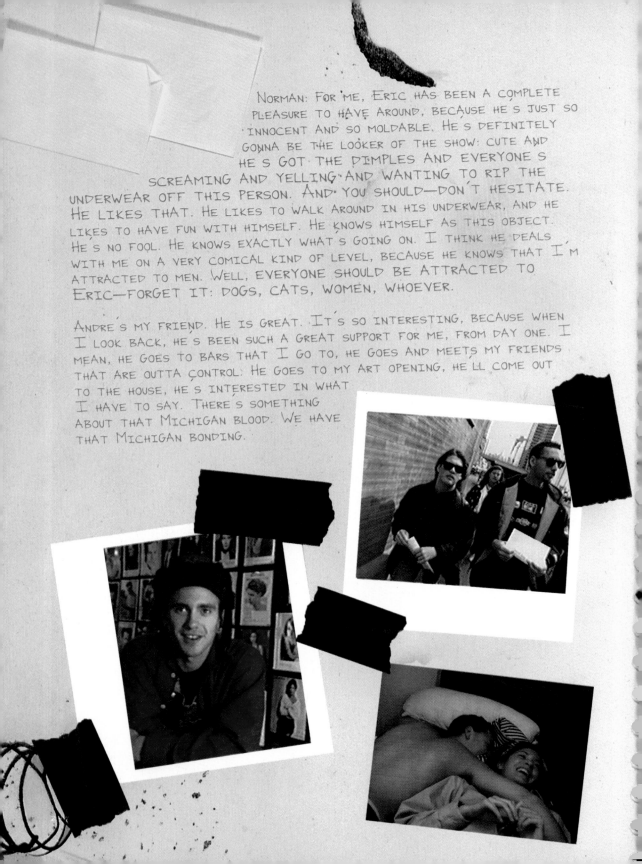

ADVICE

Andre: Advice to new people: Don't hold anything back. Don't let them call you kids—that is absolutely demeaning. Don't let them treat you like a child because I found myself having to fight against being immature whenever I heard someone say "the kids," or whenever I felt like I was being treated like a child.

Grow your hair, and that's about it. But I'm not a role model and I never want to be. Role models are parents, they're neighbors who've got something good to say. They're not sports stars, they're not rock stars, they're not musicians.

Becky: For anybody who wants to be on *The Real World*, I probably would say, "Get ready to be completely naked, get ready for reality," because you don't go in there and become buddy-buddy with everyone, and you don't sit around and listen and watch music videos. That's not what it's about. It's about people living together. You live your life—make sure you have a life—and if you have one and you wanna show it, go right ahead and do it, because it's really important. And it's a lotta fun, and that's mainly why I did it. I thought it was a great time. It's a complete hoot.

HOW to Get on THE REAL WORLD

(From the Producers)

To apply to be on The Real World, you need to show us that you are an open, honest and sincere person who's dealing with issues of concern to The Real World audience. How can you do this? Read on for step-by-step directions.

1. Call The Real World hotline:
(818) 754-5790 This number will give you the latest information on applying. It will tell you where to send your application and when the deadlines for the next season are. Be sure to call this number first to get the most up-to-date information.

2. Write a cover Letter:
We want you to tell us a little bit about yourself and what you plan to do in Boston. (Yes, the sixth season of The Real World will be filmed in Boston, MA.) Why do you want to spend six months in a house full of strangers? What activities will you pursue? Please also include a snapshot of yourself in this cover letter.

3. Make a videotape:
We would like to see you as well as hear from you. Make a ten minute videotape of yourself talking about whatever you think makes you a good candidate for The Real World.

Remember, we want to see if you are a person who is open and willing to express what is important to you. Sometimes the best videos are very simple: someone sitting on their bed talking about what makes them tick. Try to be honest, and sincere. Don't overthink it. (Also make sure there's enough light on your face and that you are close enough to the mike to be heard.)

4. Fill out the enclosed application:
Answer all of the following questions as best and as honestly as you can. Please keep your answers to a paragraph in length. And please be sure to type your answers or write legibly.

APPLICATION FORM

THE REAL WORLD

DATE RECEIVED

NAME

ADDRESS

PHONE

BIRTHDATE   AGE

SOCIAL SECURITY NO.

PARENTS' NAME

ADDRESS

PHONE

SIBLINGS (NAMES AND AGES)

ARE YOU OR HAVE YOU EVER BEEN A MEMBER OF SAG/AFTRA?   HAVE YOU EVER ACTED OR PERFORMED OUTSIDE OF SCHOOL?

EDUCATION: NAME OF HIGH SCHOOL   YEARS COMPLETED

NAME OF COLLEGE   YEARS COMPLETED AND MAJORS

OTHER EDUCATION

WHERE DO YOU WORK? DESCRIBE YOUR JOB

HOW WOULD SOMEONE WHO REALLY KNOWS YOU DESCRIBE YOUR BEST TRAITS?

HOW WOULD SOMEONE WHO REALLY KNOWS YOU DESCRIBE YOUR WORST TRAITS?

DESCRIBE YOUR MOST EMBARRASSING MOMENT IN LIFE

DO YOU HAVE A BOYFRIEND OR GIRLFRIEND? HOW LONG HAVE YOU TWO BEEN TOGETHER?
WHAT DRIVES YOU CRAZY ABOUT THE OTHER PERSON? WHAT'S THE BEST THING ABOUT THE OTHER PERSON?

IS THERE ANY ISSUE, POLITICAL OR SOCIAL, THAT YOU'RE PASSIONATE ABOUT? TELL US ABOUT ANY EXPERIENCES WHERE YOU'VE PUT
SERIOUS TIME IN HELPING PEOPLE LESS ADVANTAGED THAN YOURSELF

DESCRIBE A MAJOR EVENT OR ISSUE THAT'S AFFECTED YOUR FAMILY

WHAT IS THE MOST IMPORTANT ISSUE OR PROBLEM FACING YOU TODAY?

DO YOU HAVE ANY HABITS WE SHOULD KNOW ABOUT?

WHAT DO YOU DO FOR FUN?

DESCRIBE A TYPICAL FRIDAY OR SATURDAY NIGHT

WHAT WAS THE LAST UNUSUAL, EXCITING, OR SPONTANEOUS OUTING <u>YOU</u> INSTIGATED FOR YOU AND YOUR FRIENDS?

DO YOU SMOKE CIGARETTES?

DO YOU DRINK ALCOHOL? HOW OLD WERE YOU WHEN YOU HAD YOUR FIRST DRINK? HOW MUCH DO YOU DRINK NOW? HOW OFTEN?

DO YOU USE STREET DRUGS? WHAT DRUGS HAVE YOU USED? HOW OFTEN?

DO YOU KNOW A LOT OF PEOPLE WHO DO DRUGS, OR NOT? WHAT DO YOU THINK OF PEOPLE WHO DO DRUGS?

ARE YOU ON ANY PRESCRIPTION MEDICATION? IS SO, WHAT, AND FOR HOW LONG HAVE YOU BEEN TAKING IT?

DESCRIBE YOUR FANTASY DATE

WHAT ARE YOUR FAVORITE MUSICAL GROUPS/ARTISTS?

HAVE YOU EVER BEEN ARRESTED? (IF SO, WHAT WAS THE CHARGE AND WERE YOU CONVICTED?)

WHAT IS YOUR ULTIMATE CAREER GOAL? WHY? DO YOU HAVE A GAME PLAN AS TO HOW TO ACHIEVE WHAT YOU WANT?

ARE YOU LIVING ALONE RIGHT NOW, OR WITH A ROOMMATE?

IF YOU'RE LIVING WITH A ROOMMATE, HOW DID YOU HOOK UP WITH THEM? TELL US ABOUT LIVING WITH THEM

HOW IMPORTANT IS SEX TO YOU? DO YOU HAVE IT ONLY WHEN YOU'RE IN A RELATIONSHIP OR DO YOU SEEK IT OUT AT OTHER TIMES?

HOW DID IT COME ABOUT ON THE LAST OCCASION?

DO YOU BELIEVE IN GOD? DO YOU PRACTICE A RELIGION?

OTHER THAN A BOYFRIEND OR GIRLFRIEND, WHO IS THE MOST IMPORTANT PERSON IN YOUR LIFE RIGHT NOW?

WHAT ARE YOUR POLITICAL BELIEFS?

WHO HAVE BEEN YOUR ROLE MODELS? WHY?

WHAT IS YOUR GREATEST FEAR (AND WHY)?

WHAT ARE YOUR PERSONAL GOALS IN LIFE?

DESCRIBE A RECENT MAJOR ARGUMENT YOU HAD WITH SOMEONE WHO USUALLY WINS ARGUMENTS WITH YOU? HOW?

HAVE YOU EVER HIT ANYONE IN ANGER OR SELF-DEFENSE? IF SO, TELL US ABOUT IT (HOW OLD WERE YOU, WHAT HAPPENED, ETC.)

WHAT BOTHERS YOU MOST ABOUT OTHER PEOPLE?

IF YOU COULD CHANGE ANY ONE THING ABOUT THE WAY YOU ARE, WHAT WOULD THAT BE?

IF SELECTED, IS THERE ANY PERSON OR PART OF YOUR LIFE YOU WOULD PREFER NOT TO SHARE?
IF SO, DESCRIBE (E.G., FAMILY, FRIENDS, BUSINESS ASSOCIATES, SOCIAL ORGANIZATIONS, OR ACTIVITIES)

ARE YOU NOW SEEING, OR HAVE YOU EVER SEEN A THERAPIST OR PSYCHOLOGIST? IF SO, WHY?

	RATING	COMMENT
READ BOOKS		
SLEEP 8 HRS.		
WATCH TELEVISION DAILY		
SHOP		
GO OUT/SOCIALIZE		
SPEND TIME WITH FRIENDS		
SPEND TIME ALONE		
WORK/STUDY		
TALK ON THE PHONE		
COOK		
CLEAN		
ARGUE		
WRITE		
READ NEWSPAPERS		
STATE OPINIONS		
ASK OPINIONS		
CONFIDE IN YOUR PARENTS		
VOLUNTEER		
PROCRASTINATE		
EAT		
DRINK ALCOHOL		
DIET		
SMOKE		
CRY		
LAUGH		
GO TO CINEMA		
GO TO THEATRE		
GO TO CONCERTS		
GO TO CLUBS		
GO TO PARTIES		

**LIST 4 PEOPLE WHO HAVE KNOWN
YOU FOR A LONG TIME AND WILL TELL US
WHAT A GREAT PERSON YOU ARE**
(EXCLUDING RELATIVES)

NAME	ADDRESS	PHONE	HOW DO THEY KNOW YOU?
1.			
2.			
3.			
4.			

SIGNED _____ DATE _____

[PLEASE BE SURE TO SIGN AND DATE YOUR APPLICATION!!!]